Praise for Roderick Kalberer's first novel The Seahorse

'Cracking thriller, which carries the stamp of authenticity'
Manchester Evening News

'Intricate and powerful tale of revenge … unpredictable turns in the plot … an exciting debut'
Yorkshire Post

'A tale to meet the most exacting demands … he handles the very topical theme with consummate skill'
Colchester Evening Gazette

'A good, well-written thriller'
Liverpool Daily Post

Also by Roderick Kalberer

The Scam

About the author

RODERICK KALBERER was born in Lagos, Nigeria and educated in England. He now lives on a small island off the East Coast. He races classic yachts and has sailed from the Red Sea to the Grand Banks. His first thriller, *The Scam*, was a compelling insight into the world of the drug smuggler. *Lethal* is his second novel.

Lethal

Roderick Kalberer

CORONET BOOKS
Hodder & Stoughton

Copyright © 1999 by Roderick Kalberer

The right of Roderick Kalberer to be identified as the Author of
the Work has been asserted by him in accordance with the
Copyright, Designs and Patents Act 1988.

First published in Great Britain in 1999
by Hodder and Stoughton
A division of Hodder Headline

A Coronet Paperback

10 9 8 7 6 5 4 3 2 1

All characters in this publication are fictitious and any resemblance to
real persons, living or dead is purely coincidental.

A CIP catalogue record for this title is available
from the British Library.

ISBN 0 340 62824 3

Printed and bound in Great Britain by
Mackays of Chatham, plc, Chatham, Kent.

Hodder and Stoughton
A division of Hodder Headline
338 Euston Road
London NW1 3BH

For
Elizabeth

ACKNOWLEDGMENTS

I would like to thank my agent, Barbara Levy,
and my editors, George Lucas and Philippa Pride,
for the care, attention and patience they have shown
since this book was first commissioned.

Chapter One

━━━━◆◇◇◆━━━━

I

Leon Garrick collected the envelope from the courier at Heathrow Airport and was on the Iberia flight to Bilbao an hour later. He experienced a tremor of excitement whenever he boarded a plane. A few years ago he'd have been heading for a fire-fight in some unfamiliar country, but these days his engagements were of a more delicate nature.

He sat in an aisle seat, tried to make himself comfortable and immediately regretted not travelling business class. He winced as his right knee complained at the cramped conditions. It had been smashed by a bullet from some narco-terrorist during a clandestine operation in Colombia, and as a result had terminated his tour with the SAS. The most able volunteers were always selected for the most dangerous missions and consequently incurred higher casualties. Now he was only a statistic in an élite force's selection-destruction cycle, and his days of active service were over. He'd expected to lose the leg, but the doctor who pinned the bones had inserted a stainless-steel knee-joint and told him the technology was developed as a result of the IRA's predilection for knee-capping. The irony was lost on Leon. He was aware only that his career had ended prematurely, and he'd been jettisoned into a civilian world which had little need for someone with his skills.

During the next eighteen months he learned not to admit

he'd done two tours with the SAS because there was always some joker at the bar who wanted to find out how tough he was. 'Royal Green Jackets,' was all he admitted when questioned about his military background. He'd almost despaired of finding a decent job until he was approached by a friend who asked if he'd like to negotiate kidnap, ransom and extortion claims. He jumped at the opportunity. Life turned around. Now he was thirty-five years old, tall, tanned, good-looking and could make the mortgage repayments again. He was beginning to feel good about himself. For the first time since the bullet shattered his knee he thought he had something to offer and wanted to share his life with someone, although he hadn't met anyone suitable yet.

Leon had joined the army as soon as he left school. The transition from Cadet Corps to the real thing was easy. He never felt he had a choice. He'd been sent to boarding-school when his parents separated, and it became the most stable influence in his life. During the holidays he was shunted between his mother and father so, when he was finally signed up for activity camps, he came to the conclusion he wasn't really wanted by either of them. They both had new families and he was an unwelcome reminder of their past. The problems had begun early when his father recorded his name as Leonard on the birth certificate, objecting to his mother's choice of Leon because he thought it was effeminate. From then on his mother called him Leon and his father called him Len. In the army his mates called him Trotsky, which he preferred.

The bullet changed his life. It was as close an encounter with death as he wanted to experience before the real thing. It put life into perspective. It made him think about starting a family. He thought he'd gained sufficient insight into his own upbringing to make more of a success at it than his parents had.

Leon smiled at the stewardess who offered him some wine and shook his head. '*Agua con gaz, por favor,*' he replied. She passed him a can of water, a glass and a packet of nuts. He watched her wrestle the drinks trolley along the aisle and looked at her legs. He thought for a moment. He'd never slept with a Spanish girl. Perhaps he'd put that right one of these days. Then, irritated by his thoughts, he opened the envelope the courier had given him.

John Fraser's company, Shadow Insurance Services, provided Leon with the majority of his assignments, but there was something unusual about this job. It was odd for the Americans to contract out to English companies. However, Leon knew better than to expect any further explanations. Fraser had worked for the Foreign Office and MI6 before branching out on his own, and his subsequent success was a result of connections in the shadier corridors of power.

Leon removed the papers from the envelope and looked at the insurance policy which covered Raphael Guttman against kidnap and ransom for two million sterling. He studied the passport-sized photograph and learned little about Guttman. He was sixty years old, had grey hair, a square face, and wasn't smiling. It was as if he had anticipated why the picture was being taken.

Important man, Guttman. The chairman of a pharmaceutical company made a good target. His salary would be around four million. Share options probably doubled it. Leon stared out of the window at the clouds below and tried visualising that kind of money, and shifted uncomfortably in his seat. His knee ached in the chill of the air-conditioning. He would have to stand up soon to ease the pain. He looked back at the pages in front of him and at Guttman's physical description. Height: 1.9 metres. Weight: 106 kilos. He was a big man who would take some handling if he didn't want to come quietly. Leon looked at the date on the file. It was two years old. He flipped the page and looked at Guttman's distinguishing features to flesh out the photo. Eight gold-crowned molars. Scar on the left knee from a cartilage operation. Another small scar, one centimetre long, over the left eyebrow. Nothing too personal there, but there'd soon be little that he didn't know about Guttman's private life.

Guttman's blood group and fingerprints were recorded near the bottom of the page in case the worst happened, but it was best to ignore that scenario. Finally, there were the code words 'Les pêcheurs de perles'. Leon wanted to hear that title before the ransom was paid. It identified the hostage as Guttman, a man who liked opera and for whom the pearl fishers obviously had a particular meaning. Those words would mean that he was still alive.

As he read the details, Leon's mind was working. The choice of a victim often gave clues as to the identity of the kidnapper. How and where the victim was abducted was significant. Kidnappers planned meticulously, sometimes waiting for a year before carrying out the abduction. They did their research. They made sure the target could pay. They didn't take pot luck, thumbing through *Who's Who* in search of some likely victim. Targets were chosen on practical grounds. They were invariably rich, accessible, available and convenient. Someone knew about Guttman's business interests, and knew he was going to be in Bilbao. Leon guessed it was ETA. Barely a month passed without the Basque separatist movement making some kind of statement.

The pain lanced up the femur from his knee. Leon jerked himself to his feet and plunged into the aisle. He limped up and down the aircraft trying to ease it before he grabbed a blanket from the overhead locker, wrapped it round his leg and sat down again. He closed his eyes, and dozed.

He woke as the aircraft hit an air pocket and encountered turbulence where an Atlantic low-pressure system met the high pressure of the Spanish mainland. He fastened his seat belt and looked down at the Cantabrian Mountains. He thought about Guttman's daughter, Karen, waiting for him in a hotel room. He wondered how she would be feeling. Frightened and insecure, he guessed, like the rest of them. Negotiations could take up to six months, and during that time the victim's family became emotionally disorientated. It wasn't unusual for a wife or daughter to try to clamber into his bed. He tactfully reminded them they might later regret it, and then had to assure them the rejection wasn't personal. Dealing with the emotional fallout was often the hardest part of his job.

2

Michel Ardanza opened the throttle of the Moto Guzzi on the Bilbao-to-Behobia highway as it descended into a valley before snaking up the side of a mountain again. The howl from the exhausts disappeared, and all Michel heard was the roar of wind. Buried beneath this road lay the farm where he had grown up. Sometimes, when he rode along this stretch, he felt he had died as a child and that he was riding over his own grave in some other incarnation. The farm had been compulsorily purchased by the Spanish government to make way for the highway when he was eleven, but his grandparents had only been tenants, so they'd received no compensation and were rehoused in a concrete apartment in Gernika.

Michel didn't remember his father, who'd been killed by Spanish troops when he was four years old. He had been a guerrilla who continued the fight against General Franco for sixteen years after the Civil War ended. Michel was conceived during one of his father's clandestine visits home, and the only picture he had of him was taken long before the war. It was hard to distinguish his father's features in the black-and-white photo. His mother died of cancer when he was eight, and he was brought up by his grandparents.

Michel turned off the highway and rode slowly through the countryside. Here, the trees and the rock face which he had known as a child were familiar, but any intimacy had disappeared. Things were different. Now he was an adult these mountains weren't so big. Pine trees had been planted where once there had been fields. He stopped the bike, turned off the engine and wandered into the woods.

He remembered lying on the forest floor with Theresa, staring up through the branches and leaves at the sky. That had been twenty years ago, but it seemed like yesterday. They fell in love with each other that day as the world spun round under the swirling clouds. Nothing was ever so sweet as that first love – or so bitter. It was still vivid, moments away, so close he felt he could almost call her name and she'd come running. He could walk four hundred metres down into the ravine and find the spot where they'd made love; but he felt no desire to revisit the place. He preferred the memory. He wondered how he could have let her slip away.

But Theresa had died a year ago, killed by a disease that attacked the nervous system, damaging the motor neurons which carried the signals between her brain and her body's muscles. At first the disease attacked her fine motor control, causing her to twitch uncontrollably, but within weeks she was seized by spasms. She became a grotesque parody of her former self. Her body and limbs were permanently contorted into abnormal positions. She slowly wasted away and the drugs didn't help. No sooner did she lose one set of muscles than another would fail. Within six months her speech was incomprehensible. She lost the ability to swallow, and in the end she couldn't breathe.

The doctors diagnosed motor neuron disease, although it was unusual in women and rarely progressed at such speed. They didn't know what had caused it, but thought it might have been a virus which lay dormant in her nerves before being triggered by some trauma. Her husband, Bernal, disagreed, and suspected it was the result of a faulty vaccine. He organised other families who'd lost relatives in similar circumstances and they took the manufacturers to court. They lost the case.

Michel stood up irritably. He hadn't come to terms with Theresa's death. He still felt anger and frustration that he'd been unable to do anything for her when she was ill. He started the bike and a few minutes later he was turning on to the dirt track that led to Bernal's *baserria*. The farmhouse faced south and had a shallow roof which curled slightly at the eaves. It needed painting. On either side the fields were untended; the road hadn't been maintained and the tiles on one of the outhouses had disappeared over the winter. The place had run to ruin during Theresa's illness, and now she was dead it felt abandoned.

The rear wheel skidded as Michel dropped into first gear and wove his way through the ruts up the side of the hill. He'd known Bernal for a quarter of a century, and if he owed a debt to anyone it was to him. Bernal had introduced him to politics and encouraged him to join EGI, the youth movement of the Basque Nationalist Party. If Bernal had been the *eragile*, the instigator, then Michel became the *ekintzaile*, the activist, ever mindful of his father's legacy.

Michel was seventeen when Txiki was executed by the government, and he still remembered the words Txiki wrote on the eve of his death. 'Tomorrow when I die, don't come to cry over me; I won't be beneath the ground. I am the wind of freedom.' When he heard those words Michel knew that his future was mapped out. It had seemed so romantic.

But that was a long time ago. Things had changed, and Theresa, who had inadvertently been responsible for it all, had gone for ever.

Michel parked the motorcycle in front of the farmhouse and removed his helmet. He opened the front door.

'*Kaixo*, Michel,' Bernal greeted him. Michel stood at the threshold and peered into the gloom.

'How are things, Bernal?' He ducked through the low doorway and went inside.

'They won't allow the appeal,' said Bernal.

Michel shrugged. 'I'm sorry,' he said. Theresa was dead and winning a court case wouldn't bring her back.

Bernal had a few days' growth on his chin. Michel joined him at the table. 'There was a cover-up,' said Bernal. 'We should have anticipated that Guttman-Tiche would fight dirty. They suppressed evidence.'

'I don't know enough about it,' said Michel.

'Exactly. People aren't told the truth about vaccines. They're brainwashed into believing they need them by the pharmaceutical companies. If the truth came out things would be different. Ninety-eight million polio vaccines were contaminated by a simian virus because they were grown on the kidney cells of infected monkeys. The virus was so similar to HIV that it was once suspected of starting the AIDS epidemic.'

Michel shrugged. He'd heard these arguments before. Bernal was clutching at straws.

'I can show you papers which substantiate what I'm saying. Even when it's uncontaminated, the polio vaccine is responsible for paralytic diseases, encephalitis, leukaemia and multiple sclerosis. How can Guttman-Tiche be so sure their vaccine wasn't flawed? They wouldn't allow us access to their records.'

'I'm sorry, Bernal. But no one wins against the multi-nationals.'

'Not in the courts, they don't,' Bernal said.

Michel wondered what he meant. He waited for an explanation, but none came.

'The pharmaceutical company bought off the judge anyway,' Bernal concluded.

Michel said nothing.

Bernal fiddled with a fork, scraping some grime from a crack in the table-top. 'You must have heard how people were picked up at night, given injections and released.'

'I heard that in the bar. Just rumours. Why would anyone do a thing like that?'

'Guttman-Tiche might.'

'Why?'

'To carry out experiments.'

'Don't be ridiculous, Bernal. No way that sort of thing happens. It's just another conspiracy theory.'

Bernal stood up. He changed the subject. 'Do you want something to eat?'

'Sure.'

'It's just soup.' Bernal took the saucepan off the stove and poured two bowls. He tore a piece of bread from a loaf, threw it in the air ceremoniously, caught it and dunked it in the soup.

'Still celebrating that victory,' Michel commented on Bernal's actions.

'Of course,' said Bernal defensively.

Michel nodded. 'I guess it's still worth remembering,' he said. They'd both been kids when ETA had blown Carrero Blanco's car forty metres into the air with an excess of high explosive, but vividly remembered the excitement it had caused.

'If we hadn't got rid of him we wouldn't have anything resembling democracy now.'

'It happened a long time ago,' said Michel dismissively. Blanco had been General Franco's intended heir. 'Time to move on, Bernal.'

Bernal didn't comment. He was preoccupied with other thoughts.

Michel looked around the room. Theresa had been proud of her home, but it felt empty and unloved without her. He remembered the argument when Theresa wanted to convert the stable into more rooms. Bernal refused. One day he'd have livestock again and the animals would live under the same roof and they'd become as one with nature. He believed that Basque ideology lay in its recognition of the past, and he wanted his *baserria* to symbolise that.

'What's on your mind?' Michel asked.

Bernal shook his head, ignoring the question. He stood up and pulled out a leg of ham from the meat safe and carved a few slices.

'How's business?' he asked. There was a hint of resentment in the question.

'The bars run themselves pretty well,' Michel answered. 'I'm concentrating on the theatre, trying to turn it into a cultural centre. We're putting on Basque plays. I want to use it as a springboard for a film company to sell programmes to the new television channel.'

'Still trying to win hearts and minds for the cause?' asked Bernal, disparagingly.

Michel smiled. He wasn't going to get drawn into a political argument. Bernal believed in propaganda by deed. He'd been a member of ETA's military wing until he was caught and sentenced to ten years. He was released in an amnesty and came home to a hero's welcome and retirement, but his face was known and he was off the active list. His complexion had never lost the pallor of incarceration. 'I provide an atmosphere where people can discuss politics and explore their culture,' explained Michel.

'Waste of time,' said Bernal. 'You're walking on thin ice. There are people who won't forget you betrayed them.'

'They're dinosaurs,' said Michel. 'And I didn't betray anyone. I turned my back on the violence because it wasn't working.' He'd never tell Bernal the real reason for his change of heart.

'If you refuse to participate then you lack personal commitment. That's all. No need to dress it up in fancy words. Institutional violence is all around us in the form of state repression, and any response to it, including pacifism, is violence,' said Bernal. 'Violence is the basis of social change. Always has been.'

'It depends whether you think educating the masses is more important than individual acts of violence.'

'You're forgetting the basic rule. Exit from the group is only possible through the cemetery.'

'I pay my dues.'

'Some people put in a good word for you as well.'

'I don't think it's escaped their notice that in the last ten years green politics have replaced red politics as the voice of rebellion.'

Bernal grunted. 'Don't talk to me about green politics. My whole philosophy is based on that. There's a big difference between speaking or imagining and the concrete deed.'

'You're fooling yourself, Bernal. All you're doing here is watching the seasons change. Once it had a meaning when there were crops. There was a time to plant and a time to harvest. Now it doesn't mean anything at all. The routines of the farm have gone. You watch the shape of the clouds and speculate on whether it will rain or not, but it doesn't mean anything because there isn't any hay to bring in from the fields.'

'The land is a living thing. It has cycles, rhythms and needs. I don't need television, films, theatres or bars.' Bernal fell silent for a moment or two, then added contemptuously, 'I can't believe I shared my first *ekintza* with you.'

Michel remembered the first symbolic action which proved they were sincere in their revolutionary zeal. They'd blown up a police car. It hadn't been particularly spectacular, but it had been a start. He wondered why Bernal was reminding him of the things that bonded them in the past when they were more surely bound by the memory of Theresa. 'You've earned your peace and quiet out here, Bernal. You did your bit for the cause. You've done your time.'

Bernal didn't respond.

'I had this idea on my way out here,' said Michel. Bernal needed to get involved with the real world. He had to stop mourning Theresa's death. 'I thought you could invite kids out to the farm. We could stock up on animals. We could tie it into one of the activities I'm running out of the theatre. What do you think?'

Bernal grunted. After a moment or two he said, 'I made a contact inside Guttman's pharmaceutical company during the court case. I'm not letting this thing drop.' The tone of his voice changed. 'I'm going to get even with them,' he declared.

Michel knew that Bernal was threatening violence. 'Don't even think about it,' he warned him.

They stared at each other.

'You've got a nerve saying that to me,' said Bernal.

'If anything happens to that company you're their first port of call. The husband of one of the victims. A man with a history. Think about it, Bernal.'

'No. You think about it, Michel. Think about Theresa, and then decide if your conscience rests easy.' He waited for Michel to answer. 'Theresa was young and healthy. She was given a vaccine against something they dubbed Pirineo influenza. She died as a result. I don't accept it was a coincidence.'

'I came out here to make you an offer. I'd like to have you on board. We could do something for the community together.'

'Forget it, Michel. You disappoint me these days. I don't want to be in partnership with you,' Bernal said, and stood up. 'All you're interested in is money but you dress it up with words,' he added as he disappeared upstairs. Their conversation was over.

Michel picked up his bike helmet wearily and made his way outside. This wasn't the first time he'd been rebuffed by Bernal and it wouldn't be the last. He'd keep trying to bring his friend in from the cold.

3

It was dusk when Leon Garrick left the airport. The taxi journey to the centre of Bilbao took fifteen minutes. The road skirted an industrial wasteland where steel cranes clawed at a darkening sky. Now and then he caught sight of the river between the buildings. The water was dark, rolling lugubriously against the banks. Its surface was a skin, slick with oil, lazily reflecting the city's lights and hinting at industrial pollution. Something, perhaps an arm or a piece of wood, broke the surface tension for a brief second. There were no ripples.

The city sprawled along the riverbanks, but to the north and south the hills seemed close, suggesting that this was no more than a small town set in a valley. He caught sight of a huge modern building and guessed it was some kind of shopping arcade. Finally the taxi crossed the river.

The Parc Hotel lay in the centre of the new town. It was hard to determine whether the hotel's façade was original or had been built to blend with the nineteenth-century architecture that surrounded it. A doorman in livery guarding the entrance sprang to open the door of Leon's taxi as it drew up, then took his suitcase and led him to the reception desk.

Leon followed the porter to his room and tipped as generously as he imagined the well-heeled guests did. He didn't want the staff wondering why he had chosen to stay there. The kidnapper might have an accomplice in the hotel monitoring Karen Guttman's movements. He noted that the tip didn't impress the porter, who'd obviously surmised from the cheap suitcase that this guest wasn't the genuine item.

Leon quickly surveyed the room. He looked out of the window at the plaza below. There was a floodlit pedestal in the middle, but no monument. He wondered whether the city council had removed a statue of Franco and was waiting to replace it with some more appropriate effigy. After a moment or two he picked up his briefcase, left the room and went downstairs to the bar.

He didn't hang about for long. The place was empty. He took the lift to the third floor and knocked on Karen Guttman's door. It opened, and a young woman with a round face and cheeks dappled with tiny freckles confronted him. She was tall, with boyish looks accentuated by short brown hair cut into a bob. Mid-twenties. He wondered if he had the wrong room. She looked too fresh. He'd expected a face taut with anxiety.

'Excuse me,' he said, 'I'm looking for Miss Guttman.'

She nodded. 'I'm Karen Guttman.'

'Leon Garrick,' he identified himself. 'I believe you're expecting me from London.'

Karen Guttman let him in. She was younger than the

expensive tailored clothes suggested. He caught sight of a Cartier wristwatch as she closed the door behind him.

'Thank you for coming so quickly, Mr Garrick,' she said with a nervous smile.

'I'm sorry I couldn't get here sooner,' replied Leon. 'Please call me Leon ...' He hesitated. '... or Len.' He extended his hand. She shook it perfunctorily. Maybe if they got to be good friends he'd let her call him Trotsky.

He took in the hotel suite, which was more impressive than his own. He caught sight of a silk nightdress and briefly imagined her in it. 'Have the kidnappers contacted you again?' he asked.

'No,' she replied. She sat on the edge of a chair. 'Please sit down.'

Leon sat on the sofa. 'Did you manage to record the initial demand from the kidnapper?' he asked.

Karen Guttman shrugged and gestured towards the telephone.

It was a foolish question. 'Can you tell me what he said?'

'It was a woman,' she replied.

'A woman?' repeated Leon, surprised. He didn't like the sound of that. Women were tough negotiators. They didn't lose sight of the objectives. The German police had learned that lesson: in armed confrontations they had standing orders to shoot the women first.

Karen nodded impatiently. 'I asked her who she was. She told me not to ask questions. She said my father had been kidnapped and she'd call again in twenty-four hours with further instructions. She told me to arrange for the equivalent of four billion pesetas in three different currencies: French, German and Spanish. She said they'd kill my father if I contacted the police.'

Leon shook his head. 'Not very pleasant,' he commented. 'But in my experience the bark is worse than the bite,' he tried to reassure her. 'How do you think she knew how to contact you?'

'They knew where to find my father,' she answered bluntly. 'He was staying in the room next door.'

Leon nodded. It had been another dumb question. 'What are you doing here in Bilbao?'

'My father donated a painting to the museum. I accompanied him for the official ceremony.'

'Who knew you were going to be here?'

'Everyone and no one. The event had been arranged for a long time. It was advertised.'

'How did your father disappear?'

'He left the museum to come back here and disappeared on the way. The driver of the car that the museum put at our disposal says he never turned up after his meeting at the museum.'

'What language did the kidnapper speak?'

'Spanish, at first. But I don't speak it well. Then she spoke English.'

'How was her English?'

'Good. It sounded like she'd been to school in America.'

'Sorry about all the questions,' said Leon. 'I need to get up to speed.' There were also some formalities which needed attention before he went much further. 'I am obliged to recommend you tell the authorities that your father has been kidnapped. However, I should warn you that the Spanish police are sensitive about kidnappings. Here, the laws don't allow ransoms to be paid. They reason that if we pay out it encourages other kidnappings. They take a hard line, which affects our negotiations.' He waited for her reaction.

'I'll leave the decisions to you,' she said.

'OK. I'll assume you don't want to contact the police. Consequently, it's important that your father's abduction remains secret. The police have extensive powers. They can freeze all your assets in Spain. They can also imprison me for acting as an intermediary. On one level that makes my job more difficult, but easier on another. The police won't help trace phone calls or provide access to their files. Our chances of finding where your father is being held, and by whom, are remote. However, we won't be under pressure from the police to set a trap for the kidnappers when they collect the ransom. The most dangerous part of these operations is when the ransom is collected. That's when the kidnappers are at their most wary and most volatile. Nevertheless, I anticipate a straightforward deal. I want to reduce the ransom demand and secure your father's freedom.'

'How long will it take?' asked Karen.

'If we're lucky it'll be over in six weeks. But it might be six months. Maybe more.'

'What?' she said in disbelief. 'My father's insured. Why should it take that long?'

'There's a lot of ground to cover. I have to establish the kidnapper really has your father. We need proof of that before we agree the ransom. If we concede too much, too early, the kidnapper may get greedy and want more money. Finally we have to arrange how the exchange will take place. It all takes time.'

Karen nodded, but she didn't look convinced.

'Do you have any other questions?' asked Garrick.

Karen shook her head.

'I'd like you to make a list of all the people your father employs in his household, detailing their references, ages and how long they've worked for him. I also need a list of any people who worked for him in the recent past and have been dismissed. If you've noticed anything odd over the past year, write it down. I'm interested in anything out of the ordinary.'

'I don't live with my father, you know.'

'Anything you tell me could be useful.'

'All right.'

'Have you told anybody else that your father's been kidnapped?'

'No.'

He detected the slightest hesitation. 'No family or friends?'

'No.'

'Good. The fewer people who know, the better. One of the nastier aspects of this business is getting false ransom demands. Sometimes the money gets paid to people who have nothing to do with the kidnap.'

'I understand,' she said.

Leon stood up. 'I doubt we'll hear anything until tomorrow. I'd suggest we dine together, but I think it's best you're not seen in my company for the moment. Someone may be watching you.'

Karen nodded.

'I need to attach some machinery to the telephone so I can record the kidnapper's demand,' he said.

'Go ahead,' she replied.

Leon examined the phone line. He opened his briefcase and took out some tools. He cut the line where it disappeared into the wall and inserted a jack so he could connect a recorder within seconds of the phone ringing. He doubted the chambermaids would notice his handiwork.

'Finished?' Karen asked.

Leon nodded.

Karen stood up and walked to the door. Leon watched her hips sway in the loose linen trousers. He always found women most attractive when they were vulnerable. It brought out the best in them. 'I'll see you in the morning,' she said.

As Leon walked downstairs he thought about the job. He was surprised that the kidnapper was a woman and looked forward to hearing her voice so he could form an opinion of his own. In a few days he and Karen would move out of the hotel and rent an apartment where he'd be able to set up his tracer equipment on the telephone. After making their demands for a couple of months the kidnappers would become lazy and start calling from the same telephones because they were convenient. As soon as that happened Leon would call London for help to stake out the phones. Then they'd find out who was holding Raphael Guttman.

He wondered what living with Karen would be like. She was out of his league, but the anticipation of being with her for a few months caused a frisson of excitement to ripple up his spine.

4

It was late afternoon when Michel Ardanza reached his theatre. The meeting with Bernal had unsettled him, and he was irritated by the suggestion that he'd done nothing for Theresa. He entered through the stage door and found that the children's play had finished and the kids were fooling around on the stage while their parents talked at the bar. He watched them for a few minutes and felt the accompanying pangs of guilt. However hard he tried, he'd never be able to atone for what had happened in the past.

He watched a six-year-old girl with pebble glasses cautiously climb the stairs to the stage. She turned and he recognised her. He looked around the room for her mother. Her father had been killed five years ago in Iparraldea, the Basque region of France. The Spanish paramilitaries who carried out the execution had been arrested but released by the French government. Sometimes, like now, Michel felt like taking up the cause again and seeking vengeance. It wouldn't be hard, but he had other plans. The little girl was now on the stage and suddenly timid at finding herself so high. He knew she was about to cry and he stepped forward to reassure her, then stopped as he caught sight of her mother calling out to her.

Michel looked around the rest of the room. He would always feel uncomfortable there. A wolf in sheep's clothing. He left.

It took three minutes to cross town. He parked the bike outside his bar and pushed his way through the crowd. It was busy for an early Sunday evening. He looked around and noticed a few unusual faces. There was a cluster of students. The politicos were huddled in a corner smoking furiously. There was tension in the air. Michel sat at the bar and waited for the manager to approach him. 'Everything OK?' he asked.

'The lunch-time session was busy. I've asked a couple of extra staff to come in tonight.'

'Why's that?'

'The police have been busy. A few people have been picked up.'

Michel shrugged. Whenever there was police activity it brought people into the bar in search of gossip. 'I'll have a coffee when you're ready.' The manager went to serve some new arrivals, then brought the coffee.

Michel looked around the room again and felt a sudden compassion for the people in it. It was disturbing to think that he had once believed that violence was the only way to effect change. He imagined their bodies being blown apart by some bomb and shuddered. It was strange how things turned out. He'd never thought he'd reach his thirties. He'd expected to go out in a hail of bullets ten years ago.

There was a time when his bar would have been turned over by the police because it was a known haunt of radical Basques and students, but things had changed and now the police left it alone. He had an agreement that they could frequent his other place, Café Deusto, by the river. It was the kind of place where they liked to hang out whether they were on or off duty. Michel barely went there these days. They'd filled it with tarts and the odour of corruption gave him the creeps.

Café Deusto had been his first venture, but when it opened the police monopolised it, driving away other customers with their presence. Michel started closing early to indicate they weren't welcome. In retaliation they stopped and searched his regular customers. What they wanted was a place of their own in a hostile city. Michel negotiated with them. They could use the place so long as it made money, and he'd open somewhere else on the condition they left it alone. The police were happy with the deal, and so was Michel. He put in a manager, and before long Café Deusto provided plenty of intelligence. The undercover cops used it as well as the odd informer, or *chivato*. They even gathered there before embarking on an operation, unintentionally advertising whether the operation was antiterrorist or otherwise.

Michel looked around Txistu and realised he was unconsciously waiting for someone. The girl came in on Sunday nights. She'd been doing so for the past few weeks. She sat alone, had a couple of drinks then left. A few of the locals tried talking to her, but she brushed them off. She aroused his curiosity. If she came in perhaps he'd take a turn behind the bar and see if he could start up a conversation.

His thoughts returned to Café Deusto again. Now he was no longer active in the movement and didn't need the intelligence, maybe it was time to turf the police out. The place had turned into a potential gold mine since the new Guggenheim Museum had been built. Once the tourists turned up it would be worth a fortune. If the museum projections were right, half a million annual visitors by the turn of the century meant there was a load of money to be made. He wondered how the police would react to being moved along. They wouldn't harass the foreign customers, but they'd retaliate. Michel wondered whether it was worth taking the risk, and whether he could stand up to an investigation. He'd been straight for over five years now. He also had to consider this place. Most nights of the week Txistu was so crowded that people spilled out on to the streets. It was a bar where only Basque was spoken and where politics were discussed openly. It would be too easy for the police to put a spanner in the works.

The Guggenheim development wasn't universally popular. Sooner or later it would be bombed. The building had been funded by local taxpayers, which meant that less money was available for health and education. It was run by an international institute which had promised that some provision would be made for Spanish art. When Gehry, the architect, had been specifically asked about Basque art, he had said dismissively, 'We're a world culture. We'd better get on with it.' He had made a big mistake saying that. The Basques weren't a world culture. They spoke one of the oldest languages on earth and were proud of it. There were cave paintings which were dated fourteen thousand years before Christ. They were the original inhabitants of Spain who had never been conquered, not even by the Visigoths, Charlemagne or Franco. They possessed the lowest frequency of blood-type B and the highest frequencies of types O and Rhesus negative of any population in Europe, and had retained that genetic characteristic in the face of later Rhesus positive migration waves. They had dominant genes, and there was scientific evidence of their racial purity, although Michel didn't much care for the argument.

The authorities should have thought about how strongly the Basques clung to their identity before trying to put Bilbao on the cultural map at the expense of the people who lived there.

Michel finished his coffee and ordered a brandy. He thought about Bernal. The mourning had taken place while Theresa was still alive. They'd all known she was going to die. The trouble was, Michel couldn't tell Bernal it was time to get on with his life because Bernal had always been resentful of his relationship with Theresa. They'd argued bitterly when Bernal wanted the doctor to perform a mercy killing.

'Only one thing's certain,' Michel had told him. 'Time will heal the pain you're feeling now. In two or three years you'll remember all this but forget how terrible it is. You'll forget all the intensity. You'll wonder what would have happened if you hadn't asked the doctor to kill Theresa. You'll still remember how much you loved her. You'll know she would have lived longer and regret the days you didn't have with her. Maybe you'll read that researchers have isolated some gene or other and think Theresa might have lived long enough to take advantage of the discovery. You'll doubt yourself. Then you'll start to destroy yourself because you killed someone you love. Just think about it.'

'You're living in a dream world,' retorted Bernal, turning to the doctor. 'What about it?' he asked.

The doctor refused, and as a result Bernal blamed Michel for Theresa's final agony.

Shortly afterwards Michel believed his intervention was justified when another doctor, baffled by the speed with which the disease was progressing, compared it to Gulf War Syndrome and made the connection with a vaccine against Pirineo influenza which Guttman-Tiche had rushed out four years previously. There had been hope of a breakthrough. But soldiers in America claimed that the vaccines they were given to protect them from biological and chemical weapons had interfered with their immune systems, and the hope died as suddenly as it had appeared. As a result Bernal attached blame to the vaccine.

'How could you let someone die like that?' Bernal accused Michel. 'You, of all people, who used to play God with other people's lives.'

Michel didn't have an answer.

A young couple came into the bar. Michel looked at his watch. It was late for the girl and he was disappointed. Suddenly he felt lonely and wished there was someone with whom he could share his life. He wondered who the girl was. Perhaps he had imagined it, but he was sure she had been watching him the previous week. It made him uneasy.

Chapter Two

I

Leon Garrick woke early. He took his time having breakfast in the hotel dining-room. He looked around, clocking the waiters, chambermaids and fellow guests. He went out, bought a newspaper and sat around in the foyer to get a feel for the hotel's rhythms. He was hoping he'd spot something unusual, but there was nothing out of the ordinary.

Finally, at ten, he made his way to Karen's suite, where he waited for the kidnappers to call. He took a couple of magazines and a book. He knew it might be a long wait. Not hours. Maybe days. He warned Karen that the kidnappers would take their time. They'd be checking to see if the police had been alerted. Kidnappers played a war of nerves, knowing that confused victims were easier to handle. A ticking clock made everyone nervous and concentrated their attention on the details.

Leon didn't tell Karen that sometimes the kidnappers didn't call until the deadline. There would be silence, then a final demand for the money without the opportunity for negotiations. It had happened with other hostages in South America. If the money wasn't ready and paid in full, then the hostage was killed. There was nothing anyone could do in a situation like that.

Leon hoped it wouldn't be like that, and there was no reason for it to be. Usually, negotiations were predictable. In the process he would endeavour to wrestle control of the situation from the kidnappers. He'd slow down the operation. He'd move out of the hotel to a clean telephone. He'd demand proof that Guttman was being held, and then ask for some evidence that he was still alive before agreeing to talk figures. He'd say he needed to refer to others before making decisions, and as the days passed the kidnappers would become desperate to end an operation that had become as much an ordeal for them as for their victim.

During the morning Karen and Leon talked, but their worlds were far apart and they found no common ground. She had an apartment in New York, but when she travelled she stayed in her father's houses in Paris, London and Geneva. She was an art dealer. Guttman also had a place in Manhattan and a ranch in Argentina. He had a private jet and a yacht in the Caribbean. The morning passed. The extent of Guttman's wealth began to disgust Leon. It wasn't exactly resentment but rather the feeling that he devoted his whole life to the defence of such riches, and it lowered his self-esteem. He was still paying off the mortgage on his two-bedroom flat. He felt a brief affinity with the kidnapper, but it was an unfamiliar and unpleasant sensation. He reminded himself that indirectly he was working for Guttman, and in these circumstances a grateful employer might turn into a generous one.

Karen obviously cared about her father, but she didn't let her emotions show. Leon knew she was angry about the situation, but she didn't have any idea how angry she would be when it was over. Experience had taught him that people were changed for ever by a kidnapping.

Now and again Karen made phone calls on her mobile, most of them rescheduling appointments with galleries. Listening to them told him more about her life than she'd revealed in conversation.

When the phone finally rang at 2.15 it was a relief. Leon let it ring three times before turning on the tape recorder and picking up the receiver. 'Hello,' he said.

'Who is this?' asked a woman aggressively. Her voice was

deep, and in other circumstances he would have described it as husky, even sexy. Good English, with an American twang.

'A friend of Karen Guttman.'

'I want to speak to Miss Guttman.'

'If it concerns Raphael Guttman, she asked me to make the arrangements on her behalf.'

'I talk to Miss Guttman. No one else. Make sure she answers the telephone next time.' The woman rang off.

Leon turned to Karen, who was staring out of the window. 'They'll only speak to you,' he said. 'I was afraid of that. Now remember what I told you earlier. Try to slow down the conversation. Tell her you need proof that she's holding your father. Ask for her name.'

'I know,' Karen said irritably.

Leon was surprised that she didn't seem nervous. He wasn't used to someone so young exuding such confidence.

The call came through half an hour later. 'Remember,' said Leon, 'to speak slowly. Take everything slowly.' He slipped the headphones over his ears and nodded at her. She picked up the receiver and he started the recording.

'Hello,' said Karen.

'You remember my conditions?' said the kidnapper.

'Yes.'

'No police.'

'I haven't told the police. The man you spoke . . .'

The woman interrupted. 'Have you arranged the money?'

'I'm trying. It isn't easy. Finding that much money means liquidating assets. That takes a lot of phone calls.'

Leon raised and lowered his palm slowly, indicating that she was speaking too fast. They needed to gain control of the situation, and controlling the pace was a key element. Success was based on acknowledging such tiny details.

'You have three more days,' the woman interrupted again.

'Are you in charge?' asked Karen.

'Yes.'

Leon smiled. That was good. They didn't want to agree something with one person only to find out later that someone else was in control and the boundaries were moving.

'What's your name?' asked Karen.

'My name is not important.'

A second passed. Leon nodded, and Karen continued. 'I must be able to identify you when you telephone.' It was a reasonable request. They didn't want to give the ransom to the wrong person. Within the dynamics of the conversation they had seized the initiative. Leon scribbled a note, prompting Karen, although they had rehearsed her lines earlier.

'Marisol,' snapped the woman.

'I'll be available at this number at seven every evening,' said Karen.

'You will be available all the time.'

'I'll wait from seven until eight each night.' Karen hesitated and then returned to the previous subject. 'The money may take considerably longer to organise.'

'That is your problem.'

'No,' said Karen. 'It's our problem. We're in this together. I'm only repeating ...'

'I will call you again,' interrupted Marisol. 'Have a nice day,' she said cruelly, and ended the call.

Leon smiled at Karen as she replaced the receiver. 'You did well,' he said.

She ignored the compliment.

Leon took the tape out of the recorder and replaced it with a fresh one. He transcribed the conversation to his portable computer, then set up the voice stress analyser and played the recording. The stress analyser claimed to detect lies from truth, working like a polygraph but without the need for pads to be attached to the subject. When a person lied the fear of detection caused uncontrollable reactions in physiological areas, and these were often transmitted in speech.

Every sentence in the transcript had a positive or negative

value. Leon knew that during that brief conversation there had been a false statement. The name the kidnapper gave was a lie. He marked the question and answer appropriately in the transcript. Over the course of the operation he would have Karen ask as many questions as possible, and by a process of elimination he would be able to gauge the kidnapper's responses. At some key moment it would be critical to know whether the woman was lying. One more telephone call and he could play the conversation through the stress analyser in real time, watching the needle fluctuate, and compose questions accordingly. British intelligence-gatherers were suspicious of polygraphs and stress analysers, but Leon thought they had their uses. The Americans used them extensively, and no one worked for the FBI or CIA without taking a polygraph test. He had to employ anything that gave him an edge.

'Why did she end the conversation so quickly?' asked Karen.

'She was making sure the call wasn't traced, but she spoke for longer than she meant. Unfortunately, my machinery can't trace a call routed through the hotel switchboard.'

'Why don't I ask to speak to my father?'

'You can, but she won't let you. Your father will be held some distance from the telephone she's using. They won't put him on the line in case he tells you something in code. Anyway, they won't move him into the open until they release him.'

Karen frowned. 'I don't understand why this is taking so much time. My father has insurance for this. Surely you give them the money and that's that?'

'Your father's only insured for two million pounds. Even so, that's far higher than any recent settlements. The days of five-million-dollar let alone twenty-million ransoms are over, except in exceptional circumstances. It takes careful negotiation to agree a figure. If we offer too much the kidnappers will want more. Both sides need to be happy with the figure. The kidnappers have put a lot of effort into their work, and think they need paying for it. If we offend them they might refuse to negotiate. They might decide to increase the stakes and—' He hesitated on the word mutilate and chose another. '—hurt their hostage.'

Karen winced. 'I see,' she said. 'They won't do that, will they?'

For the first time Leon saw Karen's confidence dented. 'I'm sorry if I sound heartless,' he said. He stretched out his hand and squeezed her fingers. There was no response. 'Those are the realities of the situation. Everything takes a long time because the kidnapper communicates only briefly and sporadically. Experience tells us that the longer the kidnapper talks, the less likely he is to kill. That's why we string things out a little.'

Karen nodded. 'So when do you expect her to call again?'

'I don't know,' said Leon. 'Right now she holds the cards. We have to persuade her to become more realistic.'

Karen thought for a moment. 'How do we do that?'

'Kidnappers demand more and expect less. It's psychological. The victim's family is always relieved to settle for a smaller amount. That's why the initial figure is so high. In this case I'd be unwilling to pay more than ten per cent.'

'That's a million pounds. We can pay it now.'

'We have to convince the kidnapper it's the most we're willing to pay. Offer a million and she'll demand four million. We have to play it by ear. We'll arrange the ransom once a figure is agreed with the kidnapper. We'll probably bring the money into the country by road because it's more discreet that way. We don't want the Spanish authorities to confiscate it because you're not insured against that.'

Karen nodded.

Leon stood up. 'I think I'll take a break now. We won't hear anything until tomorrow.'

'This is going to work out OK, isn't it?' Karen asked suddenly.

'Yes,' said Garrick, realising that he now had all the power in their brief relationship. He wondered what he'd do when she threw herself at him. He was glad she hadn't panicked and tried to involve the FBI, the State Department and the Spanish police, because in those circumstances a hostage usually turned into a corpse a couple of months down the road.

2

Inspector Antonio Suarez of the Guardia Civil was tall and thin. Although he looked young, his dark hair was flecked with grey, betraying the fact that he was forty-seven years old. If he had been a doctor and not a policeman people would have thought he looked kind and gentle. Instead, he reminded his enemies of an insect, perhaps a cockroach. He knew he had enemies, and they included most Basques, who hated him on principle, as well as the policemen in Bilbao, because he was not what they expected.

Suarez came from Madrid, but had been sent to Bilbao and attached to the antiterrorist division. It wasn't a popular posting, and he'd received a number of death threats which he dismissed as an occupational hazard. He suspected some of the threats emanated from right-wing members of his own force who thought he was too liberal. Most policemen serving in the Basque regions were automatically given financial inducements. Despite this, they soon requested transfers to other regions because they caught what was known as the 'Northern Syndrome'. The men were unpopular in the streets, and their families couldn't integrate because they were shunned. After a few years the paranoia got to them, and they reacted irrationally to the slightest provocation. As a result, the police reputation was bad, and the suicide rate was high, which suited the locals. The police relieved their frustrations by torturing political prisoners in custody or using excessive force during demonstrations.

The Minister of the Interior, Agustín Hernando, had

informally suggested Suarez took the job while congratulating him on an investigation into organised crime. There was some talk of promotion. Suarez didn't remember showing much interest, let alone enthusiasm, and promptly forgot about the conversation until he received an official letter four months later. Agustín Hernando had the decency to telephone him and wish him well before he left, and to tell him he had complete operational freedom. 'All you have to do is call me. I want to know what's going on up there, Inspector Suarez. I hear rumours, but nothing concrete.' Since then Agustín Hernando had forgotten about him.

Suarez had never sought controversy, and he hadn't objected vociferously when he was appointed. He now realised it was a mistake. He had colleagues who were better suited to life in Bilbao, who approved of torture or covert killings under certain circumstances. He was an anomaly and considered as such by those on both sides of the fence. They were all waiting to see how things would turn out for him in Bilbao. He'd been there for almost two years and there was little hope of a reprieve on the horizon. If he was good at his job he stayed there; if he wasn't there was no one to replace him. His only hope was to get up someone's nose, cause a complaint and get transferred.

Suarez opened the door to the large cloakroom attached to his office. He removed his uniform and changed into a leather jacket and pair of dark cotton trousers. He left the office and told the front desk he was going home. He stood for a moment, peering past the armed guards at the entrance to the street, then retreated back into the building.

The two policemen at the rear entrance of the police station snapped to attention as he emerged, and alerted anyone who was watching to the presence of a senior officer and potential target. Suarez nodded at them irritably and went to meet the manager of the Parc Hotel who'd requested a word with him.

Outside the hotel he dodged some barricades which builders had placed for the inconvenience of pedestrians and wondered what was being erected in the square. Everywhere he looked these days something new was springing up. On the surface Bilbao was being transformed into a modern city to hide the previous grey atmosphere of a neglected industrial wasteland. A new Metro system, a new museum and new hotels to cater for the tourists didn't exactly change things. Industry had been hit by the recession, and the government's solution was to turn the place into a service city, which meant hundreds of unemployed workers and trouble on the streets. It was pointless trying to attract tourists if they were going to be confronted by beggars on every corner.

Suarez turned into the hotel. Little expense had been spared doing up the place. Plenty of marble, leather and wood. The walls were covered with local tiles to give it that authentic feel, and the management were keen to co-operate with the police because they wanted to keep it intact. A nice place like that, built with money from Madrid, made a good target. Felipe, the manager, had even offered him a room with a view for free if he had someone to share it for an afternoon.

In the bar Suarez recognised a few people from the newspapers and election campaigns, but he didn't spot any villains from his files. He ordered a beer and told the barman to tell Felipe he was there. He liked hanging out at the hotel. It was a change from the seedy depravity that dominated his usual investigations. Here he breathed the same air as the jet-setters who came to look at the pictures in the Guggenheim for an afternoon. Felipe told him if there was anyone of interest in town, and in return he vetted the employees. As far as he knew not a single teaspoon had gone missing from the hotel.

Felipe joined Suarez a few minutes later and suggested moving to a more discreet table. Suarez shrugged and followed, catching the sickly aroma of sweet cologne in Felipe's wake.

'There's something strange going on in my hotel,' said Felipe.

Suarez raised his eyebrows.

'One of my guests, a man called Guttman, seems to have disappeared. He booked in for three nights with his daughter. No one's seen him since the first night . . .' Felipe hesitated.

'Could be any number of reasons for that,' observed Suarez.

'Now his daughter's booked the room for another two weeks.'

Suarez finished his drink impatiently. Felipe fancied himself as a detective. He claimed to be a great judge of character.

'For the first two days there were phone calls for Señor Guttman from people who were expecting him. His daughter told me to tell these people that he wasn't well. The man wasn't in the hospital. I checked.'

'Have you spoken to his daughter?'

'It's not the sort of thing you do. She's holed up in her room.'

'Is her father paying the bill?'

'Of course.'

'So what's the problem? We had a drug dealer in Madrid who rented a hotel room for a year and never turned up.' Suarez let slip these sort of details to spice up Felipe's life.

'What? Never?'

'Just once or twice.'

'Good hotel?'

'The best.'

That silenced Felipe for a moment or two. 'But this is my hotel and I know there's something wrong.'

'So what's going on?' asked Suarez.

'A couple of days after he disappeared, an Englishman turned up. Señor Garrick. He took a room, but he's been seen by the staff in Guttman's suite with the daughter.'

'Might be interesting,' remarked Suarez, wondering whether to ask Felipe if he'd personally inspected the sheets for stains. 'Write the name down for me,' he said.

Felipe took out a gold-plated pen and carefully wrote the

name on the back of his card. He passed it across the table. Suarez shoved it into his pocket.

'I can smell when something's wrong,' said Felipe.

'I don't doubt it,' agreed Suarez.

'What are you going to do?'

'Wait,' said Suarez. 'I don't chase up everything I hear. You know how it is around here. Someone only has to fart and people smell shit.'

Felipe looked disappointed.

'I'll send the boys to put a few bugs in the switchboard,' said Suarez. 'Anything else?'

Felipe shook his head.

'Thanks for letting me know about it.' Suarez stood up. 'If anything else happens, tell me.'

'Of course.'

As Suarez walked back to his apartment in the old town he thought about Guttman. He was more concerned about the situation than he had let on to Felipe. Everyone who read the local papers knew about Guttman now, although he'd been relatively unknown three or four years ago, before the court case. It was strange how people who were suddenly projected into the public eye could make enemies. As the court case had progressed, the press had grown increasingly hostile. The consensus of opinion was that Guttman-Tiche's products had been responsible for some side effects in those who'd been vaccinated. Guttman was portrayed as a ruthless businessman who obtained European Union grants to establish a pharmaceutical factory on the Nervion, but far from contributing to the community he repatriated all the profits. A few articles that attempted to portray him in a better light were criticised. He might have made substantial donations to the Guggenheim, but the museum had been built with taxpayers' money and was of no benefit to them.

The obvious explanation was that Guttman had been kidnapped. It figured. ETA had been busy picking up local politicians. They were obviously hoping that Madrid would enter into talks in the same way London had with the IRA. But for Guttman's sake he hoped ETA wasn't responsible because it meant he would probably be killed. Terrorists didn't like giving up hostages. A dead body was always more dramatic.

The Basques were a hard people. They had no compassion for outsiders. They had a stockade mentality. In some ways they behaved as if they were still in the Iron Age, painting pictures on cave walls, hoeing their fields and pretending they were a simple people wanting to be left alone to pursue their simple life. Their culture was held together by the myths. Myths and history were different. Myth was the more powerful and lent itself to a people's character. Myths were dangerous. What was it that the ETA guerrillas said? 'Either you are for us or you are against us.' They also said that a people who struggled were sure of victory, which showed a blatant disregard for history.

Suarez looked across the river and saw the national flag stretched taut by a wind which whistled in from the Cantabrian Sea. Yellow and red. The colours for sand and blood. Perhaps it was the whole of Spain, not just the Basques, the *vascos*, who lacked compassion. There was little room left in the Spanish heart for humanity. During the Civil War brothers had fought against each other in an ideological struggle. When the members of one family killed each other, then it was hard for them to summon up compassion for society or humanity as a whole.

ETA, Euskad ta Askatasurra, the Basque Homeland and Freedom Party, had been going for forty-odd years, and the Spanish flag was still flying. It was time for them to give up. Franco might have banned their language and culture in reprisal for Basque Republican support during the Civil War, but they'd got that back now. They couldn't live in the past for ever. Even the French, who'd tolerated the presence of their leaders because of Franco's Fascism, had sent them packing. But terrorists who adopted such catch-phrases as 'Actions unite, words divide' weren't interested in negotiation.

There was a Basque Nationalist government in the provinces as well as a Basque opposition party. There were free elections. That was democracy. They even had their own police force, the Ertzainta, which had been accused of committing atrocities. Whatever they got they always wanted something else. Now they were demanding that their members in jails throughout Spain be moved back home so their wives and children could visit them. They didn't think about the families who couldn't visit the relatives who'd been blown to bits by the same fucking terrorists.

Suarez slipped into a bar for something stronger than a beer. Maybe he was looking on the bleak side. Maybe Guttman had been taken by GRAPO, a spin-off from the First of October group formed by the collapse of the Red Brigades. It was hard to know whether they were socialist or anarchist. Kids fighting society in retaliation for the abuses they thought their parents had inflicted on them. At least they weren't Basques. He fancied a simple case like that, without politics and demonstrations when he arrested some suspect.

Maybe Guttman was fed up with his life and had disappeared with some young woman for a holiday. Maybe this was the job that could get him out of Bilbao and back to civilisation. Maybe, if he asked the wrong questions, Guttman would complain and have him posted back to Madrid. He could only hope.

Suarez was tired of the job, tired of visiting the mayhem of bombings, tired of examining mutilated bodies, and tired of murder. He'd caught a touch of the 'Northern Syndrome' himself. He knocked back his brandy and thought about his wife in Madrid who refused to join him there. They barely saw each other now. They'd agreed on La Coruña for the holidays again. The sea air would be good for the kids, and the Atlantic coast was cooler than the Mediterranean. In the meantime he had to make do with telephone conversations which, come to think of it, had been getting shorter and shorter.

Suarez ordered another brandy and stared at the football match on the television which dominated the bar and let the commentator's voice drown out his thoughts.

3

Michel sat with a bottle of wine, staring out of the window into the night and thinking about Theresa. When he thought about her the years rolled back. He remembered the softness of her skin. He remembered the freshness of her mouth and her lithe limbs wrapped around his body. He remembered how she gave herself to him, telling him that it was the first time. He was gentle with her, and loved how she trusted him.

As Michel became more involved in the movement he knew that relationships would make him vulnerable. Relationships were dangerous because the police or others could manipulate him through his emotional attachments. In the early days the *etarras* were constantly compromised when their girlfriends or wives were arrested for being accessories to ETA actions. He knew it wouldn't be fair to expose Theresa to that kind of danger. He couldn't bear the thought of her being raped by some policeman in a prison cell because of her involvement with him.

Bernal was a commando until his arrest, but Michel moved up to become a *liberato*, a salaried organiser dedicated to the movement. He represented ETA at the International Congress in Frankfurt where he met the PLO, the IRA and the Red Brigades, and as a result was responsible for the later co-operation of various revolutionary groups in their anti-imperialist actions against NATO and American military bases.

Shortly afterwards he explained to Theresa that he was ending their relationship because it was too dangerous for it to continue. He told her about his activities, things he shouldn't have told anyone, but he felt he owed it to her, and he was sure she would understand. In those days he used to feel that actions didn't have any meaning unless he told someone about them, but he soon grew out of that.

After his confession Theresa said, 'I don't believe you.'

He was shocked. He imagined she thought he was spinning her a lie. He began to justify himself.

She interrupted. 'I don't want to believe you.'

'Why not?' he asked.

'Because if it's true you should never have told me. You should take more care with the movement's secrets. Their success depends on that.'

That had been the end of the relationship. He never gave her the option of playing her part. Now, when he thought back over the conversation, Michel wondered if she had implied that she was willing to accept the risks.

Theresa married Bernal soon after his amnesty. At the time Michel was hurt by their marriage. However, she never told Bernal what Michel had told her. Theresa was always dependable with his secrets. Tight as a drum. And the secrets held the two of them together.

When Michel retired he wondered if he and Theresa would start an affair, taking off, as it were, where they had left off. There was an unspoken understanding that their love had never been fully satisfied, but neither of them had brought up the subject.

Michel put down the empty bottle of wine. Enough of memories. He stood up and pulled off his clothes. He lay on the bed and wondered why he had never asked her if she was truly happy with Bernal. Although they had been together for ten years he knew more about her than Bernal did. They'd gone to school together at the *Iskatola*, the unofficial schools where they were taught Basque at classes held in the back rooms of bakeries and factories when the language was still banned. She'd been the one constant in his life, but now she was dead and he would never know if he'd meant as much to her as she did to him.

He imagined Theresa stepping out of her clothes. He

remembered how she used to turn her body away modestly to remove her underwear. He almost felt the bedclothes move as she slipped into the bed. For the past ten years he'd been living with a secret past and wished there was someone with whom he could share it. It was a lonely business being on the wrong side of the law.

4

It was noon when Antonio Suarez finally reached his office. He'd spent the morning checking out the death of Luzio Arrate, one of the ETA old school, active before the movement divided itself into political and military wings. Arrate had returned from exile in the French Basque provinces some years before, crippled by a car crash, and lived out in the country writing the odd article for *Deia* or *Egin*, the Basque newspapers.

Suarez took a cursory look at the body and noticed bruises on the arms which suggested Arrate had been strapped to his wheelchair at the time of death. He didn't feel much sympathy, though. Arrate had been responsible for a few murders in his day. Another terrorist was permanently off the register.

'What do you want me to write down?' asked the police doctor. 'Death caused by a massive stroke when the wheelchair tumbled down the stairs?'

'No,' said Suarez. 'We'll take a closer look at this one.' The police doctor raised his eyebrows. 'Seal off the house and call in forensics,' ordered Suarez. Under normal circumstances he'd have taken the easy option and done as the doctor suggested. He'd have made a mental note that Arrate's death was probably the result of some internal ETA power struggle and that would have been the end of it.

However, Arrate's death was part of a pattern. During the past few days a number of ETA sympathisers had come to Suarez's attention. A couple had even been reported missing by their families, which was unusual considering local antipathy to the authorities. He was hoping this wasn't the first in a series of murders.

'Who do you think was responsible for Arrate's death?' Suarez asked his driver on the way back to town.

'Looks like GAL.'

'Huh?' responded Suarez, taken aback. Grupos Antiterroristas de Liberación had been set up fifteen years ago and was run by a former chief of police in Bilbao. It was funded by the Ministry of the Interior, and composed of mercenaries to target ETA militants hiding out in the French-owned Basque regions. Responsibility for their actions was denied at all levels.

The driver didn't elaborate.

'GAL doesn't exist any more,' Suarez said emphatically, leaning forward. When the French right-wing government came to power in 1986 there was no further need for GAL because the French police agreed to hand back all known militants.

'The organisation might not, sir, but some of the people are still around.'

'That's true,' said Suarez. There had been assassinations until the last few years, but no one had been brought to justice for them, which was a sure sign of the government's involvement.

Suarez thought about it. The government had paid GAL to do their dirty work but when things started going wrong they slammed a couple of its members in jail. Five years ago shit hit the fan and it landed on González's government. The Ministry of the Interior was found to be paying a couple of GAL mercenaries while they were in prison. The men were accused of killing twenty-seven members of ETA, and civil libertarians didn't like the idea of convicted murderers sending out for whores and dinners. The scandal helped bring down González's government.

'Are you telling me that GAL are back in business?' Suarez asked.

'Between you and me, sir?' asked the driver cautiously.

'Of course.'

'Someone's been trying to put them back together.'

'Any names?'

'Just rumours, sir. You know the kind of thing. If you're interested make it known and you'll be contacted.'

'I asked for names,' insisted Suarez.

'I don't know.'

'Thanks,' said Suarez, and leaned back in his seat. Things were taking a nasty turn if GAL were back in action. They wouldn't have any trouble finding recruits in the police barracks. The problem would be uncovering their agenda. He'd make a few calls to Madrid and ask some questions. That would remind Agustín Hernando of his existence.

Suarez congratulated himself for choosing the driver, who had become his eyes and ears in the department. At the initial interview the man had apologised for his weight. 'I wasn't always fat like this,' he said. 'I had an accident and then my metabolism changed.'

Suarez was so taken aback by the excuse that he appointed him immediately. However, he soon discovered that the man was just plain greedy. Sometimes he was tempted to make him walk to lose some weight.

Back at police headquarters, Suarez immediately arranged for the telephone taps to be installed in the Parc Hotel. He then decided to inspect the subterranean cells to see and speak to the detainees. If the police were involved in some kind of purge it would include the rounding up of suspects.

When he first discovered that the practice of beating prisoners was a matter of course he included the details in his reports to Agustín Hernando. There were few things he found more disagreeable than people deprived of their dignity. Unfortunately, Hernando didn't reply and there was no inquiry. It also became clear that Hernando had no intention of honouring the promise of operational freedom. News of the report was leaked back to Bilbao, which consequently made Suarez unpopular among the men. Sometimes Suarez wondered if Hernando had sent him north to prevent him from stumbling on some scam that he was involved in back in Madrid. The investigation into organised crime had embarrassed a few officials in charge of public works.

Suarez steeled himself for a journey into the cells.

5

Arnault Lafitte made his way down to the copse four hundred metres from the farmhouse to relieve the Spaniard who'd been watching it for the past six hours. He smelled the cigarette smoke before he saw the man and wondered why the Hispanic races were addicted to tobacco. Maybe it was a death wish. He got up close, clamped his hand over the Spaniard's mouth and put a knife to his throat. 'You could be dead,' he whispered. He docked him the day's pay and dismissed him.

Lafitte didn't smoke or drink alcohol and was strictly vegetarian. He didn't believe in a sixth sense. If someone turned around seconds before being greased it was because they smelled something. They smelled cigarette smoke, washing powder in clothes or soap on skin. In a life-or-death situation, scent was a factor. Scent told a story. Even kissing a girl left traces of perfume. Sex. He could smell sex a mile off. He didn't take chances with his life. Cigarettes. He'd shot a couple of bad guys out in El Salvador, waiting for their smokes to glow in the dark when they took a drag before squeezing the trigger. Cigarettes were a killer whatever people did with them.

Lafitte buried the cigarette butts and chose another vantage point. When he got back that night he'd lay down some rules for the team. No smoking on duty. If any of them were picked up, that was the end of the operation. This was enemy territory out here. The peasants knew the countryside like the back of their hands, and nothing escaped their notice.

He focused his binoculars on the farmhouse. It was little more than a ruin. These people were living in the Dark Ages.

However, he was encouraged by the evidence of activity. He wished he could get closer so he could note the number plate of the motorcycle, but there was no cover and he didn't want to take risks. He had an inkling that this was the place he was looking for. Intelligence suggested that Bernal Lasturra would be at the centre of things, but if not then he'd have a good idea of who was. Maybe Guttman was being held in that hovel.

Ever since the liberals had tried to associate the last Prime Minister, Felipe González, with the discovery of a few Basques in a limepit, things had been easy for ETA. Now the liberals had a conservative government for their efforts, and it served them right. Trouble was, when the heat was off ETA, the intelligence stopped flowing. Everyone lost sight of the sympathisers and the suspects. Addresses changed. The players changed. It took time to catch up with them again. But Lasturra stood out like a sore thumb from the bunch of suspects. There were a couple of other suspects – correction, had been a couple of others – until Arrate checked out in the middle of a lively discussion the previous night.

It hadn't taken Lafitte long to find that key members of his old team were still around when he got word from Colonel Jackson in Washington that Guttman had gone missing. He wasn't surprised to find they were eager for another crack at the Basques. It was better paid than minding consignments of smuggled cigarettes or dope coming into Galicia.

Bernal Lasturra had been an ETA activist ten years ago. He'd been locked up in prison until the liberals granted him an amnesty. He disappeared from view until the court case against Raphael Guttman, when it turned out that he was one of the instigators.

Lafitte wondered why Guttman was so important, but he knew better than to ask. His reputation was based on discretion. The news that Guttman had been snatched hadn't hit the papers, which meant that whoever was running this show had plenty of influence.

At dusk Lafitte took out a mobile phone and made a call. It was time to get to know Bernal intimately.

Chapter Three

I

Bernal woke in the early hours. He listened. Something was wrong. He thought he heard a footstep outside the window. Then the night closed in again. He'd been mistaken. The silence rang in his ears.

He'd left the Kalashnikov downstairs. Now he couldn't sleep. He swung his legs out of bed. He wanted the gun next to him. Last night he'd pulled it out of its hiding place and assembled it. He had a feeling that things were coming to a head. Although he hadn't looked at it for over a year, it was still in perfect condition. Its loose mechanical tolerances made it reliable, and that was what made it so good. It was a gun for the people. It was the revolutionary's favourite weapon, which was why America thought that every insurrection was communist-backed. Modern weapons might fire more quickly and be more accurate, but they had more moving parts to go wrong. In this game there were no second chances.

Bernal heard voices whispering outside and knew they were coming for him. He jumped off the bed, ran down the stairs and snatched the gun from the cupboard. He swung it towards the door as it burst open. The flashlight blinded him as he pulled the trigger. The sound of gunfire was deafening in the kitchen. He knew he'd hit one of them from the scream, but then they were on top of him. He was slammed against the wall, handcuffed and bundled out of the house to a car. He fought back, but his head was smashed against the door frame and he was crammed between two men. A hood was pulled over his head and his head was forced between his knees. The car skidded away, sliding on the dirt road, before reaching the asphalt.

Bernal prepared himself for torture. He'd been through this before, years ago. He couldn't expect any mercy from these people. They weren't wearing uniforms, but he knew they were operating with the knowledge of the authorities. The last time, he'd been taken to Madrid and tortured in the Dirección General de Seguridad on the Puerta del Sol. His skin crawled, and his stomach heaved at the thought of what was about to happen.

His past had come back to haunt him. His only hope was that Michel would hear what had happened and instruct a lawyer to make enquiries. The police would deny they were holding him but a lawyer could make things difficult for them. Under the antiterrorist laws they could hold him for nine days incommunicado. They'd have their way with him but Michel was his insurance policy. If people asked questions there was less chance of his disappearing permanently.

Bernal prepared himself to pace his resistance. He needed to keep his strength in reserve. He wondered if he'd be able to avoid naming those who'd retired or who sympathised but were innocent. He'd gone through this the last time he was arrested. He didn't break that time, and he wasn't any weaker. Although he was acting alone he reminded himself that he was still part of a larger organisation, a community that would support him to the end. Yet again he was about to become a victim of state violence, as he had always been, as his family had been, as his people had been.

He knew they'd reached Bilbao from the length of the journey. The process of disorientation began as soon as the car stopped. The men pulled him out feet first, and his head hit the ground. He was dragged up steps and into a building. A door slammed. He was hauled up another flight of stairs.

For a few moments he lay on a wooden floor and listened to the footsteps echoing as furniture was moved. This wasn't the police station on Calle de Gordoniz, and it confirmed he had been taken by GAL.

'Stand up!' ordered one of the men.

Bernal tried. It was impossible. His hands were tied behind his back. He couldn't see. He was kicked and fell on to the sharp corner of a table. He was jerked to his feet. He didn't regret a single one of his previous actions. Not now. This was the enemy. There was no place for guilt in revolutionary violence. It was necessary for the struggle. Bernal remembered executing the police informer, the *chivato*, Juan. Responsibility for violence lay with the movement. His responsibility was to his friends. The enemy – the soldiers and policemen in this room – felt no guilt either, because they were acting for the state. Their actions were condoned by the Ministry of the Interior, which was still paying the wages of two assassins in prison who'd been found guilty of murdering his fellow commandos.

'Fuck you!' he shouted.

He heard laughter. Then he was punched. He stumbled and fell. There was no escape. He felt blood creeping down his chest. There was an explosion at the back of his head and he sank into unconsciousness.

Bernal woke, confused at first, but remembered where he was after a moment. He had no idea how long he'd been out. Water was drowning him. He spluttered, betraying his consciousness. He was rolled on to his back and hoisted by his feet.

There was no disgrace in breaking under torture. No one was expected to withstand it.

'Who are you associates?'

Bernal tried to think of names. He felt a boot pushing down on his spine. His vertebrae cracked. He screamed.

'We want names. We want to know about your operations. We want to know where you're hiding the hostage. Tell us and we'll let you go.'

Bernal tried to think. There were too many questions. Too many answers. He didn't know where to start. He searched for the half-truths.

'You think you're tough. Well, think about this. How many of your friends have died under interrogation? Not many, huh? Do you know why?'

Bernal didn't answer.

'Come on!'

The pain was bearable when he only had to listen to words. 'Article twenty-five . . .'

'Speak up.'

'Article twenty-five of the Spanish Constitution stipulates that no one will be subjected to torture.'

Someone laughed.

'That's the wrong answer. I'm the answer. I'm the reason. My job is to take you to the point of death. It's a delicate procedure. I have to keep you conscious and alive. One wrong move and you escape into the peace of death.' The man was speaking slowly. 'In the end you'll beg me to kill you but I won't give you that pleasure, because I take a pride in my profession. It's one of the oldest. There was a time when the torturer was killed if his victim died. Believe me, it takes skill and patience to break every bone in a body and keep a man talking.'

The man stopped speaking. For a moment it sounded as if he were coughing. Then he continued. 'Do you know how many bones there are in your body?'

Bernal realised the man had been laughing.

He felt the fingers of his left hand being prised apart and his index finger was clamped in a vice.

'There are two hundred and six. Let's say that this metacarpal is the first bone.'

The finger snapped. Bernal screamed.

'Now you have two hundred and seven separate bones.'

Waves of pain shuddered up Bernal's arm.

'Or should I say two hundred and five left intact. It's easier to count down.' He paused. 'Tell me where you're holding Señor Guttman.'

Bernal didn't answer. Something was wrong. Last time they'd been careful not to leave marks on his body.

'Then we'll try another time.'

Bernal felt the vice grip another of his fingers.

Arnault Lafitte looked down at Bernal's writhing body with some pleasure. He was exacting retribution of a sort for the member of the team who'd been shot earlier. He knew that Bernal would talk. It was only a matter of time.

2

Leon Garrick was woken by a cramp in his leg. He glanced at his watch then got out of bed. He drew the curtains and looked at the dawn. It would be a few hours before the kidnappers called. Criminals were seldom early risers. They waited until the streets were busy before making their demands from public telephones. He'd soon have them conducting their business at the same time every evening. When they all settled down to a routine things would be better. Hanging around like this got on his nerves. He dressed quickly and went downstairs. A brisk walk would put some life back into his leg.

When Leon returned he ordered breakfast in his room, then called London. It was six in England, and the voice that greeted him tried hard to sound alert but was betrayed by the slur of its speech.

'Did I wake you?' he asked.

'I was just getting up,' replied Fraser quickly. Men at the top didn't like to be caught sleeping. 'How are things at your end?'

'Business as usual. I've opened negotiations. The managing director is a woman.'

'Don't sound so surprised. Equal opportunities apply to all professions,' said Fraser. He'd woken up.

'What's the strategy?'

'The paperwork will be dispatched but we need a final figure. Make it clear we'll meet the taxman's deadline.' Fraser indicated that they were prepared to accept the kidnappers' agenda. The paperwork referred to the ransom.

'Has the accountant been through the figures?' asked Leon. He wanted to know if the banknotes were ready for shipping.

'Yes. But he'd like a phone number. He thinks he's got a crossed line.' Fraser was concerned about the size of the ransom demand. 'Check it and let him know. Nevertheless, we're still acting on the taxman's initial estimate.'

'OK,' said Leon, with little enthusiasm. He didn't like the idea of a quick payment, but at least Fraser was concerned about the size of the ransom and was allowing him to negotiate. In his experience, kidnappers treated a quick settlement as a down payment, reneged on any agreement and held out for a further sum.

'Call me when you've arranged a meeting with their managing director,' said Fraser, and hung up.

Leon sat on the edge of the bed. This was turning out to be more interesting than usual. If someone was prepared to stump up that kind of money, no questions asked, there was more to Guttman than met the eye. He was disappointed with his instructions, though. He was on a daily rate and a quick settlement wasn't in his interests.

There was a knock on the door. He opened it, and admitted the maid with his breakfast. She placed it on the table by the window. He studied her carefully, but she didn't look the type to be involved in a kidnap. Years of service had made her invisible. She left the room.

Leon ate his breakfast quickly, then went to Karen's suite. She acknowledged his arrival with a grunt. There were dark rings under her eyes. The strain was taking its toll.

'How did you sleep?' he asked.

'OK.'

'Maybe you should get out into the city for a while. Try to relax and take your mind off things.'

Karen looked at him with disdain. 'Get real,' she said.

'Don't let them get to you,' said Leon. 'Not yet. Not this early. It's far from over. You have to pace yourself.'

Karen ignored him.

'We're going to take control now. We told them we'd be here at seven in the evenings. So we'll keep to that.' Leon waited for some response, but there wasn't one. 'We're going to agree to their deadline.'

Karen snapped. 'I didn't know there was any question of that.'

The telephone rang. Their eyes met. Leon shook his head. The telephone rang a second time. Karen's eyes didn't flinch. Leon shook his head a second time. Karen reached down and picked up the receiver.

'Yes,' she said.

Leon grabbed his headphones.

'Good morning, Karen Guttman. This is your friend Marisol.'

'I want to speak to my father,' said Karen. Leon frowned at her.

'That is not possible.'

'I want proof that you're holding him.'

Leon touched Karen on the shoulder, reminding her to adopt the tactics they'd discussed the previous day which would dictate the course of the conversation. She ignored him. Leon closed his eyes and shook his head. Karen was ruining everything. For a moment he thought she was going to ask the kidnappers to ask her father for the code words. *Les pêcheurs de perles*. Guttman would reveal the code words when he was asked for the name of his favourite opera. The code words were his life insurance. They indicated he was still alive. If the kidnappers knew them, they wouldn't need to keep him alive. They could make arrangements for the delivery and collection of the ransom and quote the code words at the appropriate moment.

'Ask him for the name of the puppy I had as a child.'

'OK,' said Marisol impatiently. 'Now listen carefully. You have only two more days to collect the money.'

'If I arrange everything too quickly there will be publicity.' Karen reverted to the tactics they'd agreed. 'The banks are obliged to tell the government. I need more time—'

'Don't try to bargain with me,' the woman interrupted.

Leon grinned. Karen had drawn blood inadvertently. The kidnapper had introduced the idea of negotiation. 'I'm not bargaining,' said Karen. 'I'm just repeating what I was told. I can't collect the money in two days.'

'That's your problem.'

Karen didn't have an answer. She'd run out of steam. 'Please . . .' she said. 'I don't know if we have that much money.'

'That's also your problem. Señor Guttman's company will make up the difference. I suggest you call them immediately.'

'Please, I can't arrange these things and stay by the telephone all the time,' pleaded Karen.

The kidnapper broke off the connection.

Leon leaned forward and took the receiver from Karen and replaced it on the cradle.

'What else could I do?' she demanded defensively.

Leon shrugged his shoulders. 'Not much,' he said. There wasn't any point remonstrating with her. 'They hold all the cards.'

'Is this normal?'

'Yes.'

'Are you always successful?'

'I've never lost a hostage,' said Leon. Sometimes it had been close, when the police had insisted on setting a trap, but he'd always rescued his man. This time the police wouldn't be involved and things would be simpler.

'What if they won't accept less money?'

'I spoke to London this morning. They've agreed to pay up.' He anticipated what she was feeling. 'You're not responsible for this, Karen. I see this all the time. Some sick person has chosen to play God with your life. It has nothing to do with you. You're standing up to the strain very well. You wouldn't be normal if it didn't have some effect on you.'

Karen looked at him. She frowned. 'I know that,' she said abruptly. 'Don't try your amateur psychoanalysis on me, Mr Garrick. For that I have a professional in Manhattan.'

She's turned, thought Garrick. Now he'd have to be careful she didn't screw things up.

3

The theatre had been bombed and the children were laid out on the stage. Michel walked between the rows of bodies, looking down at the faces. A pile of shoes lay in a corner. The dead always lost their shoes. He started matching the shoes to the feet. If he did it correctly within the time limit they'd all come back to life. He picked up a pair of pebble glasses and looked for the girl. She couldn't see without them. He was wasting time. She was dead.

Michel woke from the nightmare.

Someone was knocking on his door. He grabbed his watch. It was eleven in the morning. His mind flashed back to the previous evening. He'd closed the bar in the early hours and come home. If there had been any problems the manager would have telephoned him.

He threw back the bedclothes, pulled on his jeans and grabbed a shirt. He guessed whoever was at the door wasn't bringing good news. No one visited him at home. If they wanted him they telephoned or found him at Txistu. He opened the door.

It took Michel a moment to recognise the girl. He was too surprised to say anything.

'I need to speak to you,' she said in Spanish.

'Come in.' Her presence excited him more than he had imagined. As she walked into the room his body thrilled. He closed the door, turned around and found her standing awkwardly. For a brief moment he wondered if she was throwing herself at him, consumed by some unbridled passion, but knew she was too old to make such a gesture.

'You know who I am?' she asked.

'I've seen you before,' he replied. It seemed an inadequate answer. 'I've noticed you in Txistu.' She was wearing jeans, shirt and a loose jacket. Her black hair was tied back. Her fingers betrayed her nervousness as she played with her car keys.

People noticed her. That was the thing about her. She did little things to gain attention. She always wanted what wasn't on the menu. She dropped things clumsily and picked them up gracefully.

'I'm a friend of Bernal's.'

'Oh,' said Michel. He was confused. He wondered, with a hint of jealousy, whether Bernal had been having an affair.

'He told me I should contact you if anything happened.'

Michel froze. His internal alarms sounded. He wondered what she meant.

'What's your name?' he asked, picking up his cigarettes and lighter from the table.

'Abene,' she replied. He waited and she added, 'Abene Izura.' Sometimes the full name indicated where someone came from.

Michel nodded. The name meant nothing to him. The girl wasn't stupid. She knew the atmosphere in the room had changed. There wasn't any point pretending it hadn't. He shouldn't have reacted so badly when she explained her presence. He'd revealed himself.

'You're not from here?' he asked.

She nodded, holding his gaze.

'*¿Badakizu euskaraz?*' He asked if she spoke Basque.

'*Euskaldun naiz.*' She confirmed she was Basque-speaking. The language had no other way of defining a Basque. The language was the land.

'So, what is it?' Michel asked brusquely, continuing the conversation in Basque.

'Bernal's been arrested.'

'Why?'

'I don't know. He was supposed to call me this morning. He didn't. His neighbours say he was picked up in the middle of the night. The usual thing. An unmarked car. Plainclothes cops.'

'Is that the usual thing?' asked Michel innocently.

Abene shrugged.

'Why don't you call a lawyer? Why come to me?'

'Bernal told me to speak to you. He said you'd know what to do.'

'I don't know why,' said Michel. He wondered what Bernal was playing at.

The girl said nothing.

'Was he expecting trouble with the police?'

Abene looked at the ground.

Suddenly Michel was irritated. He stubbed out his cigarette in a saucer. 'Let's get to the point. I can't help you unless you tell me what he was doing.'

'He kidnapped Raphael Guttman,' she replied.

'Jesus!' Michel swore. 'When?'

'Four days ago.'

That meant Bernal had already snatched Guttman when he went out to the farmhouse. 'Are you involved?'

The girl nodded. Michel walked to the window. 'Why did you come here?' He looked down at the street to see if she'd been followed. Nothing was out of place. There weren't truckloads of police.

'He said you had connections.'

'There's nothing I can do for Bernal,' snapped Michel. 'What about the rest of your cell?'

'They're safe at the moment.'

'What about your controller?' Michel asked.

Abene said nothing. The truth struck Michel. Bernal wouldn't have been included on an official operation because of his past. Anyway, members of a *baserria* didn't get involved in the struggle. Looking after the land usually meant they were fully occupied.

'We did this because of Theresa and everyone else who was affected by the vaccine,' explained Abene. 'The idea was to pay out the ransom to all the families who had suffered.'

Michel shook his head. It was the sort of thing that could attract unwelcome attention to ETA. It could ruin some other operation that had been planned for years. 'You won't get any support from the movement,' he said curtly. 'And there's nothing I can do. I'm not in the loop any more.'

'The movement knows about this,' she said. 'They advised us to kill Guttman,' she added angrily.

They stared at each other. He knew she was lying.

'Kill him and you kill Bernal,' he said softly.

'Bernal told me about you,' she said. 'He was right. You're not what you appear to be. You're cold and ruthless.'

'Is that all he told you?'

'No. He trusted you. But unfortunately the trust was misplaced.'

Michel nodded.

'I'm going,' she said. 'I've wasted enough time. Maybe I can find someone else to help us.'

'Don't advertise it too widely,' advised Michel.

The girl was at the door when Michel asked, 'How did the police get on to Bernal?'

'I don't know.'

'Had you demanded a ransom?'

'Yes.'

'How did you make the demand?'

'I did it. By telephone.'

Michel nodded. 'And where is Guttman now?'

'We have him somewhere safe.'

There was a long silence. Michel broke it. 'There is someone I know who could help.'

The girl smiled as if she'd known all along that he was going to relent.

'Come back and sit down. I need you to tell me everything, right from the beginning.' He needed to know how they'd organised it. He needed to know how many people were involved and if their security was tight.

Michel knew he was going to help. He had no option. He owed it to Theresa.

Half an hour later Michel was on the street. He'd told Abene to move Guttman immediately and arranged to meet her later. He felt safer when he'd left the house. He felt something stirring inside him. He was waking from a long sleep, returning to a world he knew and understood. There had been times in the past few years when he had ceased to live. He'd walked down a road wondering what motivated other people. Sometimes he pretended he had a destination. He took buses, and when he alighted he crossed the road to catch a bus in the opposite direction. Such empty gestures provided an illusion that he was a part of humanity, although deep down inside he felt he'd lost the will to live. He'd been killing time, he realised now, waiting for something like this to happen. He was a fixer. He was good at solving problems. He'd have Bernal released.

He started his bike and rode out of town thinking about what Abene had told him. He had found himself liking her as she told him about Guttman's kidnap. She told him proudly how the operation had been her idea. She explained how the pharmaceutical plant had polluted the river, killing what little life was still there, and how Guttman deserved to pay for that. She had targeted him long before Theresa's death and the question of the vaccine had been raised.

Abene was good material. Political activists had to be childlike in their beliefs. Anything more and they might doubt or hesitate. They had to be recruited when they were young. As they grew older they became more cautious and objective. They learned compassion and became less extreme in their beliefs.

Security on the operation seemed to be tight. And so it should have been. Bernal knew about cell security. He'd been in the game long enough. Each cell had a single controller, who knew only the controller on either side of him. No one knew the identity of cell members not under their command. Each member of the cell worked on a different day in a different location so none of them ever knew of the existence of other cell members. If people kept their mouths shut a husband and his wife wouldn't know they both worked for the same controller.

When the central committee decided on an action, the surveillance cell carried out early reconnaissance while a planning cell decided what weapons and safe houses were needed. The operations controller received the report from the planning controller and consulted with the central committee, who agreed the target. The operations controller passed the planning cell's data to the target controller, who refined the target list and checked the information. Meanwhile the reconnaissance cell prepared a detailed operational plan for the trigger cell, which would execute the action. It was fail-safe, so long as no one talked.

Michel remembered it all from the years he had spent establishing contacts between the disaffected revolutionary groups in Europe. He'd operated as a broker transferring weapons, papers and intelligence between these isolated organisations. What kept the groups alive were their politics, their actions and, most important, money. But in 1992 things had changed when the French police arrested Pakito, Txelis and Fiti, the ETA leaders in exile, and Michel's link with the high command disappeared. ETA's new leaders lived in Algeria.

Michel came down to earth. Bernal had managed Guttman's kidnap on his own, without resources. He'd recruited a few friends and acquaintances. Abene was lying about ETA's involvement. An official operation was run very differently from the way she'd described things. This one was a shambles. Abene knew everything. She knew how Guttman had been picked up by Bernal's contact inside the pharmaceutical company. She knew where Guttman was being held. She was handling the ransom negotiations. It was pathetic. If she was picked up, everyone was finished. No wonder she and Bernal had to call him in when something went wrong.

Bernal had made too many errors of judgment. He was naïve to think he wouldn't be suspected. He'd kidnapped before and was known to be a member of ETA who'd done time. He had been publicly outspoken about Guttman's pharmaceutical company, accusing it of a cover-up.

Now Bernal's life was hanging by a thread. The police were unlikely to give him the option of repentance, because he'd already been granted an amnesty once before. Bernal would never become an *arrepentido*. ETA didn't allow former commandos to renounce their beliefs. It was bad for business. If the state provided him with a new identity, police security was so bad that his whereabouts would soon be leaked out. There was only one way for him to get out of this alive.

Michel stopped the bike and walked out to the cliffs of Algorta and stared at the Atlantic swell breaking on the beach below. A coaster was rolling out of the river. He pulled out his mobile phone and spent a few moments wondering whether he'd overlooked something. Courtesy of modern technology, the number he was dialling five miles away was beamed through the German switchboards, transferred into a radio signal, and directed back to Spain. His precise location remained secret. The security forces had worked out how to track mobile phones, but they had to be in constant use for that. Here the contents of the conversation would be known only to some radio hacker, and there weren't many of those around the Cantabrian Mountains. Even if the call were intercepted the message wouldn't make much sense to an outsider. If it was traced, the phone was rented and paid for by a man who didn't exist in Frankfurt. It was an expensive phone, but it was safe.

4

When Suarez inspected the prisoners in their cells he found them as happy with their conditions as might be expected. There were no signs of an unofficial purge afoot, and they were being held under a wide range of charges, not spurious conspiracy charges. They made no complaints about their treatment, except for the usual claims of innocence and false imprisonment. At first he suspected the men were too frightened to admit they'd been assaulted in case they received more punishment. It was so suspicious that he asked two prisoners to remove their clothing. At that point the prisoners became extremely agitated, expecting the worst, but when he reassured them they complied with his request. He knew how beatings were administered so as to leave no marks and he examined the prisoners carefully. However, there were no signs of brutality.

As a consequence Suarez went to lunch optimistic. He liked to think he was responsible for the change in the prisoners' fortunes. He celebrated by eating at one of his favourite restaurants. The only good thing about being posted to the Basque region was the food.

When he returned from lunch he found a tape waiting on his desk and was momentarily pleased that the bugs he'd ordered to be planted in the Parc Hotel were already paying dividends. He slipped the tape into the player and listened to the conversation.

A minute later Suarez realised that something had gone very wrong. He rewound the tape and listened to the recording again.

'Hello?' It was a man's voice. Suarez assumed it was Garrick.

'I must speak to Karen Guttman,' said the caller. It was another man.

'She's not here at the moment. Can I take a message?' Garrick again.

'I have a message from Marisol,' said the caller. Suarez thought there was something familiar about the voice.

'Who?' asked Garrick.

'From Marisol.' The caller sounded irritable. 'Karen Guttman is playing with her father's life. Tell her to stop playing games before it is too late.'

'She has already agreed to your terms,' said Garrick. 'We will ...'

'We understand you have taken a hostage,' interrupted the man. 'I will telephone again to make arrangements for the exchange.'

'I don't know what you're talking about.'

'Then find out.' The line went dead.

Suarez pressed the replay button. A shiver went down his spine. Raphael Guttman had been kidnapped, but the situation was more complex than that. It sounded as if a hostage had been taken in retaliation. What had started out the previous night as mere conjecture when he talked to the manager of the Parc Hotel seemed to have turned into a major crime. A cycle of violence was about to commence.

He listened to the recording again and again. He knew the man's voice. He was sure of it, although he couldn't quite place it. It was deep. A voice with controlled power. The syllables were measured. A hard voice, not unattractive. A voice which sounded as if it had a bag of gravel in its throat. The voice of a man who knew his own power.

Suarez ordered Archives to send him whatever recordings of terrorists they had in their files, then turned his attention to more immediate issues. He needed to organise a rapid-reaction team in case an exchange of hostages took place. He needed round-the-clock surveillance on Garrick and Karen Guttman. He wanted more information.

As he spoke on the telephone to brief the members of

his team, he wondered who'd carried out the kidnap. He thought about their motives. If it was mere extortion, then there was a reason for choosing Guttman as opposed to some other businessman. In general, extortionists were greedy. They'd have chosen Guttman because he received extraordinary press coverage over the court case, but they usually selected low-profile targets.

Somehow he wasn't convinced it was an ETA operation. Terrorists were usually motivated by one of two things. There were those who acted out of hatred and revenge, and those who wanted to change things. Guttman's kidnap didn't help fulfil either of these criteria. He was American, and ETA was generally careful to keep its activities in the local arena. When they'd killed Blanco they could have killed Kissinger the day before when he drove over the identical spot. They didn't avail themselves of the opportunity because the last thing they wanted was America pouring funds into Madrid demanding their extermination.

There was another possibility. The people who lost the court case against Guttman-Tiche might be seeking revenge. Suarez had followed the case. The evidence that the plaintiffs produced concerned a faulty vaccine. The case seemed conclusive until the defence had delivered the results of independent trials which showed the vaccine wasn't dangerous, although it had been used without being fully tested. Indeed, the vaccine was now credited with having stopped the spread of a dangerous and contagious flu epidemic. He remembered seeing a picture of the scientist who'd been the main witness for the defence. Not only that, he remembered that the scientist's name was Miller. He made a note to telephone the court and request a list of the plaintiffs.

He savoured the thought of interviewing Garrick in the near future. Like all policemen, he was intolerant of those who broke the law. He was especially intolerant of foreigners whom he expected to respect and honour the laws of his country. At the very least Garrick would know it was against Spanish law to negotiate with kidnappers.

Suarez looked at his watch. The policemen who worked the street would be reporting back to the station. According to his driver they were the ones who'd first heard that GAL were looking for new recruits. He went downstairs to ask a few questions.

5

The police doctor looked at the naked man lying on the blood-soaked mattress. It was the second victim he'd inspected that day. The other had been in a coma, and as he hadn't been able to do much he'd suggested the man was dropped outside the hospital if no one wanted to finish him off. The doctor didn't have any sympathy for terrorists, but torture on this scale was unnecessary.

'At the very least you could have cleaned him up for me,' he growled.

'Get on with it,' said Lafitte. He was pissed off. Bernal had been tougher than expected, but he'd finally broken and told them where Guttman was being held. When Lafitte reached the cave in the hills, the kidnappers had gone, and he found nothing but some cold shit and a few newspapers. Now he needed to talk to Bernal again and get a few leads.

The doctor opened his bag, took out a pair of gloves and pulled them on. The body stank. Bernal had responded to the *submarino* treatment. He hadn't liked having his head pushed into the bucket of piss and shit which stood in the corner.

Lafitte took out his mobile phone and dialled a number. 'That you, Carlo?' He paced the room while he listened to the report from his other team. 'Good. Good. Now let the creep go. Let's have him on the street. I want the word spread that we want Guttman back.'

He snapped the phone off.

'What's the point of doing this?' the doctor asked irritably. 'He's half dead.'

'Just bring him round,' said Lafitte.

'The intensity of pain isn't necessarily proportional to the amount of tissue damage. There are better ways to make people talk,' said the doctor. 'You could disorientate him with a drug like haloperidol.'

'Yeah, yeah, if I had time,' said Lafitte. The last thing he wanted was a lecture on morality from some dead-beat doctor who was so compromised he did jobs like this.

'The fact that I'm here suggests you didn't get what you wanted.'

'Get on with it!' hissed Lafitte. 'That's what you're here for. Not to teach me medicine.'

The doctor lifted his patient's wrist and felt the pulse. He looked at the shattered fingers on the hand. Pieces of bone pierced the skin. The pulse was quick but very weak. He lowered the arm on to the bed. It lay at an awkward angle. The doctor didn't need to examine the body any further to form an opinion. He looked at the face. It was bruised and swollen. The skull was covered with ugly cuts. The doctor shook his head involuntarily. The skin was white and clammy, and he guessed there was internal haemorrhaging. He lifted an eyelid.

The doctor looked up and his eyes locked with Lafitte's. He looked back at his patient.

Chapter Four

I

Karen sat in the lounge of the Parc Hotel with Garrick and sipped a glass of wine. He was drinking water. The place was busy. Local businessmen obviously used it as a watering-hole after a day's work. It was the first time she and Garrick had allowed themselves to be seen publicly together at the hotel. She flicked through a magazine.

'The trouble with working in a foreign country is that you can't tell if the opposition are around,' said Garrick.

Karen looked at him. 'What do you mean?' she asked.

'If I were in England I'd know if this lounge was full of undercover policemen. I could probably tell if there was anyone suspicious in here. In your own environment you know whether people merge against the background.'

Karen looked down at her magazine again and wondered why Garrick hadn't hired someone with some local knowledge, in that case. There were a lot of things that bothered her about the way this kidnap was being handled. She sipped her drink and looked around the room. No dark suits or men in shades. Men in black — that's what she was looking for. She'd called the chief executive officer of Guttman-Tiche as soon as her father was kidnapped and he passed her on to the security consultant, McFarlane. She was immediately assured that her father's kidnap would be handled by the best people in the world. She had been tempted to call her friends and involve the FBI, except McFarlane warned her not to involve another agency. His specific use of the word 'agency' appeared deliberate and implied the FBI were already involved.

Karen looked at Garrick and wondered whether he was really one of the best negotiators in the world. She wished he were an American. She didn't care for the English. They were supercilious. They might speak the same language but that was all the two nationalities shared. She decided that she'd cut up rough if there wasn't any progress during the next twenty-four hours. Garrick was far too laid-back. At the beginning he'd assumed her father's release would take months. She didn't want someone with that kind of attitude. It might suit him, but it didn't suit her, and it certainly wasn't in her father's interests.

Over the past few days Karen had thought constantly about her relationship with her father. When her mother died she just accepted that her father had retreated into himself and his work. From time to time he invited her to join him on important occasions, as he had this time in Bilbao, because he'd donated a picture to the Guggenheim. She responded because she thought he wanted her to be there. She felt it was a duty of sorts because her mother was no longer there to accompany him to functions. Now she realised that she'd been hiding her feelings behind labels. When she imagined her father being held in a room somewhere, she didn't imagine him angry. That wasn't something that came naturally to him. She imagined him being sad and bewildered, and the image upset her. Her father was a good person. He'd done good things with his life. He provided jobs for people. He manufactured drugs to cure diseases. He was a patron of the arts. He was on the board of two charities. He donated art to museums.

She'd never been particularly close to her father, but he'd encouraged her interest in the world of art. They had different tastes, but he'd never tried to dictate what she should or shouldn't like. He'd bankrolled her when she first started buying and selling art, and she saw this as a way of paying him back and showing him how much she loved him.

Karen finished her drink and signalled the waiter for a refill.

'Relax,' said Garrick. 'Things are going to work out fine. Nothing's going to go wrong.'

'I don't like this,' said Karen. She'd been nervous ever since the call that had mentioned a hostage earlier in the day. Garrick had been unperturbed about it but she didn't like complications. He said it could only work in their favour and that it looked like there were other people trying to secure her father's release.

'We have to play along with the kidnappers,' said Garrick. 'We do what they say.' He looked at his watch. The kidnappers had issued them with an itinerary in another phone call, and they were due at the Arriaga Theatre in half an hour. Garrick didn't know whether it was because the kidnappers wanted to contact them in person or just wanted to identify them.

'Something's wrong,' she said suddenly.

'What?' Garrick looked up sharply.

'I've got this feeling. Too many people are looking at me.'

He smiled. 'You're attractive. You're the best-looking person in the room.'

'I've been around.' Karen dismissed his remark. 'They're looking at me in the wrong way. I know when men are looking at me. I'm a woman. They're looking at me for the wrong reason.'

'Who?' he asked.

'Don't look now.'

'Of course not.'

'There are two men at the bar. There was a man by the telephones when I came in. They avoided eye contact. They're not admiring me. They're watching us.'

'Don't worry. Nothing's going to happen here,' he said. There was a long pause before he spoke again. 'Of course, the kidnappers might be here, in the room with us. That's why they told us to wait here. They want to see you, and see what's happening. They want to see if we've contacted the police. They're amateurs. They're making mistake after mistake. They're getting too close to us.'

Karen looked past Garrick and saw the man with sad eyes watching her. He glanced down at his drink again. The tall, thin man with the sensual lips by the telephone had disappeared.

'Something will happen,' continued Garrick. 'They'll want you to take a walk alone somewhere so they can see if you're being followed.'

'I'm not doing that,' Karen snapped. The thought of being alone on a dark street terrified her. Then she immediately felt guilty. She had to do it if her father's release depended on it.

'Don't worry,' said Garrick quickly. 'I'm not going to let you out of my sight. We're perfectly entitled to reject unreasonable demands.'

For the first time Karen was grateful for Garrick's presence. Then the hotel receptionist approached and said there was a telephone call for her.

2

Abene breathed a sigh of relief as she left Michel's apartment. It hadn't been easy persuading him to get involved, but then she had never expected it to be. She had played on his conscience about Theresa and he agreed to help in the end, but only because she led him to believe that ETA had sanctioned the operation. He was professional, and that impressed her. He insisted on knowing anything that might be relevant and demanded complete control of the operation.

Abene knew he'd check whether Bernal had really been kidnapped. Once he'd done that he'd try to find out where he was being held. She knew Michel had connections. Bernal had told her that intelligence was one of his strengths, but she still didn't understand why they hadn't involved him from the very beginning. That morning the kidnap had gone wrong and the world had threatened to collapse in on her. Now she felt they could pull it off again.

Abene had gone to Michel's bar, Txistu, five weeks ago out of curiosity so she could check him out. Theresa had talked about him a long time ago, and admitted that they had once been lovers. Something in the way she spoke suggested that Michel had been a good lover, and it made Abene inexplicably jealous.

She was attracted to him from the start. Even though he was the owner of the bar, she never saw him throw his weight around. He kept his distance from the customers. On one occasion he broke up a fight that erupted in a corner. He was slightly built even though he was tall and she thought he'd be hurt, but she was surprised by how he took control of the situation. He simply grabbed the biggest man, immobilised him, led him away and talked to him. He didn't throw the man out like most owners would. She knew that in the first flurry of activity he'd done something, made a few moves which the men recognised, and they'd known not to push him any further.

The incident made him more attractive. His face, which she had originally thought to be too sensitive, suddenly acquired a strength. His eyes seemed darker, his lips harder. He was thin, and she had mistaken it for weakness, but now she saw that he was lean and fit. When she finally spoke to him she realised she'd been right to reassess him. He was tougher than he looked.

By the middle of the afternoon Abene had done everything Michel wanted. She moved out of her apartment, taking everything she needed for a couple of weeks because he'd warned her she might not be returning there for a while. She contacted the others and told them all further meetings were cancelled. She told the two who were holding Guttman that they were not to talk to him on any account until further orders, and that they were to move him to the second hiding place.

Finally, in the late afternoon, she checked into a double room at a hotel and waited. She found herself staring at the telephone, willing it to ring. Twenty-four hours ago she'd been at the centre of the operation, but now she'd lost control. Michel had taken charge and she wasn't sure she liked it. She turned on the radio and listened for a few minutes. She turned it down, picked up the telephone and called her friend who worked at Guttman-Tiche Pharmaceuticals. She was careful not to say anything that would give her away, but she wanted to know what reaction Guttman's disappearance had caused. 'How are things?' she asked. She listened carefully. It was chaos there. People moving things. Packing up files and folders. People over from America. Too busy to chat today. Let's have a drink some time.

Abene replaced the receiver thoughtfully. Guttman's kidnapping seemed to be causing ripples. She looked at the double bed and realised what she'd done. The more she thought about it the more attractive the idea became. She glanced at her watch. Michel had said he would be back in an hour's time.

3

Bernal returned to consciousness. There was a moment in limbo when he wasn't sure where he was, before the pain screamed along his nerves. He shivered involuntarily and his muscles contracted, culminating in a spasm. When he regained control, he heard voices, picked out words indistinctly, and felt hands examining him. It reminded him of when he was a child. They were the hands of a doctor, and he felt a childish trust in the man.

Bernal winced as the fingers probed. He was in a hospital after all. It meant they must have found Guttman. He tried to open his eyes, but they didn't respond. He didn't care. If they'd found Guttman the pain was over.

He heard the voices again, floating towards him on a wave. 'What's that?' asked one of them.

'Something to take away the pain. He's been able to focus on pain to avoid your questions. Now it will only be a memory, and you'll find he's more likely to answer. This time just suggest pain and his recent experience will make it more vivid. This time you'll get your answers.'

Bernal gasped. He didn't understand. It was the pain he feared. Now they were taking it away. He felt the needle prick his arm and find a vein. Slowly he felt a warm rush up the back of his neck into his head. He felt as if he were being lowered into a warm bath.

'If you cause his body more trauma you'll kill him.'

Bernal retched unexpectedly. It was a dry gagging which tore at his throat.

'Turn his head. He'll choke on the vomit.'

Nothing came out. There was the bitter taste of bile at the back of his throat.

'Make sure his head is turned to the side.'

The warm rush up his neck became hotter. The top of his head was blowing off. His body was rigid, tearing at the straps that held him. The room spun slowly. Bernal imagined himself spinning the other way. He tried to control the sensation but failed.

His heels hammered on the boards violently.

'Shit!' shouted the doctor. 'He's having a heart attack.' He scrabbled in his bag, then plunged a needle into Bernal. There was no response. He massaged Bernal's heart without enthusiasm.

'He's dead,' the doctor said finally.

'The boss won't be happy about it,' said the guard.

The doctor shrugged. 'Tell him I did my best.'

4

The taxi driver glanced in the mirror, registered the man's

Castilian lisp and grunted in response to the instructions. He drove, horn blaring, through the rain and the dusk. These days he worked himself into a fury whenever he went out to Neguri. It wasn't because of the rich who lived there, looking down at the squalid houses and dirty factories across the polluted water. It wasn't because they were an élite who wielded their power through secret networks, imposing their will on the city and its workers. It was because the government had built a new Metro system to connect them to the centre of the city. On the other side of the river the workers, who needed decent housing as well as transport, were ignored.

Michel looked at his watch, then peered out of the taxi's window at the night sky. He guessed what the driver was thinking. He didn't like speaking Spanish. It stuck in his throat. It was the language of Castile and a nasty reminder of domination by an alien culture. He emphasised the affected lisp which was the hallmark of Castilian and had been adopted because Philip II had a speech impediment which all his courtiers imitated to make him feel at ease.

He'd dined at the Parc Hotel that night and seen Karen Guttman when she was paged for the telephone call Abene made. She was accompanied by a man whom he guessed he'd spoken to earlier in the day and who was the negotiator. He'd also noticed that the place was swarming with undercover cops. Guttman's people were taking a lot of chances with his life. They'd been told not to contact the police. On top of that they appeared to have taken a hostage. Under normal circumstances that would have been enough to sign Guttman's death warrant. It didn't make sense. But he was confident he'd be able to exchange Guttman for Bernal.

His awareness was coming back. It was as if his senses had been dulled all these years. He was noticing people on the street, the clothes they wore and how they walked. He was no longer a part of the crowds; he was apart from them.

He wondered what he would do if he spotted surveillance

around the hotel where he'd told Abene to meet him later. It would prove he was well and truly compromised. He'd have to leave the country and find somewhere safe to live. There had been a time when he would have gone to France, but he didn't trust the French any more. The days when Mitterrand declared that France would adopt its traditional role as the land of exile for political prisoners were long gone. The French had abandoned their sympathy for the Basques, who'd fought the Fascists during the Second World War, and now they expelled anyone whose politics might offend the Spanish government. So much for De Gaulle's promise that the allies wouldn't stop at the Pyrenees but would destroy Fascism wherever it was found.

The world got smaller all the time.

Right-wing governments were in power throughout the northern hemisphere. Socialism no longer existed. It was a dirty word now. Newspapers didn't report the activities of revolutionary groups. For years the government and the television stations had agreed there wouldn't be any coverage of the ETA campaign, so the only alternative was to take out a few tourists from time to time in order to gain publicity through the international press. Everywhere it was the same. The alliance between the Red Army Fraction and Action Directe, caused by the cold-blooded killing of a Red Army member, was ignored. Nothing was changing. The press didn't even take the trouble to get the names right half the time, thus missing the political distinction between Red Army Fraction and Faction.

Devolution was the future political landscape of Europe. Empires that had been built on the exploitation and subjugation of minority populations were now falling apart. But democracy no longer existed. Governments silenced awkward questions with money and were propped up or funded by the capitalist multinationals. Ordinary people no longer had a voice and needed to find new ways in which to organise themselves.

The taxi stopped outside a restaurant, ending Michel's train of thought. He paid, and the driver sped away without acknowledging the tip. Michel opened his umbrella and walked briskly down the road. He stood for a few minutes in the shelter of a tree, checking that he wasn't being followed, then entered the bar across the street from the hotel where he had told Abene to wait in her room.

He watched the hotel while he drank a cup of coffee, and when he was satisfied that it wasn't being watched he slipped inside through the entrance from the carpark in the basement. He used the public telephone in the foyer to call Abene, told her he'd be there in half an hour. He waited to see if his call had prompted any undue activity before he walked up the stairs.

Abene opened the door. He was surprised to find her wearing nothing but a towel wrapped around her body. Her hair was wet; she had obviously just stepped out of the shower. He locked the door behind him and went over to the window, looking down at a courtyard. He felt trapped.

Abene was brushing her hair in the mirror.

Michel took off his coat, opened the minibar, rummaged through it and found a bottle of wine. He poured a couple of glasses. He leaned forward to put the glass beside her and felt her hand behind his neck. She pulled him towards her and kissed him on the lips. For a second she forced her fresh tongue into his mouth, before he pulled away. The unexpected made him nervous. This was the moment when he was caught off guard and the police burst through the door.

Abene smiled. 'If you live dangerously, love is more easily given. You never know if there will be another time,' she said.

'They say that every time you make love to another person you lose a little more of yourself,' replied Michel.

'No,' said Abene. 'Each time I think we find a little more of ourselves. We don't have time for relationships. We must live for the present. Take what we can, when we can. Who knows what the future holds?' She took a step towards him. 'But if you don't want me, Michel ...' she whispered. 'Well, that's another thing.'

Michel felt uneasy. The previous night he wouldn't have thought twice about sleeping with Abene. Now it was too easy. There had to be a catch. She might, after all, be a police agent. He knew nothing about her.

He slipped his hand beneath the towel and caressed the insides of her thighs. 'Wait,' she ordered. She let the towel slip away and began undressing him slowly.

When he was naked she pulled him on to the bed. She reached under the pillow and retrieved a contraceptive, and Michel realised that she had decided to sleep with him long before he'd arrived. He wasn't sure he liked his acquiescence being taken for granted. She unrolled the condom down his penis.

'Did you ever sleep with Bernal?' Michel asked.

'No,' she answered. 'Theresa was my friend.'

'Good,' he said.

Abene pulled him on top of her and guided him into her. There was none of the fumbling he associated with making love to strangers. She made it feel natural.

They made love for a long time, until finally he came. He was suddenly tired and exhausted.

Abene sat up, startling him. He opened his eyes. She sat cross-legged on the bed. Her dark hair framed her face and tumbled over her breasts. It was tousled by their lovemaking. Her muscles were firmly toned, her breasts just a little too big. He closed his eyes again. Somehow it seemed that he was starting over again, but instead of having Theresa in the bed, he had Abene.

He wondered what he was doing. He couldn't have a relationship any more than he could have a home. He was denied anything he couldn't leave at a moment's notice. It didn't make sense that he kept thinking of Theresa, though. She had been the first sacrifice he'd ever made for the cause.

'Please,' he said, 'I need to sleep for a minute.'

Abene was pretty. Much prettier than Theresa. When she

smiled the small scar that ran from the corner of her mouth to her chin puckered. Imperfections made people more beautiful. In their business scars were the only medals. He felt Abene touch his lips. He tried to ignore her fingers which ran through his hair. He stretched up, pulled her face down and kissed the corner of her mouth to stop her.

'How did you get that scar?' he asked.

'I fell off my bicycle when I was six.'

'Come here,' he said, nestling her in the crook of his arm. 'Be still for a moment.'

'Forget it,' she said. 'You've had your minute of sleep.' Michel didn't respond. 'How long have you been a terrorist?' she asked.

'Don't use that word,' he snapped. He was defensive. He'd have to teach her not to ask questions like that. 'Terrorism is an emotive word. When there's no democracy you can't pursue democratic methods. I'm not a terrorist. Gaddafi might be, but I'm not.'

'In that case Gaddafi isn't,' she contradicted him. 'He overthrew King Idris in a military coup and transformed Libya from a feudal to an industrial state in ten years. He demanded a market price for the oil exports to America, and when the oil companies complained America played some dirty tricks on Libya as a result. Gaddafi retaliated by supporting individual terrorists who would take the war back to America. It was OK for America to employ the CIA against Gaddafi, but it wasn't OK for him to fight back.'

'But Gaddafi doesn't promote the freedom of his people,' said Michel. He was wide awake, irritated by the simplicity of her observations. He wondered where she had learned that stuff.

'Doesn't he?' responded Abene. 'I'm not aware of any Libyans in exile who complain about his regime. The papers aren't filled with reports of Libyans wanting to become political refugees.'

'That's because they don't want to draw attention to

themselves. Or haven't you read about the assassination of Libyan exiles?'

'Gaddafi is still in the business of political philosophy,' Abene said earnestly.

'That's crap,' retorted Michel. 'And I don't think this is much of a post-coital conversation.'

Abene didn't like that. 'What are we going to do with Guttman?' she asked.

'Nothing until the morning. We don't drive at night.'

'That wasn't what I was asking,' she said. 'Do we still collect the ransom?'

Michel didn't answer. It would be suicidal to collect the ransom now. The Parc Hotel was staked out by the police. Guttman's people had told them about the kidnap.

'I want to know what you're thinking,' she said. 'I want to make the decisions with you.'

Michel didn't share things. He didn't like talking because it created the illusion that he was sharing something. It reduced the anxiety levels he needed to stay sharp. Angst had kept him alive all these years.

'We'll send them Guttman's ear. We can retaliate,' she said suddenly.

'Don't be naïve,' he said.

Abene turned away from him, and he knew he'd hurt her feelings. She was proving to be a curious mix. Sensitive people shouldn't get involved in this game, he thought.

'Let's not make any decisions until we talk to Guttman,' he said.

Abene turned towards him again. 'My contact at Guttman's laboratories says that people have been causing chaos all day in the offices. They're digging out old files and packing up boxes.'

Michel frowned. He'd told her not to make any telephone calls. 'Did you mention Guttman?'

'Of course not.'

'Who are these people your contact mentioned?'

'They're from the head office in America. They flew in after we snatched Guttman.'

Michel's curiosity was aroused.

5

Antonio Suarez sat in the fourth-floor apartment he rented overlooking Plaza Miguel Unamuno. The shutters were open and he sat in front of the window, feet on the sill. He rocked his chair on two legs backwards and forwards. His shoes had worn through the paint over the past two years.

The apartment had come unfurnished and it remained so, with the exception of two chairs, a table and a bed. A few books lay along the sill of the other window. He had no intention of making the place comfortable.

Home was a house in Madrid where he couldn't relax because he'd been restoring it to its eighteenth-century splendour for the past twenty years. Here in Bilbao he found time to think, but he knew if he started taking an interest in these surroundings he'd be doomed by his obsessive nature. He wished his wife would join him, just for a week or two, but he couldn't blame her for staying in Madrid among her friends. She hadn't put up much objection to his posting, though, and he noticed that over the past few months there hadn't been the usual protestations of affection and complaints about his absence. When he'd first arrived here they'd had a bout or two of telephone sex, which was something they hadn't done since they first met. Now his attempts to seduce her down the telephone line were ignored, and he wondered if she was seeing someone else. It wasn't the kind of conversation he wanted to have over the phone, but the thought of her having an affair made him realise how important it was that he get out of Bilbao.

He stared at the night sky, oblivious to the noises rising up from the square below, and listened to the voice he had first heard on a recording that afternoon. Among the hundreds of voices stored in the police archives was that of a man delivering a bomb warning nine years ago in Barcelona. The warning had come too late, and the bomb had killed ten people, seven of whom were children.

Suarez had been the first policeman on the scene. He was turning into Calle de Ribes when his car was rocked by the explosion. Everything stopped as if it were the end of the world. He continued on foot, searching for the centre of the blast, and found a group of injured schoolchildren who'd been on their way to the Museo Zoológico.

Suarez wasn't surprised that no one claimed responsibility for the atrocity because it would have alienated people from the cause they espoused. No one was ever brought to trial, despite a large reward. Terrorist groups lived and died every day. People were brought in to do a job and never saw other members of the cell again.

Suarez used to hope that the man responsible for the bomb had been punished by his own people, but now he knew that hadn't happened. He'd identified the voice of the man who spoke to Garrick that morning. The inflections and speech patterns were the same as those of the Barcelona bomber, and he wondered how the bastard had lived with the knowledge of his mistake for all these years.

There had been rumours about the man responsible. Word bubbled up from the underworld as people tried to claim the reward. Two separate sources said the man's name was Lopez, but Suarez suspected this was a *nom de guerre*. The only Lopez who was still at large in the department's records had been a guerrilla who fought against Franco's government for ten years after the Civil War had ended, before he disappeared. At best Lopez would be seventy years old now. The voice Suarez had heard on the recording was that of a younger man. Of course, they'd never found him because they believed he was a Catalan, not a Basque, and looked in the wrong direction.

Suarez had a hunch he'd soon meet this terrorist because things were going wrong for him. Guttman's kidnap wasn't the easy fund-raising operation the man had obviously expected. One day Suarez looked forward to hearing how the man justified his struggle against the government by bombing a group of schoolchildren in Barcelona. Talking to him was the key to understanding him. Terrorists had to mythologise the origins of their conflicts in order to justify the killing, and how they did it determined whether or not they were psychotic.

Myths again. The Basques weren't short of myths. They'd been painting caves fourteen thousand years before Christ was born. They'd kidnapped and killed two engineers to stop the building of Lemoiz nuclear power plant because they thought the radiation would destroy their links with the past. Justifying a few murders with that sort of logic made it hard to define psychosis.

Suarez peered down at the square below, where a crowd milled around the bars. For the first time during this posting the city made him nervous. GAL were back, and that made him apprehensive. GAL were also terrorists, and no less worthy of his attentions. They'd assassinate him as soon as they would an ETA commando. He didn't care for mercenaries, because they were trained to kill, devoid of morality or a sense of obligation to society or civilisation. At least ETA derived some kind of legitimacy for their terrorism from the Basque cause, which was a start, albeit a meagre one.

Agustín Hernando had definitely abandoned him. When he called, Hernando was never in his office and didn't return calls. Suarez even mentioned GAL in a message, hoping to elicit some response. It didn't. He wondered whether he ought to move into an official residence. He was exposed out here in the public domain. The police housing units were basic, but at least they were guarded round the clock. Better to be in a concrete police bunker than on a marble slab. Except it would be an inside job when they came for him.

Outside there was a clap of thunder and rain started to fall. A chill gust of wind lashed through the window and Suarez closed it with the heel of his shoe. Things didn't look good for Señor Guttman. He shook his head unconsciously, leaned forward for his beer and raised it to his lips. He'd been to the hotel earlier that evening and watched Karen Guttman with the man called Garrick. He'd left after a while, leaving a couple of plainclothes cops in the bar to keep an eye on things. He'd thought of speaking to Guttman's daughter but decided that when they eventually found Guttman's body it would be better to pretend he'd known nothing about the business. After all, if he knew nothing he could hold the moral high ground and claim that the outcome would have been different had he been informed of the kidnap in the first place. He had no illusions as to how things would end up.

Holy Mary! This was one hell of a place to be posted. He was surrounded by enemies. It had taken three hours for the second recording of the Barcelona bomber's brief conversation with Garrick to be delivered to him. Then, when he'd made enquiries about GAL with the policeman, the face that stared back at him conveyed an innocence bordering on insubordination.

Chapter Five

I

Michel woke early in the morning and disentangled himself from Abene's limbs. She moaned, turned over and went on sleeping. For a moment he thought of making love with her again, but instead got up and took a shower. Another twelve hours and this whole mess would be over. He'd leave the country for a few months to let the dust settle. The bars and the theatre would run themselves. He'd tell his accountant and his managers that he was heading for the Himalayas. They all knew his passion for mountain-climbing. He'd call in now and then to check things were running smoothly and find out if the authorities were making any enquiries. He'd take Abene with him. She knew too much in any case. It was dangerous to leave her where she could talk to others and tell them what had happened. He had to bond with her.

He stepped out of the shower, wrapped a towel around himself and went into the bedroom to wake her. He sat on the edge of the bed and let water drip from his hair on to her skin. She pulled the sheet over her head.

'Wake up,' he said. 'We've got to get moving.'

Abene didn't respond. He shook her. Irritation was building inside him. It was time to hit the road. Important things were at stake. He turned on the television to listen to the news, then pulled the sheet off her. She sat up and tried to grab it. 'Fuck you!' she said.

'We don't have time for this,' said Michel.

'What difference do a few minutes make?'

'Sometimes it's the difference between life and death,' snapped Michel.

'Don't be so melodramatic,' she responded. 'And stop looking at me. Haven't you seen a naked woman before?' She got out of bed and pulled on her clothes. 'I'm ready,' she said. 'Now what? I thought we were in a hurry. I'm waiting for you.'

Michel ignored her. He was watching the news. The cameras showed a street he recognised. He turned up the sound. 'The body of Bernal Lasturra was found here after a tip-off to the newspapers. He was a known member of ETA, imprisoned ten years ago, but released in an amnesty despite his refusal to renounce an allegiance to the politics of violence. Police have not yet commented on whether he was involved in terrorist activities, but his death can only lead to the mounting atmosphere of tension which surrounds this year's regional elections.'

Michel snapped off the television. 'That changes everything,' he said.

Abene's face was white. 'What do we do?'

'We talk to Guttman. I'll leave the hotel the way I came. You pay the bill, then pick me up at the Iruña Café. Before you meet me dismiss Guttman's guards. If they question you about it, tell them it's out of your hands and the operation is now under official control.'

'That's not true.'

'I know the movement never sanctioned this operation. But it's better they think that. They're less likely to talk about it,' said Michel.

Abene stared at him.

'I'm sorry if you don't like it. Do as I say. There's no alternative. Tell the guards they're dismissed.'

'All right.'

'Thank you,' said Michel. He felt her resentment but didn't have the patience for it.

On the street he checked the hotel for signs of surveillance and took a circuitous route, jumping on and off trains and buses. Eventually Abene picked him up as arranged and drove along the river.

'You don't have any curiosity, do you?' she said suddenly.

'That depends,' replied Michel. He guessed she was irritated that he hadn't asked where Guttman was being held.

'Don't you want to know anything about me?'

He looked at her in alarm. 'No,' he said. 'Knowing too much about your friends can be dangerous for them.' He knew all he needed to know about Abene.

'You've judged me,' she said.

He shook his head.

'You don't have to come from a deprived background to have any decent convictions,' she said.

Michel didn't say anything. But she was right, he had judged her. Her accent gave her away. It wasn't easy to trust people with her sort of background. Private education. They had the money to buy themselves out of trouble, not to mention connections in the right places to help them out when the going got tough. If Abene was caught she'd probably do a year of rehabilitation under some psychologist in a private hospital that resembled a leisure club. Meanwhile he'd be doing life in a prison cell on the Canaries.

They crossed back over the river heading out for Getxo.

'We're going to kill Guttman, aren't we?' said Abene.

'I don't know,' Michel told her. He hadn't decided.

'It's the deal. They killed Bernal. We kill him.'

Michel shrugged. Things weren't that easy. Killing Guttman wouldn't wipe the slate clean.

They were driving between a row of run-down buildings. Some were boarded up and others had been converted for light industrial use. Garage services, architectural salvage, automobile dismantlers. Abene pulled over. A few rusty cars littered what passed for the forecourt of a body workshop. The place looked deserted.

Abene got out of the car. Michel followed her. She looked around uncertainly before going down the side of the building. She searched under a rusty bucket, found a key and opened the side door. 'He's in the van,' she said.

Michel shut the door behind them and looked around the workshop. There was a car in the process of being welded. A blue plastic sheet hung down from a rail and divided the room. He looked behind the sheet and found himself in a primitive spray shop. The business was running on a shoestring. He looked at the van. It had received a coat of grey primer. The windows were masked.

'Who else knows about this place?' he asked.

'No one,' Abene answered. 'Just the two who were looking after Guttman. It's their business.'

'What about Bernal?' he asked.

'He wouldn't have known that we moved him here.'

Michel nodded. The answer didn't reassure him. He picked up a pair of gloves and a balaclava from the bench and handed them to Abene, then impatiently pulled on another set. He took the gun out of his jacket pocket and opened the back of the van.

He found Guttman lying on a mattress in the gloom. An inspection light dangled from the roof. He plugged it into the socket of the extension cable that lay on the ground.

Guttman blinked in the bright light. He was naked but for a pair of underpants. He shivered. His wrists and ankles were chained together. His wrists were bleeding where the metal links had chafed. Michel could see Bernal's fingerprints on the operation. Guttman had been stripped to dehumanise and debilitate him psychologically.

'Let's talk,' said Michel.

Guttman didn't respond.

Michel searched for words. It was a long time since he'd spoken English. 'This morning everything changed. Our friend who was making the arrangements for you has been killed by the police.' Guttman's cheek twitched. He seemed to be struggling to comprehend what was being said. 'We have a problem,' said Michel. 'I hope we can help each other.'

Guttman blinked.

Michel turned to Abene and asked in Basque, 'Is he drugged?'

She nodded. 'I think they gave him something when they moved him here.'

Michel looked back at Guttman. 'In my experience it is not normal for the authorities to react like this when someone is kidnapped. It is dangerous for the hostage. With you many strange things have happened. There has been much—' He hesitated, searching for the words. '—activity at your headquarters here in Bilbao also. People are taking away papers.'

'I don't know anything about it,' said Guttman weakly.

'Of course not. But how do they know you are kidnapped? Your daughter was told to say nothing.'

Guttman didn't respond.

Michel grew impatient. 'This is how it goes now. While I am wearing this mask you have the chance to be free. When I remove it I must kill you because you have seen my face. You understand?'

Guttman licked his lips.

'Do you understand?' repeated Michel. He reached up with his left hand and tugged the bottom of the balaclava free.

'I have insurance against kidnap and ransom. Karen would only contact the insurance company. You can't tell them I told you about the policy because that would invalidate it.'

Michel nodded. 'If you have insurance the money is not the problem. But your people, they took a hostage. And this changes things. It is dangerous for us to collect the money now. As a consequence your life has no more value for us.'

Michel waited for the information to sink in.

'You know why we wanted the money?'

Guttman shook his head.

'We wanted to give it to the people who lost their family because of the vaccine.'

'What vaccine? What are you talking about?'

'The court case here in Bilbao. The drugs your company manufactured.'

Guttman said nothing. He stared at his hands.

'You have to trade something in exchange for your life.'

Michel waited for Guttman to crack. He glanced at Abene but could only see her eyes. He sensed her anger and frustration.

'You have no choice,' repeated Michel. 'Tell me about your company.'

After a long pause Guttman started speaking. He was pulling himself together. Michel was impressed by the way he was able to focus on the issues under the circumstances, but then people didn't become captains of industry through luck.

'My company is involved in mapping genomes to create microbiological agents and genetically targeted therapeutic agents.'

'We're concerned about the vaccine that was associated with the Pirineo influenza.'

'I don't have a personal involvement in research or development.'

'So this was just research?' asked Michel.

'You could say that all vaccination programmes are research-based.'

'Does your company specialise in vaccination programmes?'

'We have a long association with the American Department of Defense. We supplied vaccines against chemical and biological weapons during the Gulf War.'

'Veterans are claiming the vaccines caused side effects – Gulf War Syndrome. What about the Pirineo influenza vaccine?'

'I don't know about that. There's certainly a connection between some Gulf War symptoms and the use of the vaccines but the Americans have already authorised payments to soldiers so it's been decided not to reveal this.'

'Even if people are dying you are not prepared to tell the truth?'

'You have to consider whether more people are saved by a vaccine than are adversely affected by it. There are always going to be casualties.'

Michel wasn't getting anywhere. Guttman was deflecting his questions. Suddenly he had an inspiration. 'If you supply the vaccines for biological and chemical weapons then you must also have the weapons.'

Guttman didn't reply. The silence sounded like an admission.

'What did you say about targeted agents?' asked Michel.

Guttman still didn't reply.

Michel's thoughts were racing. He was making the connections. 'You develop weapons,' he said finally. 'That's what it is.'

'No,' objected Guttman.

'Yes,' said Michel. 'Remember you are negotiating for your life now.'

Guttman licked his lips nervously. 'The company has been involved in genetically manipulating viruses for the defence industry. It's only a very small part of our operation. Our microbiologists are mostly involved with creating a genetic library for commercial purposes.'

'I'm not interested in them,' said Michel.

'The research for defence is carried out by one of our subsidiaries.'

'Who runs it?'

'Dr Miller. Paul Miller.'

Abene grabbed Michel's arm. 'Wait!' she said, in Basque.

'He was here. He's the one who gave evidence in the court case.'

Michel nodded.

Abene's urgency had transmitted itself to Guttman. He knew something had changed. He panicked. 'I'm not a scientist. It was classified. I don't know about it.'

'Tell me all you know,' ordered Michel.

'They developed discipline-breakers. The intention was to make viruses active for specific lengths of time, programming them to stop replicating after a predetermined number of divisions.'

'Tell me about the test they did here.'

Guttman spoke quickly and softly. The words poured out as if he were glad to be rid of them. 'It was a double-blind test. The doctors didn't know what they were giving. The patients didn't know what they were given.'

'And what was the result?'

'I don't know. Something went wrong. Somehow the Basque patients were affected.' Guttman shivered. 'I told them we ought to settle.'

Michel picked up a blanket and put it around Guttman's shoulders. It was time to give the man a reward. 'So, start at the beginning. Tell me why the virus was used in Spain, then we'll release you.'

Guttman looked more pathetic huddled in the blanket. He shook his head. 'I don't know any more. That's all I was told. I'm not involved in research.'

Michel questioned him for another hour but learned little more. Finally he was convinced that Guttman was telling him the truth. 'I'm going to make the arrangements for your release now,' he said.

Guttman sighed with relief. He relaxed. The ordeal was over. Suddenly he looked older. 'Don't leave me alone,' he said suddenly.

Michel caught Abene's eye. Now Guttman had told them

everything he was beginning to feel remorse. He was seeing things from another perspective. He was identifying with his captors. What the authorities would call the Stockholm syndrome had set in. The drugs they'd slipped into his food had done a good job of disorientating him.

'We have to make some arrangements,' Michel said, and closed the doors of the van.

2

Antonio Suarez sat at his desk. He was baffled. He'd just received a call from the Ministry of the Interior. He hung about on the line expecting Hernando when all of a sudden he heard a voice he didn't recognise.

'How are things, Antonio?'

'Who is this?' asked Suarez.

'Baltazar de Souza. Deputy director.'

Suarez was on his guard. He'd never met the deputy director and all of a sudden they were on first-name terms.

'Agustín asked me to check up on things.'

'We have some activity up here,' replied Suarez cautiously. 'No clear picture has emerged yet.'

'I heard a policeman and some terrorists had been killed. Sounds like a war to me. What's going on?'

'Just for the record, sir, not all the deaths are connected.'

'Officially, you mean. Yes, of course that's the way to play it,' de Souza hurried on, jumping to his own conclusions. 'You must release the policeman's name immediately to the newspapers. Give details of the family he left behind. Give his wife and children some column inches. Organise a memorial service. Get a decent photographer round there. Build up some local sympathy. Maybe a collection. Mention how they used to support the Bilbao football team.'

'Bilbao Atlético only use Basque players,' said Suarez.

'Huh?' The irony was lost on de Souza. He'd obviously

never spent a night in Bilbao. He was probably running his finger down the Zen Plan – Madrid's programme to win the hearts and minds of the Basques. Painting a human face on dead policemen was one of the items that came near the top of the list. 'Well, I don't suppose I need to tell you how to do your job,' de Souza finished lamely.

'It's rumoured there's some unofficial activity here, sir,' said Suarez, referring to GAL.

'We have to play a strong hand with kidnappers,' responded de Souza without surprise.

That was the bit that confused Suarez. There'd been no word of a kidnap, but Madrid seemed to know all about it.

'How did you hear about it, sir?' he asked innocently.

There was a grunt. 'From the Minister, of course. I've just spoken to America. They want to know what steps we're taking. I told them we're taking it very seriously.'

'I don't think we'll have a satisfactory outcome,' said Suarez.

'What do you mean?'

'The chances of Señor Guttman being released are slight. Doesn't exactly look like peaceful negotiation.'

'That's a pity. But in any case keep it quiet. That's what the Americans want. They don't want terrorists taking revenge on their citizens.'

'Why should they do that?'

'We keep it quiet, Suarez. Understand! We don't report these things. You know that. It gives the terrorists too much publicity.'

'Well, of course, sir.' Suarez buttoned up.

'So keep in touch, Antonio. We want to know everything. That's why you were sent up north.'

'Of course, sir. It will be in my report.'

'Before your report. You understand?'

Suarez hesitated before acknowledging the veiled threat. 'Absolutely, sir.'

Baltazar de Souza, Deputy Director of the Ministry of the Interior, put down the telephone without further ado.

Suarez looked out of the window at the faded yellow paint on the building opposite. He shouldn't get too used to the view. He could be on his way out of Bilbao within a few weeks. Threats didn't exactly work out here. He didn't know where he might be sent, but it could only be up from where he was sitting. Hernando had conned him well and good. 'You're my man, Antonio,' he'd said in Madrid. 'You're going to be my eyes and ears. You'll have a roving commission.' It was all rubbish. The bastard was just using him.

There was a myth that long ago even the Devil had left this region because he couldn't understand the Basques and they couldn't understand him. The Devil had obviously gone back to Madrid.

Suarez wondered when the killings would end. Bernal Lasturra's body had been dumped in a disused warehouse in La Ribera and a call had been made to a journalist. Someone wanted publicity. And the message was clear. An eye for an eye. Out at Lasturra's farm they'd found a dead policeman. The Kalashnikov which the barely recognisable Lasturra was grasping had killed the policeman two days before.

Baltazar de Souza was right. It was a war.

Suarez returned to his desk and once again listened to the tapes from the Parc Hotel. It was time to question Leon Garrick.

3

Michel pulled aside the plastic curtain and left the paint shop. He laid his gun on a workbench and pulled off the balaclava. Abene did the same. 'I want you to stay with Guttman,' he said.

Abene shook her head. She'd been responsible for targeting Guttman in the first place. She wasn't going to be ordered around — she'd had enough of that as a child. Twenty years ago Spanish women weren't allowed bank accounts, but things had changed since then, or maybe Michel hadn't noticed. She hoped he wasn't like all the other men in her life, just paying lip-service to the idea of women's equality. When it came to getting things done, it was the women who sorted things out. It was the women in Algeria who won freedom from the French, although the men had them back in purdah and chains in no time at all.

'What are we going to do?' she asked.

'Release him. We can't collect the ransom,' said Michel, misunderstanding her. 'We'll make him sign a statement. We can publish it and expose what he's told us.'

'You're missing the point,' said Abene. 'They killed Bernal because they wanted Guttman dead. They were frightened about what he might tell us. If they think he talked, we're going to become targets and there's no way we'll get his statement made public.'

'That's one interpretation,' said Michel. 'What do you propose?'

'We kill him because we have to. That was the threat in the beginning. That's what kidnaps are about. Any statement we get out of him will be worthless. It's going to be denied, whatever happens to Guttman.'

'His murder will escalate the situation.'

'I don't think so. If Guttman's dead they'll think he never told us anything.' She waited for Michel to speak. 'It doesn't end here,' she added. 'You know that, don't you?'

Michel still didn't answer.

'How far does this go?' Abene asked. 'I don't think either of us can ignore what we've just heard. I might have been able to stand by while Iraq used chemical and biological weapons against the Kurds. I'm not going to do that while someone experiments on us and our friends.'

'We're out of our depth,' said Michel. 'The whole world

knows that the West sold Iraq the biological weapons which it used against the Kurds. They never said anything. They won't give a damn about us.'

'We have privileged information and we have to make use of it.'

'How?'

'We decide that after we kill Guttman. Don't forget they killed Bernal,' she said.

Michel nodded. Abene was right. They'd killed Theresa too, in the course of some experiment.

'In order to get where you want you have to walk over corpses,' said Abene. She took the gun off the bonnet.

'Don't give me that crappy dogma,' Michel said angrily.

Abene hesitated. Doubts crowded in. She questioned her motivations. She no longer knew if she was being objective.

Michel looked at her. For a moment he was tempted to let her kill Guttman. Have it over with. It would bond her to him. It would be proof of her commitment. A bombing or a kidnap was done at arm's length. It was easy. The target was the result of months of research, and had been dehumanised long before. This was different. If she killed Guttman she'd graduate into another world. He remembered what it had been like the first time he killed someone. The world changed. Boundaries shifted.

But Michel had lost any enthusiasm for killing. He was older now and not so sure about absolute solutions. Anyway, killing was invariably a messy operation.

'No,' he said, and took the gun from her hand. 'We'll let him go.'

4

Inspector Suarez looked at his watch. Leon Garrick had been waiting in the interview room for an hour. That was long enough to demonstrate who was running the show. Long enough for Garrick to realise that things were serious and to cut out the bull. He straightened his uniform and went down to the basement.

'How's he been?' he asked the policeman in the corridor.

'He shouted for attention at first, but he's got the picture now.'

'Good,' said Suarez.

He peered through the spyhole and saw Garrick sitting on the bench glowering at the door. There wasn't much to occupy his attention in there. The bench and the table were both bolted to the floor. The atmosphere was generally conducive to thought. It brought out the best in people who were concerned that their next view might be a cell wall.

Suarez unlocked the door and stepped inside. 'My name is Antonio Suarez. Inspector Antonio Suarez,' he introduced himself.

Garrick remained seated and ignored the offered hand. He was making his displeasure apparent.

'Do you speak Spanish?' Suarez asked, sitting on a corner of the desk.

'Only a little,' replied Garrick.

Suarez accepted the lie. 'A pity,' he replied. 'In that case I shall speak English.' He waited a moment before continuing. 'It is strange that you come to my country on a mission of delicacy without understanding its language.'

Garrick's angry expression dissolved into confusion.

'Negotiation for the return of someone who has been kidnapped is a delicate matter. I understand that is the purpose of your business in Spain.'

Suarez watched as Garrick wrestled to deny it. 'How did you know?' he asked weakly, in the end.

'I have my informants,' said Suarez dismissively.

'Raphael Guttman insured himself against kidnap. I have an obligation to my client.'

Suarez nodded. 'Tell me about your company.'

'It was established twenty years ago to handle the kidnap

and insurance market at Lloyd's. The market is worth in the region of two hundred million. Premiums start at half a per cent of the insured sum, depending on the country. South America is running at two per cent.'

'How many cases do you have each year?' asked Suarez.

'Three or four. It depends where they take place, and whether I am qualified to work in those countries.'

'What qualifications?'

'Language. Knowledge of the country.'

'But you do not speak Spanish,' insisted Suarez.

'Just a little,' admitted Garrick. 'It doesn't compare with your English. I was the only person available at short notice, and anyway we were told the kidnapper was negotiating in English.'

'Why do you not work with the local police in the countries you visit?'

'I do, on occasions. The trouble is that you and I have different agendas. I want my client out for the least amount of money, and you want the kidnapper. When you set a trap for the kidnapper you place my client in danger.'

'So you are prepared to hand over the money for Señor Guttman's return?'

'I would prefer not to answer that question.'

Suarez clicked his fingers irritably. 'So don't answer me. You have broken the law. I will put you in prison now and we can forget this conversation.' A part of Suarez begged Garrick not to answer so he could carry out the threat.

'Yes,' replied Garrick. 'I will authorise the ransom.'

'How much?'

'Perhaps two million, sterling. It's an insurance risk. Our company makes a gross profit of seven million a year. It doesn't leave a large margin for error. The fact that we've been in business so long shows we know our stuff. Of course, once our client has been released we try to find the money as well as the kidnappers.'

'Do you have any success?'

'We note all the serial numbers of the notes. We put electronic tracers in the handles of the suitcases. That sort of thing. We would have passed the information on to you.'

Suarez snorted. He didn't believe that for a second. 'You are playing into the hands of terrorists by offering insurance?'

'The people who take out kidnap and ransom insurance are wealthy. In fact, they could probably pay the ransoms without having to sell any assets, but they choose to take insurance. These people control industry. If they didn't go to places like Brazil and Colombia there would be no growth in those countries. They are entitled to some kind of protection, in the same way you're entitled to insurance from the drug addict who breaks into your car and steals your radio.'

'Of course,' said Suarez.

'Don't you think that the Spanish policy of allowing an amnesty to terrorists lets them off lightly? They kill a few people, then give themselves up.'

Suarez was irritated by Garrick's moral tone, but he wasn't going to let it show. He didn't need to. He had the upper hand. 'Oh yes,' he agreed readily. 'But we think it is better to take them out of circulation that way.'

'A terrorist goes free, and a bank robber spends twenty years in prison?' asked Garrick.

'But the terrorist has a political agenda,' explained Suarez.

'What's the difference?' Garrick asked smugly.

'More than half the governments represented at the United Nations won their seats through terrorism. Today's terrorist may be my government's ally tomorrow.' Suarez smiled coldly before he continued: 'But there is another reason. No government wants a terrorist in prison. He becomes a symbol to his sympathisers. There are bombings to remind people of his existence. Better have him repent and renounce his beliefs. Then his own people kill him, or forget him. Usually they kill him after he has accepted an amnesty.

'The terrorist in prison is only trouble. Your country knows that. She does not advertise her policy. Your policy is to shoot terrorists if they are caught in the act. Sometimes they come back to haunt you—' He gave a wry smile. '—like that business in Gibraltar.'

Garrick bristled. He felt obliged to defend his country. 'That was an anomaly. Our policy is to avoid conflict. Leila Khaled is a better example. We deported her within twenty-four hours.'

'Very clever. The last thing your country wished was for the Palestinians to fight their cause on British soil.'

'Exactly,' agreed Garrick.

'But it is better the police don't kill a terrorist. If he is killed by the state then he becomes a hero. A whole new problem starts.' For a moment Suarez wondered why he was bothering to discuss the subject, then remembered he was putting Garrick at ease.

Garrick nodded. 'I know. I did a few tours in Northern Ireland.'

'So why do you think an ETA commando would kidnap Guttman and not want publicity?' asked Suarez suddenly.

'You don't know it was an ETA operation,' said Garrick. 'But, if it was, then the only reason would be to raise money. Why are you asking me?'

'Because something is not right with this case. Perhaps you know more than you are telling me.'

'What would I have to gain by hiding information from you?'

Suarez shrugged. 'We shall see. But first understand my position. Everything is quiet in Bilbao. Then one day there is ETA activity and questions from Americans wanting to know if terrorism is under control. They reach me from the Ministry of the Interior. These are not the FBI who normally investigate the kidnapping of Americans in a foreign country. Something else is going on.'

'I don't know anything about that.'

'You know the special thing I don't like?'

'No.' Garrick shook his head.

'It is like they know what has happened before me. Then I find someone like you, who thinks he does not have to obey our laws. What are you thinking?' Suarez glared at him. 'Do you suffer some illusion that Spain is the Costa Brava, and our only economy is from the *turista*? Do you think our country is like the beach where you drink *sangría*, eat some *gambas* and kick sand in our face?'

'Of course not.'

'Good.' Suarez allowed a long silence. 'So, tell me everything that happened since you arrived here.'

He listened carefully as Garrick told him about the telephone conversations. There was nothing he did not already know.

When he had finished Suarez said, 'Now, I must ask that you do not leave Spain until this matter has been completed.'

Garrick nodded.

'Please. Your passport. I will keep it for you.'

Garrick stared at Suarez for a moment. He reached into his jacket pocket slowly and withdrew the passport. He put it on the desk.

'Thank you. Now, I have work to do.' Suarez opened the door.

Garrick was angry, but there was nothing he could do. 'I'd like a receipt for my passport.'

'Show him to the front door,' Suarez told the policeman outside, 'and give him a receipt.'

5

The scenery flashed past in a blur. All Michel saw was the black road and the grey sky in front of him. He hustled the motorcycle round the sweeping bends of the toll road that cut through the Pyrenees and led to the northern regions. The faster he rode the harder he concentrated. He changed down through the gears and cranked the bike on to its side through an unexpected hairpin. Sparks flew as the centre stand grounded. He felt Abene's arms tighten around him. He accelerated out of the bend and changed up. The back end twitched. At that speed there was no margin for error and no time to think about what had happened back in Bilbao. The road was empty. He glanced at the speedometer. The needle touched two hundred kilometres an hour. It was dangerous to ride so fast. He was a sitting target for a police car. He throttled back for a moment.

Travelling at half the speed, he began to think about what had happened after he had released Guttman on the cliffs at Algorta that night. He remembered the man's grateful face, tears of relief rolling down his cheeks. Guttman had shaken his hand and promised not to retract his statement. It was pathetic. He'd have promised anything. It was hard not to respond to the man's gratitude, but Michel knew he'd recant in due course. He told Guttman to stay where he was and not to try to find his way back to the road in case he fell over the cliffs. Then he drove back to Bilbao, made the call to Guttman's daughter and told her where she'd find her father in the morning.

Michel changed down, twisted the throttle and the rev counter hit the red line. The engine howled in protest. He changed up again. The motorcycle accelerated. Drizzle smeared the screen of his fairing. He lifted his head and the wind buffeted his helmet. He switched on the lights. The rain made the road slick.

He knew more about Abene after their second night together. Her mother was one of four thousand orphans who were evacuated to England when Franco defeated the Basques. Her grandfather was executed with three hundred thousand others for opposing the Nationalist forces. They had more in common than he had expected. She confessed, 'I've always been searching for something which has a meaning. For some way in which I can make a contribution to the world around me.'

He made love to her for the second time. Her lovemaking

was wanton, her energy boundless. Sex with her was convenient, available at all times, in all ways, without question. She was a curious mixture of child and adult. He wondered how things would work out between them.

It was late afternoon when the news hit the streets. Guttman was dead. He'd been killed, shot in the head, and dumped by his kidnappers. The whole country was up in arms, horrified by the brutality.

At first Abene thought Michel had changed his mind and killed Guttman before releasing him, but he put her right. There were two possibilities. One was absurd. Karen Guttman killed her own father. The other possibility was more sinister. Someone had intercepted Michel's call to Karen and found her father before she did. Whatever the truth, Michel knew they had to leave the country immediately. ETA were being blamed for the murder and they wouldn't be pleased. They'd be looking for whoever was responsible.

The road dipped down towards the sea. Ahead lay the French border which separated the Basque regions. A stream of cars loaded with luggage and children approached from the opposite direction, coming for the Easter processions and the passion plays.

Michel slowed down as he approached the border. He felt a moment's trepidation, and wondered if he'd ever return to Spain. He would soon be wanted by the police and by ETA: life expectancy would be limited to a matter of days if he stayed in Spain. Over a million and a half Spaniards must have felt the same when they emigrated to escape Franco's regime.

6

Antonio Suarez knew the kidnappers would have left the country. Guttman's body had been found in the bottom of an old chest. He was interested in the chest. It was his best clue. It was a coffer of English extraction, probably early nineteenth century. It was beyond repair, although a desperate antique dealer might describe it as distressed. None of the other policemen had commented on it, but then none of them knew about antiques. A coffer wasn't an unusual object in Spain, but one carved with an English coat of arms told another story. In Bilbao the Industrial Revolution had begun earlier than in the rest of Spain, in the middle of the nineteenth century. There had been considerable trade between the Basques and England. Iron ore and wool were exported, and in return came manufactured goods like wrought-iron beds. The industrial barons developed a taste for houses after the English style, and along with that came a demand for their trappings and furnishings. These owners of the blast furnaces, the shipyards and the paperworks lived up in Neguri, and in those grand houses, some of which were dilapidated, Suarez expected there would be items of English furniture that matched the coffer.

A close examination showed that it had been kept in a moist atmosphere. There was a musty odour, and a thin layer of mould was fast disappearing as the wood dried. Probably the coffer had been removed from the house years ago because of an infestation of woodworm, and left in a barn; there was no doubting its origins, but the problem would be finding its owner. In due course he would advertise it in the newspapers, but before that there were other matters needing attention.

Two policemen escorted Leon Garrick to Suarez's office. 'Close the door and wait outside,' said Suarez. He stared at Garrick.

'This is getting to be a routine. In future you could just telephone and dispense with the escort,' said Garrick.

Suarez nodded. He wasn't in the mood for banter. 'Raphael Guttman is dead,' he said bluntly

'Are you sure?'

'Of course.'

Garrick winced. 'When did it happen?'

'Twelve hours ago. Maybe more. The doctor will tell us.

The body was moved from the place of the killing. It was found by a man looking for some carpet material in a refuse site.'

'I received a call last night telling me that he had been released,' said Garrick. 'I went to the location as soon as possible, but he wasn't there.'

'You received a telephone call?' asked Suarez. He'd heard nothing about that.

'That's right.'

'The kidnappers were willing to release him without the ransom?' Suarez was surprised.

'Yes.' Garrick knew it sounded strange. 'How was he killed?' he asked.

'Two shots to the head. An execution.'

Garrick said nothing. Suarez stood up and paced to the window, looked down at the street and watched a police van disgorge some suspects. 'I will let you tell the news to his daughter. It is your responsibility, naturally.'

'Have you made a positive identification?' insisted Garrick. He hoped there was some mistake.

'His passport was with his body. You will go with Señorita Guttman to identify him.'

'Of course.'

'You have broken Spanish law. Negotiation with kidnappers is illegal.'

'I was doing my job,' replied Garrick defensively. 'I would have contacted you if necessary. If there had been any publicity you'd have heard from me.'

'You realise that this business could have ended differently if you had informed me of the situation?'

Garrick shrugged. 'Perhaps.'

Suarez let Garrick sweat for a few moments, then said, 'I have decided to ignore the fact that you broke the law and negotiated with kidnappers. To my mind it would serve no purpose to bring you before a judge.'

Garrick nodded cautiously.

'For now, I will keep your passport. You will need to remain here to help Señorita Guttman with the paperwork. In situations like this there is much to do. She will be grateful for your help.'

'That's considerate of you,' said Garrick.

The sarcasm was lost on Suarez. 'My men will now take you to collect your client and deliver you to the mortuary,' he said.

Garrick was going to help him find the kidnappers. Suarez needed someone outside Spain to make enquiries. He would never be given the time or allotted the expenses to go looking for the murderers. He'd already been told by the Ministry of the Interior to keep things quiet. Foreign police authorities were always difficult about investigations that crossed national boundaries. They had to be cleared at the highest levels. Paperwork proliferated like confetti. It was far better to have someone like Garrick do the legwork.

They'd told Suarez to keep it quiet, but they hadn't yet pulled him off the case or posted him out of the region.

7

Back at the Parc Hotel, Garrick called Fraser in London to tell him that Raphael Guttman was dead. He hoped Fraser would have some clue that would explain why things had gone so wrong. He wanted some kind of excuse to offer Karen.

'It appears there were other parties trying to obtain Guttman's release,' he said, not bothering to talk in code this time.

'Not to my knowledge,' said Fraser, defensively.

'That's what the police here are suggesting.'

'So they're involved.' Fraser sounded disappointed.

'The kidnappers told us they were going to release Guttman. They told us where to find him but he wasn't there. They killed him instead.'

'Sounds like things are getting messy. How did the police get on to you? You didn't contact them, did you?'

'Of course not. And they're not pleased at my presence.'

'Have you told the daughter?'

'Not yet.'

'You'd better do it. I'll see what I can do from this end to smooth things over. I'll be in touch.'

Garrick went down to Karen's suite. She opened the door. There wasn't a good way to deliver the news. 'Karen,' he said, 'your father's dead. They didn't release him as promised.'

Karen stood up. She stared at him.

'I'm sorry,' he blurted.

'You promised me you'd get him back,' she said.

'No—'

'Don't argue with me. You promised. That's why I didn't involve anyone else. You said you'd always negotiated the return of a hostage.'

'I accept it was my responsibility but—'

'I don't want your pathetic excuses,' Karen said. 'You fucked up.'

That hurt Leon. He winced. Fucking up hurt his pride. He shook his head. He'd already wondered whether he'd overlooked something. He'd fucked up when he bought the bullet in his knee. He'd not taken care of the details then. He should have known that a terrorist who was wired on drugs wouldn't drop dead like a normal person after a burst in the chest. In this instance he didn't know what he'd overlooked.

'You fucked up,' Karen repeated.

'The police want us to identify your father,' he said. 'They're waiting,' he added.

Karen opened the closet door and took her coat off a hanger. She put it on. 'Let's go,' she said, and followed him out of the room.

'It's the first time I've lost someone,' said Leon.

She ignored him.

There was a funereal atmosphere as they walked through reception. The police car was waiting at the front of the hotel. They drove in silence to the hospital, waited a few minutes for the mortuary technician and then descended into the basement.

A body-bag lay on a gurney. The technician unzipped it. Leon looked at Karen. She was staring at her father. The body was still in the state in which it had been found. Dried blood was caked down one side of the face. It had been preserved intact with its microscopic clues for forensics and the pathologist.

'Is this your father Señor Raphael Guttman?' asked the policeman who'd accompanied them.

'Yes,' replied Karen quietly.

The policeman passed her a clipboard and a pen. 'Please sign here,' he said, rubbing a finger along the bottom of the page.

Karen signed and handed back the clipboard. She turned to Leon. She held his gaze. Her eyes were cold, her face expressionless. 'I will give you one million dollars to find the people who did this to my father,' she said.

Leon blinked. He was embarrassed. He glanced at the policeman and wondered if he'd heard or understood. 'Let's talk about it outside,' he said.

'No,' said Karen. 'I want to do it here, in front of my father. I want him to know we're going to avenge his death.'

'I understand how you feel ...'

'Do you?' she interrupted. Her voice rose. Anger broke through the control. 'How could you understand? You don't know me, Mr Garrick.'

'No one's going to let this rest, Karen. The police here will be looking for the killers. Your father's an American citizen. He was important. The FBI will investigate his death. Their combined resources will be far more effective than mine. You don't need to offer me a reward.'

'I like certainties, Mr Garrick. I know how these things turn out. The police run out of time. They don't have the money. They have different priorities. I want to sleep at night knowing there's someone on the case all the time.'

Leon looked down at Raphael Guttman. It seemed inappropriate to argue about the details over his body. It was time to get out. 'Yes,' he said. 'Of course I'll try to find them for you.'

'Not try, Mr Garrick. You will find out who was responsible.'

Leon nodded. 'Let's go,' he suggested, quietly.

Karen looked back at her father. 'I'll be taking my father back to America with me,' she said, and led the way out of the mortuary.

Chapter Six

I

Leon Garrick was back in Bilbao at the Parc Hotel six weeks after Guttman's death. The place made him feel uncomfortable. He still wondered if any of the hotel's employees had been involved in Guttman's kidnap and looked around suspiciously. The barman smiled at him before remembering why he recognised him, then substituted a more sombre expression. Leon took his beer over to a table in the corner and waited for Inspector Suarez to arrive.

He'd spent two weeks after Guttman's murder helping Suarez with his enquiries. Spanish bureaucracy moved at a snail's pace. Finally, his passport was returned and he flew back to England and another inquisition from his employer, Shadow Insurance Services. Fraser had not been pleased by the company's first major loss in two years and suspended Leon until the case was satisfactorily concluded. Leon didn't tell him that Karen Guttman had employed him to investigate her father's death, because he knew Fraser would object.

By the time Leon was ready to start his enquiries on Karen's behalf, Suarez had disappeared on holiday, and a month slipped away. When Suarez returned he wanted a week to pick up the pieces before they met. Now he was late and Leon was impatient. He flicked irritably through the newspaper he found on the table. Things had changed in the short time he'd been away. ETA had announced an indefinite truce and were calling for peace talks to end the bloodshed. He wondered whether Guttman's death had played a part in their sudden willingness to negotiate. It would make his investigation more difficult. No one would want him digging up the past now.

Leon looked up and saw Suarez approaching. He quickly put down the newspaper and jumped to his feet. They shook hands. He followed Suarez's eyes down to the newspaper and smiled sheepishly.

'Your Spanish has improved since we last met,' said Suarez.

'I've been working on it,' Leon replied.

Suarez nodded. 'Would you like a drink before lunch?'

'I'll have another beer.'

They sat down. Suarez signalled to the waiter and ordered drinks.

'Did you have a good holiday?' asked Leon politely.

Suarez hesitated a second. 'Yes, thank you,' he said.

'Where did you go?'

'La Coruña. We usually go there. It is a matter of habit. Perhaps it is time for a change.'

'I've never been there.'

'It is on the Atlantic coast. Cooler than the Mediterranean. My wife's family has a small villa there.'

Leon nodded. He wasn't interested in Suarez's private life, but the policeman's willingness to talk about it indicated that their relationship had changed. They were on equal footing. 'Have there been any developments since you've been away?' asked Leon, straight to the point.

Suarez frowned. 'Maybe. It depends how you interpret the information,' he said. 'The Ministry of the Interior tells me that they are looking into the matter. It is no longer my problem.'

'How does that suit you?'

'It is a political decision.'

'Are you pleased?'

'No. They won't find Señor Guttman's killers in Madrid.

But maybe they are not interested in finding them. The Minister of the Interior told me he believes that the kidnap was an attempt by ETA to raise money, but it went wrong.'

'Do you buy that?'

'No. The politicians are trying to cover up what happened. We know the kidnappers probably left Señor Guttman on the cliffs at Algorta and others took him so you would not find him. I know this because you recorded the instructions. However, I was also recording your conversations, except the machinery apparently failed on that evening, which is convenient for some people.'

'You knew about the kidnap all along?' asked Garrick.

Suarez shrugged and smiled. 'Most of the time.'

'Tell me about ETA,' Leon said.

'For many years the official story was that they were finished,' said Suarez. 'The newspapers said their cause was lost in 1992 and stopped reporting their activities. That was when the French arrested the organisation's top commanders, Pakito, Txelis and Fiti. Now they are suddenly in discussion.'

'How strong is the movement?'

'ETA is stronger than ever. Their leaders are in Algeria now, and the fact that the IRA have entered discussions with the British government gives them hope. They have also joined in the elections. Before, they refused to participate in the democratic process.'

'Basically they're criminals, using a political agenda to cover up their actions,' observed Leon.

'Not all political violence is terrorism,' Suarez corrected him. 'The Geneva Convention allows prisoner-of-war status for captured guerrilla fighters so long as they do not harm civilians. ETA states that the Spanish government is a force of occupation. It targets the military, the police and the politicians. If you think that terrorists are criminals then you must understand that they see their crimes as actions of retaliation. We should not underestimate the skill of these individuals in justifying their actions. The Ministry of the Interior is still paying money to those secret police who have been convicted of anti-democratic activities, for killing twenty-seven suspected members of ETA in four years. We must try to understand the terrorist because otherwise we cannot accommodate him. Things are not necessarily what they appear.'

'What was ETA's motive in kidnapping Guttman? They must have wanted the ransom. When a terrorist steals dynamite you expect a wave of bombings.'

Suarez nodded. 'Perhaps they wanted publicity. The news blackout in the national papers was too effective so they tried to get international publicity. Maybe they are angry with what they think is American involvement in Spanish affairs.'

'What are the Americans doing?'

'ETA was always anti-American. After the war the countries of Europe imposed sanctions on Spain because Franco was *fascista*. But America wanted military bases in Europe so they made a treaty, and afterwards it was impossible for Franco to fall from power. Then, in 1982, Spain joined NATO, but the Basques thought it meant more involvement by the United States in their affairs. America is a nuclear power, but Spain and especially the Basques refuse the nuclear option.'

'It's absurd to think America would target the Basques.'

'America never forgets an enemy. Maybe they built the Guggenheim Museum here as a challenge.' Suarez shrugged. 'But I also hear other things. It is rumoured that those who were involved in the unofficial attempt to rescue Señor Guttman are complaining. The people who organised them are late in making payments.'

'What people?'

'I don't know.' Suarez thought for a moment. 'If the Spanish government is behind an operation, then the police-men and mercenaries are usually compensated anonymously and win some prize from a bank, or a draw for a car, or even a local lottery prize. This time there have been no payments, not even to the family of the policeman who was killed.'

'Our investigation is getting off to a bad start,' observed Leon.

Suarez shrugged. 'I checked the names of those involved in the court case against Guttman-Tiche and who were known to be associates of Bernal Lasturra against the Wiesbaden files. They returned what I will call a list of associates of associates. I have a copy here for you.' He opened his briefcase and passed two pages across the table.

Garrick took them and looked at them with interest. The Germans would never have given him the list. The Wiesbaden database was legendary. Information about terrorism was recorded in two parts. The first contained non-evaluated information about people, institutions, objects, events and addresses suspected of being connected with terrorism. The system automatically made connections between the five categories without being prompted. The second was a file of people who were under suspicion but were not to be arrested. Once recorded they were registered whenever their papers were checked by police, especially when crossing borders.

'I tried other agencies without success,' continued Suarez. 'Unfortunately the professional terrorist does not advertise his politics or his movements.'

'Bernal Lasturra?' questioned Leon, reading off a name that was marked on the list.

'He was a former ETA activist who was released in an amnesty. He was killed around the same time as Señor Guttman. I suspect he was the hostage taken in retaliation for Guttman's kidnap.'

'That explains why the negotiations failed,' observed Leon, relieved that he had some clarification.

Suarez nodded. 'He was also involved in the court case against Guttman-Tiche here. I have the details and will show them to you later.'

'Did you follow up any more of these names?' asked Leon.

Suarez shook his head. 'Not yet. Many of the terrorists use aliases or adopt their identities from the false passports they use. I think we will be wasting our time at this early stage looking through all these names.' He changed the subject. 'And do you still have contact with Karen Guttman?'

'Yes. She returned to America. I have her address.'

'Let me ask you something,' said Suarez. 'Do you not think it strange that here in Spain they have closed the book on Señor Guttman? *Finito.* Just like that.'

Leon nodded.

'We will find out the answers to this, you and I,' said Suarez, with a conspiratorial smile. 'Maybe the answer lies in America. There is a connection between the Basques and the New World. Do you know about the two major migrations of Basques? The first was in the middle of the sixteenth and seventeenth centuries when the Basques dominated the fishing fleets off the Grand Banks. But the most recent was after the Civil War. Now ETA receives support from the Basques in America in the same way the IRA does from the Irish Americans. It is also possible that the kidnappers came from America and not from Spain.'

'That's a big jump,' said Leon.

'My contact from ETA denies the organisation was involved in the operation,' said Suarez suddenly. He looked at his watch. 'We can think about that while we eat. I have booked a table for us at Gorrotxa.'

Leon drained his glass and they stood up.

'Have you ever eaten traditional Basque food?' Suarez asked.

'Just at the hotel,' answered Leon.

'That is not the same,' said Suarez. 'Basque food is famous. Nowhere else does a country have gastronomic societies like they have here. You will see.' Then as an afterthought he added, 'It is the only good thing about the place.'

Leon ignored the remark. He felt apprehensive. His idea of

a good lunch was a prawn cocktail followed by steak. Invitations to sample the local delicacies usually involved eating things like chicken's feet and turkey gizzards.

2

Paul Miller worked for Korbett Biotek Inc., a subsidiary of the Guttman-Tiche Corporation, in upstate New York. Although his work was funded by the Pentagon it would take the most dedicated of investigators to trace the links.

It was Miller's birthday, and as always he thought how appropriate it was that he was born in 1953, the same year in which Francis Crick and James Watson discovered that deoxyribonucleic acid, DNA, contained the genetic code for life. For as long as he could remember he wanted to learn about life's delicate machinery. He attended the Bronx School of Science, and went to Johns Hopkins University in Baltimore in the same year that the first genetic experiments took place and genes were placed into harmless viruses to infect organisms, but it was another ten years before he became involved with genetic engineering.

Now Miller was forty-five years old and at the top of his field. He was tall, but stooped awkwardly as if perpetually apologising for his height. His fair hair was thinning, and the pallor of his complexion betrayed a sunless existence. His world was one of artificial lighting, antiseptic rooms, hard surfaces and precision instruments.

There was an arrogance in Miller which others found insufferable. No one in his field disputed his brilliance, but he was a loner. At first he gained recognition from his scientific papers, but soon stopped writing them because the rapid advances in molecular biology made the traditional means of disseminating new developments redundant, and others invariably benefited from his discoveries. His self-imposed exile from scientific circles suited his employers.

'The more you know, the more there is to know,' Miller always said. New diseases were continually released as the planet's ecology was destroyed. Viruses that once lay dormant in the rainforests, inhabiting monkeys or rodents, latched on to humans. The new viruses that threatened the human immune system were of paramount importance to biologists. The road to riches, fame and power lay in understanding and controlling them.

His life had not always been perfect. He'd gone to Johns Hopkins to escape his dominating parents. Afterwards he'd worked for six long years in the field as a virologist for America's Center for Disease Control, based in Atlanta. He'd loathed the discomfort of travel in primitive conditions when he visited villages in Africa and South America where there had been some viral outbreak. There, he had worked in unhygienic conditions testing blood samples. He trapped animals and insects to find which vectors the virus used to infect the villagers. He hated working with animals because they were invariably alarmed and furious at having been trapped. Monkeys, rodents and bats were the usual culprits, and they lashed out at him, tooth and claw. He had to be careful not to let their fluids or tissues come into contact with him. The urine from mice had been responsible for the Machupo outbreaks in Central America. Villagers sweeping their floors had inhaled the urine-contaminated dust and died four days later.

Now he shuddered when he thought about some of the things he had done. In the case of humans who had been contaminated by a virus, there was always the problem of handling them while they haemorrhaged from their noses, anuses or mouths. Invariably new outbreaks would be reported at the most inclement times of the year: during the rainy seasons, in places that were hot and humid and to which he was badly suited because of his fair hair and pale skin. The humidity caused all kinds of fungal infections, and barely a day passed when he didn't think he had been infected by something or other.

He'd performed hurried autopsies in the worst of conditions – in places without electricity, by the light of a few candles – before the body decomposed and turned to mush. There was nothing like a cadaver and some blood to attract every living creature from the wild to the site. And there was always one certainty. One of the attendant creatures harboured the virus which had killed the person beneath his scalpel. Now, thank God, he left that kind of thing to others.

During those years Miller planned a future for himself. Primarily, his job was to find the virus's reservoir, where it might have lived and replicated for decades or centuries in harmony with its host until it came into contact with a vulnerable animal or human being which it could infect. Infection in humans invariably caused epidemics. How commonly viruses exchanged genetic material while inside a vector wasn't known, but they did, and Paul knew that discovering this was his way back into the safety of a laboratory.

Those who sought power looked over the scientists' shoulders. All employees from the Center for Disease Control were forbidden to talk to outside agencies, especially the intelligence agencies. When Paul was ready to make his move it was a simple thing for him to call the number on the card which someone from the Defense Intelligence Agency had given him. Within months he had trebled his salary and was master of his own destiny. He had come a long way and didn't plan on sleeping under another mosquito net again in his life.

Although Miller had heard about Guttman's death in Bilbao, he felt neither sympathy nor concern. It had no effect on his research. He'd met Guttman only briefly, when he was called as an expert witness for the company at the Spanish court case. Some lawyer attempted to prove that the influenza vaccine was faulty. If anything, Miller thought wryly, the vaccine had surpassed his own expectations in its efficacy.

He peered at the test tube and concentrated on the job in hand. It had taken six weeks to collect the pellet of concentrated virus from thousands of hamster cells. The tube was in a glove box, and the gloves he wore were sealed into the glass front of the box. He eyed the test tube warily, even though he was wearing a plastic suit with a helmet. The suit was kept under pressure so that if he tore it, or inadvertently slit it with a scalpel, the air would flow away from his body. In a Level 4 maximum-security laboratory it was always assumed there might be aerosolised droplets that could infect him through his lungs, where the nerve fibres linked the outside world to his brain.

Miller knew what would happen if the virus entered his body. First there would be a severe fever. He would lie in pain, shivering and exhausted. Long before his immune system could counterattack the virus, his organs would cease functioning. His skin would peel away and his capillaries would bleed. He wouldn't be able to speak or swallow. He'd vomit blood and rot as his internal organs collapsed. In four days he'd be dead from a massive seizure or cardiac arrest.

Miller glanced out of the laboratory window, and for a moment he felt lonely. He wished there was someone with whom he could share dinner. It was his birthday, after all. He didn't look forward to the walk across the parking lot and the drive back to an empty house.

He looked back at the test tube. Relationships were easier for viruses. Their survival was simple because replication was merely mechanical and there were no expectations. Even bacteria could share their genes, reaching out for each other in a primitive mating ritual, which was how they gained an immunity to antibiotics. Humans were different, though, and now Paul Miller yearned for someone to share his life. However, he didn't want children because he knew the future was doomed through the inevitable evolution of viruses, the warming of the planet, and unavoidable war and starvation. He saw no point in procreation. He'd leave that to the masses in the Third World. Procreation was instinct, and he scorned such base motives.

Peering into the test tube, he imagined the horsemen of the

Apocalypse astride their rearing steeds. The history of humanity was the history of war.

3

Leon Garrick stood in the hall of Karen Guttman's New York apartment on Carnegie Hill. Ahead of him a staircase rose up to a second floor. The staircase alone was the size of a downtown studio apartment. Any concerns he'd harboured about claiming for his expenses evaporated. He was shocked to find he recognised a painting on the wall that he'd seen in some book. It was obviously the genuine item.

The maid opened a door into the lounge. Karen Guttman unfolded herself from the sofa and stood up.

'Hello, Leon,' she said, extending her hand. 'Thank you for coming to see me.'

He shook her hand and sat down opposite her. Karen's greeting wasn't what he had expected. When they had parted in Spain she'd been angry, upset and resentful. She'd blamed him in part for her father's death, and when they'd spoken on the phone the conversations had been cool and brief.

'How are you?' he asked.

'I'm still in shock, but it's wearing off. It's going to take a long time to come to terms with what happened,' she said.

'I know,' said Leon. Even when a victim wasn't killed, those involved in a kidnapping spent years in therapy, and often their relationships never recovered.

'Did you find out anything in Bilbao?' she asked.

'Not exactly,' he said. He didn't want to tell her that the investigation there had been closed to all intents and purposes. 'Inspector Suarez is still on the case and suspects that there were other people involved who didn't have your father's best interests at heart.'

Karen nodded.

'Are you sure you want me to continue making enquiries?'

'Why wouldn't I?'

'You might want to put this behind you,' Leon said.

'I need to know what happened. Until then I can't move forward.'

'I understand,' said Leon. He was relieved because he also wanted some answers. 'I need to talk to the people at your father's company, and for that I'll need your permission.'

'You have it.'

'Thank you.'

'I think you should know that I had a visit from someone called Colonel Jackson.'

'Who is he?' asked Leon.

'He didn't tell me which agency he represented, but said they were taking my father's death as a matter of top priority. He said that although I might not notice much publicity that was because they preferred to play it that way. He said they were going to move heaven and earth to find out who killed him. He gave me this card.'

Karen passed Leon the card. He looked at it. Just a name, and on the back a number written in pencil. 'Not very substantial,' he commented. He made a note of the telephone number.

'No,' Karen agreed. 'He said my father was important to him, to the Department of Defense and to this country. He said they owed him a debt and that they were going to make whoever killed him very sorry.'

'That must be reassuring.'

Karen looked at him as if trying to detect some hint of sarcasm. 'Yes,' she said. 'I want the bastards who were responsible. I don't know if you've ever lost a parent, Leon. I've lost both mine. Both times it was a shock. In some strange way the death of your parents turns you into an adult, although you still really want to be a child.'

Leon looked away. He'd never had those feelings. He'd been on his own for as long as he could remember. Finding out who killed Guttman would do something for him, though. It would put his career back on track. He wasn't so sure what it would do for Karen Guttman.

4

It was late in the afternoon. The sky was deep blue and the sunlight was bright. Clouds hung in the sky. Abene watched Miller walk across the parking lot towards her, and she then ducked down beside her rented car. She'd parked it next to Miller's Lexus. 'Give me a week,' she had told Michel in Paris, 'and I'll be drinking with Miller.' She'd find out about the vaccine Guttman-Tiche used in the double-blind trial in Bilbao.

Michel didn't think it would be that easy. She had laughed at him. 'Men are vain,' she said. 'They all think they're attractive. If they're approached by a woman they don't question it. The first thing on their minds is the quickest way to the bedroom.'

'Not all men,' said Michel.

'All men,' Abene insisted. 'It's programmed into their genes.'

'I thought I was special.'

'You are. But I wouldn't trust you alone in a room with another woman.'

Abene heard Miller open the car door. It was time to prove her theory was right.

'Can you believe it?' she said, apparently speaking to no one in particular, but addressing Miller because no one else was around. She turned towards him and smiled. He caught sight of her crouching in the shade by the front wing of the Chevrolet. She was holding her sunglasses in one hand and squinting up at him. She tossed her long brown hair.

'I believe in many things,' he answered. 'Most of them are usual,' he added, awkwardly pedantic.

'Look,' she said, standing up. She'd been changing the tyre. There was a light smear of grease across her forehead where she'd wiped her hair from her eyes with the back of her hand. A pair of expensive kid gloves lay on the asphalt beside her.

'Let me help you,' said Miller.

This was going to be easy. She was over the first hurdle. He could have ignored her and driven away, but he was coming to inspect the tyre. She made room for him beside her. He bent down and touched the sidewall with his hand.

'What are you going to do?' he asked.

She shrugged. 'Telephone a mechanic.'

'I'll help you,' Miller said. 'Do you have a spare?' She nodded, looking at him, her eyes wide and her face openly grateful.

'There's no point,' she said. 'The other front tyre is also flat.'

Miller thought for a moment. 'We'll change this tyre. Then we'll take the one off the other side and leave the car on the jack. I'll take you to get them repaired and bring you back. How about it?'

'You're not too busy?' she asked.

'No. It's Friday afternoon. I've got nothing better to do than help a damsel in distress.' He knelt down and clumsily fitted the jack into the chassis. He was mechanically inept. He grazed his knuckles loosening the wheel nuts.

Suddenly he stood up and stuck out his hand, awkwardly. It was covered in dirt. He withdrew it sheepishly. She giggled. 'My name's Paul. Paul Miller,' he introduced himself.

'And I am Abene. I am very pleased to meet you, Paul. Today you are my knight in armour.'

'Abene,' repeated Miller. 'That's a nice name.' He bent down and struggled with the wheel again. Abene squatted beside him and took the wheel nuts from his hands, one by one. Her fingers brushed his hand.

'Do you live near here?' asked Miller.

'I just moved into the area,' she answered.

'Oh.' He nodded. 'I've been here a couple of years.' He

looked closely at the wheel. 'Someone removed the valve and deflated the tyre,' he said.

'What does that mean?' asked Abene innocently.

'It means that your tyres weren't punctured. Someone did this on purpose.' He looked at the other tyre. 'The same here,' he added.

'Why would they do that?'

'This mall is new, but it's got problems.'

'Problems? How?'

'Muggings. People come here to do their shopping and gangs of youths rob them. They probably did this to your car. It would have made you more vulnerable if I hadn't been here.'

She gasped. 'Then I was lucky to find you,' she said. She reached out and touched his arm.

Miller smiled. He rolled the two wheels over to his car and wrestled them into the boot. His trousers were ruined from kneeling on the asphalt. He opened the door of his Lexus for her and said, 'Let's find some place to get these fixed before it gets too late.'

They got in his car and drove for a couple of miles before finding a suitable garage. The mechanic was busy but said he would do the job in an hour. They found a diner further down the strip mall and ate ice cream while they waited.

'How did you get that scar on your chin?' Miller asked.

'I was bitten by a dog when I was six,' she told him.

Miller winced. 'I don't like dogs,' he said.

'Good,' she laughed.

'So where were you born?' he asked.

'Argentina.'

'What brings you here?'

Abene's expression changed. She looked sad. 'I was married to an American. We were divorced five weeks ago. I came here from New York to make a new start in my life. Maybe it was a mistake. Perhaps I will go back to Buenos Aires. It is hard to make friends in America, especially in the country.'

'I know what you mean,' said Miller.

When they went to collect the tyres, he asked, 'What are you doing tonight?'

'Why?' she answered.

'We could have some dinner. It's my birthday,' he said.

'Only if you let me pay so I can thank you.'

'We'll discuss that over dinner,' he said.

That night Abene reinvented herself to mesh with Miller's life. Their tastes were the same. They liked the same films, the same books, the same hobbies. Chance appeared to have thrown them together and Miller never suspected otherwise.

Abene hadn't known if Miller was married or had a girlfriend. She assumed that someone who was forty-five would have some kind of attachment. She'd prepared herself for that. She imagined herself on the outside of Miller's life, as someone he would want to keep secret. That would have suited her. Instead he was single and keen to include her in his life.

When he heard she was living in a motel while she looked for a job he suggested that she move into his house. He joked about how he rattled around in it. She protested, but he insisted. He said there was enough space for her to have her own sitting room and bedroom. He promised to respect her privacy.

Abene moved in two days later. The large colonial-style house, set back from the road, was furnished with antiques and had a swimming pool to the rear. As she carried her suitcase through the door, Abene felt apprehensive. Something was wrong. Miller had everything in his life except someone to share it. The absence of a woman in his life made her question his character.

Over the following days she learned more about him. He'd never lived with anyone before and found difficulty in adjusting. He couldn't respect her privacy, wandering in and out of her room. The novelty of having someone in the house excited him, and she knew that he wanted more from her than friendship.

They had their first argument within a week when he began clearing up her belongings.

'I won't stay here if you keep moving my things. I don't want you to hide me away. Either I live here or I don't. I don't want you to pretend I am not here,' she burst out.

'Take it easy, Abene. I didn't mean it like that,' he said.

Abene sulked. 'I have the feeling you don't want me here. You are always cleaning after me. I will go.'

'Don't think like that,' pleaded Miller. Abene looked away and shook her head. 'Please believe me, Abene.' He put his hands on her shoulders. 'It just makes me happy to have you here.'

She looked up at him and smiled. 'Do you really mean it?' He nodded, but when he tried to kiss her she turned her head away and his lips touched her cheek. 'No,' she said. 'Not yet.'

Slowly, in a subtle way, she began to control his life. He began to doubt himself. Things changed, but he didn't understand how, and he became increasingly dependent on her.

5

The plane began its descent into JFK. Michel Ardanza felt groggy. He'd slept most of the way. Two rows ahead of him someone sneezed. In the days when he thought he might hijack a plane he'd researched aircraft manufacture. In order to reduce fuel costs the amount of freezing air drawn from the outside was decreased because it required heating. It resulted in a mixture of old and new air being circulated every seven minutes as opposed to a complete air change every three minutes. A complete air change now took over half an hour. The man sneezed again, his nasal passages efficiently spraying a fine solution into the air. Michel steeled himself for the inevitable cold in a few days' time.

Clouds scudded past the wings, and condensation licked across the porthole. Michel wondered how his life could have changed so quickly. A few months ago he'd been running a successful business, his past safely locked away, but now he was jeopardising it all. It was becoming increasingly difficult to turn back.

After leaving Spain, he and Abene had rented a short-let apartment in Paris. If it hadn't been for Abene he would have waited there for a few months and tried to find out what was happening in Spain, but she wanted to track down Paul Miller, the expert who had given evidence for Guttman-Tiche in the court case. Her enthusiasm was both compelling and attractive. It reminded Michel of himself when he was younger. He saw himself in her and as a result he loved her. It was a honeymoon period. They made love endlessly, and he was flattered that a girl almost twenty years younger than he found him attractive.

He taught Abene about being an urban guerrilla, explaining how she had to pretend to go to work every morning to avoid attracting the attention of the neighbours. He told her that she would have to kill time at museums, libraries and cinemas. He showed her how to communicate with dead-letter drops, e-mail and bulletin boards over the World Wide Web using a computer, a modem and a service provider; and together they tracked down Miller's address over the Internet.

Michel felt a flutter of fear in his stomach. Far below, as the plane broke through the clouds, he could see Long Island with its pincer claws stretching into the Atlantic Ocean. He'd done only one thing which could compromise him. Finding a false passport for Abene had meant contacting someone from his past. That person knew he was active again, but there was no way of determining if that person had changed his allegiance. Information had a nasty habit of being traded. Nevertheless, he'd taken the risk and bought Abene an Argentinian passport in the name of Pehrzon.

He peered down at the end of North Fork, where he knew there was a secret military research station on Plum Island. He strained his eyes but he couldn't distinguish the island from the mainland. He looked at the sandy beaches glinting in the sunlight. Americans claimed to espouse freedom, but instead they robbed, exploited and did whatever was necessary to ensure that existing privilege was protected. A little over a hundred years before, they'd given the Indians blankets contaminated with smallpox to wipe them out. Nothing had changed. They were still playing the same game.

A wave of anger against American imperialism rolled over him. He checked himself. He felt apprehensive all of a sudden. Perhaps it was because he felt out of control. Abene had made all the decisions. She was impetuous and he would have to be careful. He remembered how he used to advise the cells to recruit people when they were young and without personal affiliations, before they knew what death meant. These days in Peru the Shining Path were recruiting orphans who were sometimes only eleven years old. It made him feel he was too old to be back in the game. He was a composite creature once again, living on stolen licences and passports. He borrowed other people's memories to make a past for himself when he talked to strangers.

The captain told the passengers to fasten their seat belts. Michel looked down the aisle of the 747. There was no way out now. The plane was going to land unless he stood up, walked to the front, pulled out the all-plastic Glock and hijacked it. He imagined the expressions on the passengers' faces and felt a shudder of excitement, but it was nothing more than his anxiety about clearing Immigration. He smiled grimly to himself, inadvertently attracting the attention of a stewardess, who looked at him enquiringly. He shook his head and turned back to the porthole.

Hijacking planes was suicidal. Even the Algerian special forces could handle a hijack with some finesse. These days the best thing was to blow the plane out of the sky. That was still easy. Four ounces of Semtex was adequate. It couldn't be detected by X-ray machines. It could be rolled flat, popped into an envelope with a miniature detonator wired to a watch, and slipped under a seat where it would explode on the next leg of the flight, after the bomber had disembarked. It was vital that the watch made the electrical connection when the plane was cruising at around thirty thousand feet. If there wasn't enough plastic, the difference between the atmospheric pressure inside and outside the plane would help blow it apart. But, thought Michel, that wasn't his way. He wasn't interested in sacrificing the innocent. Never had been.

He was sweating, nervous about passing through Immigration. He told himself there was no reason to be worried. He'd been careful with the identity he'd set up years ago in case he had to leave Europe in a hurry. He was Carl Landow. If anyone checked they'd find that Carl was forty years old and lived in the Midwest. He was a United States citizen, a second-generation immigrant and long-term inmate of some squirrel farm in Idaho. His brains had been fried for the past ten years, and the nearest he'd come to flying was a syringe full of sedative.

Chapter Seven

I

Leon Garrick swung the hired Honda through the open gates into the Guttman-Tiche plant and stopped in front of the barrier. He looked at the keyboard below a video camera, opened the car window and pressed a button. A voice squawked from the intercom: 'Please state your business.'

'I have an appointment with Tod McFarlane,' he replied.

'Follow the blue line and park your vehicle in the visitor area, then report to reception.'

The barrier rose and Leon followed the instructions. He stepped out of the Honda and looked at the research laboratories in front of him. He was impressed. There were around two hundred cars in the parking lot. The place was surrounded by twenty-foot fences topped with razor wire. He walked to the entrance of the building. The door opened automatically and closed behind him. He felt the chill of air-conditioning. A man walked towards him. He was white, overweight and in his fifties. 'Hi there,' he said, extending an arm. 'You must be Leon Garrett. Pleased to meet you. I'm Tod McFarlane, head of security.'

'How do you do,' replied Leon, wondering whether or not to correct the man's mistake concerning his name and deciding against it.

'Let's go into my office,' said McFarlane. Leon followed him along a corridor until they reached the office. McFarlane pressed his finger on a touch pad and the door opened. He beamed. 'Pretty neat, huh?' he said, referring to the security device.

Leon looked around the office, waited for McFarlane to manoeuvre himself behind the desk, then sat down.

'When did you get in?' McFarlane asked.

'This morning. I caught the red-eye,' lied Leon.

'Staying in the Big Apple?'

'If I finish my business today.'

'First time in the States?'

'No. I was here a few years ago.'

'How do you like it?'

'Great place,' said Leon. Always flatter the inhabitants of a foreign country.

McFarlane smiled. 'I don't care for the city too much,' he confided. 'It's sixty miles but I only get there a couple of times a year. Guess I'm a countryman myself.' The conversation threatened to stall. 'Hey, how would you like some coffee?'

'That would be good,' said Leon.

McFarlane stood up. He was breathing more heavily from the exertion of walking down the corridor. 'How long did it take you to get here? Couple of hours?'

'A bit longer. I took a wrong turn.'

'Sugar? Milk?' Leon shook his head. McFarlane poured the coffee from a machine in the corner. Leon watched him load his cup with sugar.

'So,' said McFarlane, sitting down again, 'you've come about Raphael Guttman?'

'That's right. He took out insurance with my company in England. I'm tying up a few loose ends so we can make the necessary payments to his estate.'

'Sure,' said McFarlane. 'That was a terrible thing happened to Raphael. By the way, you got a card or anything to tell me who you work for?'

McFarlane leaned forward. Leon reached into his pocket and retrieved his wallet. He pulled out his card and passed it across the table. He realised that McFarlane was a lot sharper than he looked.

'Mind if I call you Leon? I don't stand on ceremony too much.' Leon nodded. 'So, Leon, tell me about this outfit.' McFarlane flicked the card with his finger.

'It was established about twenty years ago. It may not be the biggest, but it's the most discreet company specialising in kidnapping, extortion and forensic accountancy. It employs around a thousand people.'

'You always worked for them?'

'No. I was in the army before.'

'You don't say. Me too. I did twenty years. This is like a second career. I come up for retirement next year.'

Leon was surprised. 'You look younger than that.'

'Left the army when I was thirty-seven. Next year I'll finish here. I'll have two pensions. Then I plan on taking some time off.'

'I guess we're in the same sort of business, Tod. Security of one sort or another.' It was time to bond. 'What's it like working here? After the army, I mean.'

'OK. The place runs itself, mostly. I keep an eye on the systems.' He brushed aside Leon's amiability. 'So tell me about what went on over there in Spain. I didn't get to hear the details. All I keep thinking about is Karen Guttman. Hell of a thing to happen to a young woman like that. You ever meet her?'

'Yes,' said Leon. 'I met her while I was negotiating for Guttman's release.'

McFarlane nodded. Leon described what had happened and how Raphael Guttman had been killed.

'That's a terrible thing to have happened,' repeated McFarlane when he had finished. 'So how can I help you?'

'Mr Guttman's insurance policy took into account the possibility of his death,' lied Leon. 'Before we pay out we have to clear some details.'

'Sure.'

'First of all, the Spanish police don't seem to have carried out a very thorough investigation. Can you tell me when you first heard about the Guttman kidnap?'

'When they found his body.'

Leon nodded. He'd been thinking this trip was a waste of time until McFarlane said that. Karen Guttman had told him she'd contacted McFarlane when her father disappeared.

'You probably heard there was a court case against your company. There were claims that something went wrong with one of the vaccines. Something like that. I wonder if I could talk with someone who was out there.'

'That was cleared up.'

'Sure. But one of the theories is that the people who murdered Raphael were also involved with the court case. When it was thrown out they decided to take direct action. Maybe someone in your Spanish operation was involved with the kidnappers.'

'Why aren't the Spanish police checking this out?'

'They are. You know how it is over there. Always *mañana*. There's an Inspector Suarez who's still interested.'

'Any suspects?'

Leon shrugged. 'He mentioned a few names, but they didn't mean much to me.' He waited for McFarlane to sound him out, but he didn't. He hurried on, 'It would help me a lot if I could find out what was going on there. Like I said, these details are holding up payments to the estate, and I'd like to sort things out as soon as possible. If it were me I'd just pay the money. Karen shouldn't have to wait about like this. How can her life move forward with this hanging over her head?'

'I don't see what happens here has to do with your company,' said McFarlane bluntly.

'Nor me. I got sent here to make a report. You know how insurance companies work. You take out a policy, forget to read the small print, and you don't get paid. They're looking for a way out. It's just a formality as far as I'm concerned.'

McFarlane nodded. 'Yeah. Sounds like insurance to me. Who do you need to talk to?'

'I'd like to get a handle on that court case in Bilbao. You know, get to understand the issues at stake. Inspector Suarez suggested I speak to Dr Miller.'

'We don't have a Miller working here.'

'He was an expert witness.'

'They must have called him in from outside. I'll make a few calls for you to see if I can track him down. Maybe our lawyer can help.'

'Any idea how long that will take?'

'You can try me Monday.' McFarlane looked at his watch and shut down his computer. 'Guess I should be moving.'

Leon realised he was being dismissed. 'I'll call you on Monday,' he said, and followed McFarlane to the front door. 'Do you know the name of a hotel around here?'

'There's the Bel Air Motel over in Bethlehem.'

'Thanks,' said Leon.

He doubted he'd learn much of interest from Miller after McFarlane had spoken to him. He turned at the last moment and offered his hand. 'The strange thing is that Karen Guttman made a call to America as soon as her father went missing. I'd like to know who she called, and why.'

McFarlane's eyes narrowed for a brief second. 'I guess you got to check every angle, Leon,' he said breezily.

'That's right,' said Leon. He walked back to his car. He drove towards the gates. A security guard was walking across the lot. Leon pulled over and opened the window. 'Excuse me,' he said.

The guard stopped.

'Do you know if Dr Miller's here today?'

The guard rolled his eyes and gestured at the cars in the lot. 'You gotta be joking,' he said. 'Better ask in the office.'

'It'll wait,' said Leon casually.

'Describe him to me.'

Leon thought quickly. 'Never met him. A friend asked me to look him up.'

The guard pulled out his radio, turned his back and spoke into it.

'Paul Miller?' the guard asked Leon a moment later.

'That's right.' Leon nodded.

'He don't work here.' The guard glared at him.

'Thanks,' said Leon, and drove back to New York City. Karen Guttman would have to use her contacts to find Miller for him.

2

It wasn't the first time Miller had stepped over the boundary. This time he'd helped himself to another whisky and as he passed Abene he grabbed her and tried to kiss her.

'No,' she said, pushing him away. 'Please, not yet.' She disentangled herself and quickly cleared up the dinner debris. She didn't know how much longer she'd be able to hold him off. She'd told him that she needed time to recover from her failed marriage. She told him that her previous husband abused and beat her. The stories appeared to make him angry, and he talked about finding out where the man lived and exacting revenge on her behalf. 'I just want to forget about him,' Abene said.

'You can trust me,' Miller insisted.

'After what happened to me your trust and faith in people disappear,' she said. 'You think you know someone, and then you find out he's seeing people behind your back.' She hesitated. 'I don't want there to be secrets between us, Paul,' she said. 'It's important that our relationship starts off on the right track.'

He looked at her. She made it sound like a promise. 'There won't be any secrets,' he agreed.

After that it was easy. She played the victim, and if he didn't answer her questions then she acted hurt. He did everything he could to accommodate her.

'Explain your work to me,' she asked him one evening.

'It's just research for a small biotechnology company,' he said.

'What sort of research?'

'Manipulating viruses. That sort of thing.'

'Is it interesting?'

'Yes. But it's secret,' he said.

Abene waited for a moment, then said, 'But we don't have any secrets, Paul. I thought that was the agreement.'

'I mean, we don't talk about it much,' he said quickly.

'Why?'

'Because other companies are interested in our developments. We have to be wary of industrial espionage.'

'It sounds exciting,' said Abene. 'But I understand if you don't feel comfortable telling me about it.'

'I suppose there's nothing wrong with talking about it in general terms,' he said. 'I'm developing fusion viruses.'

'What's that?' she asked.

'I guess you've heard of genetically engineered vegetables?'

'Tomatoes grown to have the best features of all the different varieties? The best colour and the best taste?'

'Yes, although that's a very simple concept. What I do is the same sort of thing. Except I use viruses.'

'Huh? Why would you want to do that? Aren't there enough viruses in the world already?' Abene asked.

'We're just beginning to understand the complex way in which viruses work. They can be good and they can be bad. They invade our bodies all the time and get picked up by our cells. Some have no effect; others cause cancers or latch on to our genes.'

'I don't understand.'

'Imagine your body's a computer. With a computer you move the mouse, you type the words, you print out the result. You don't care about the hidden files on the computer which make it do what you want. Your body works the same way.

You go down the road, buy some food and eat it. You don't care how your body works on a cellular level. Computer viruses are programmes which can affect the hidden files on computers. Viruses do the same with humans. You go down the road, buy some food, eat it, but then you get sick because your hidden files have been corrupted. Computer viruses are engineered by people. But natural viruses can be manipulated in just the same way.' He paused.

'Is it like chemical weapons?' Abene frowned.

'Not really. It's more precise and selective. But maybe you've got a point. In the early days of chemical weapons scientists had problems testing their weapons. In the First World War there were two scientists, a German and an Englishman. The German, called Fritz Haber, pioneered chemical weapons and won the Nobel Prize for chemistry. He called them a higher form of killing because they didn't maim people. Meanwhile an Englishman called Barcroft was looking for a chemical to use against the Germans and discovered that some were selective. He found that hydrogen cyanide killed dogs but not goats. He had no idea whether it would kill humans so he stood in the gas chamber with a dog. The dog died but he walked out with only a headache.'

'I didn't think we would be so different to animals,' said Abene.

'That's just the beginning,' said Miller. 'Soon afterwards the Geneva Convention outlawed biological and chemical weapons. However, Japan never signed, and during the Second World War their Special Unit 731 embarked on some experiments. They tried different chemicals and bacteria on prisoners to determine whether some races were more resistant than others. They vivisected them to record the effects. They even used American prisoners and they didn't use anaesthetics in case the drugs interfered with the results. At the end of the war we covered up the Japanese programme and granted an amnesty to the Japanese scientists in return for the data. The material was unique.'

'But if biological weapons are illegal then the data isn't any use,' Abene observed.

'Knowledge is power,' commented Miller. 'And things have moved on since then. Thirty years ago two scientists managed to clone genes, and that changed the whole ball-game.'

Abene bit her lip and frowned. 'I don't understand.'

'Each organism carries hereditary information passed from its ancestors through genes. Each gene contains a chemical known as DNA. When a cell divides, it creates an exact replica of itself. The process is the same for all organisms, from viruses to humans. All we need to do is snip a single gene from a virus and splice it into DNA.'

'But why would you want to do that?'

'So we can control the virus. We can decide how long it lasts, how strong it should be and even who or what it will affect. Genetic markers differentiating between one group of people or another trigger the virus.'

Abene looked at him. 'That's amazing,' she said.

Miller was encouraged. 'Lederberg put it most succinctly. The essence of a virus is its fundamental entanglement with the genetic machinery of its host. You can prevent viruses, but you can't cure them. Viruses can be used to trick the human immune system. They can even smuggle things into the body, like vaccines.' He was caught up in the excitement he felt for his subject. 'It's like myxoma, which gives rabbits myxomatosis. It affects and kills only rabbits.'

'Is that why the Human Genome Project is so important?'

Miller raised his eyebrows. He didn't expect her to know anything about the subject. 'The Genome Project's limited. When it's completed it'll tell us all there is to know about people in general. It won't tell us anything about an Indian in Bombay, except that he's human.' Miller hesitated. 'There's a much more important project called the Human Genetic Diversity Project, which takes samples from distinct racial types. Now, the DNA in that project tells us about the evolutionary history of particular populations and their resistance or susceptibility to diseases or viruses. It's a fantastic project. Race genes don't exist as such, but a cluster of genes might be shared by a group of people. Look at it from this angle. Some tribe in Borneo might have a gene that prevents them from catching schizophrenia.'

'That's not a virus.'

'There's evidence to suggest it is,' he said dismissively. 'Anyway, you take the preventive gene, put it in a virus and give it to people in a vaccine.'

Abene looked doubtful.

'Think about Anglo-Saxons, especially those fat English people with a predisposition to heart disease. That's genetic. Feed them plenty of eggs and red meat to increase their cholesterol, then put them in a room full of cigarette smoke and wait for the heart attack. Now, imagine what you could do if you had mapped the genes which were responsible.'

'You wouldn't want this knowledge to fall into the wrong hands,' Abene said ingenuously.

Miller giggled. 'I'll let you into another secret,' he said, and leaned forward. 'I work for the Department of Defense.' He was excited because he seldom talked to people about his work. Here was someone who was interested and he wanted to share the passion he felt with her.

'Other countries are already using this knowledge. We need to make vaccines that will work against engineered viruses. But it's not that easy. The engineered virus is sometimes manipulated to render current vaccines ineffective. It's like a game of chess.'

'That's awful,' said Abene.

'Sure. That's why these weapons are called the poor man's atom bomb. It costs two thousand bucks to target a square kilometre with conventional weapons. Eight hundred with nuclear weapons. But only one dollar with a biological weapon. We have to consider these things. An epidemic of dengue fever nearly bankrupted Cuba but hardly killed anyone. You don't need a sledgehammer to crack a nut. Shortly afterwards the Russians engineered a variation of the virus called D7.'

'You make the viruses as well as the vaccines.'

'That's right. We need to know what viruses might be developed so we can manufacture a vaccine.'

'What sort of viruses?'

'Like a virus I'm working on at the moment. I'm splicing an influenza strain to a rabies virus. We have vaccines to both viruses, but we haven't been able to create a vaccine to the recombinant virus yet.'

'But why did you combine those two viruses?'

'Rabies is one of the obvious choices. It's easiest to start with something that exists in the natural world. It's a severe virus, normally caused by a bite from an infected animal. It enters the skin and travels along the nerves to the spinal cord and then to the brain. Incubation takes from one to six weeks. Once the virus is full-blown, death happens in a few days. By combining it with a virulent influenza strain it becomes airborne. The object of the influenza would be to soften up an enemy, and if they capitulated then the vaccine could be administered in good time to reduce the number of casualties.'

'But you don't have a vaccine?'

'Not yet, but some day soon we will. Like I said, it's chess. We research because we'd better be sure we've gotten something bigger and better than they have.'

Miller explained how the researchers decided what viruses to manufacture and how they could be deployed. He described how ballistic missiles could be filled with frozen viruses, and how mosquitoes could be used as a vector to spread plasmodium parasites. He told her how viruses were being manipulated to target particular groups.

'You said we are all different but we are all the same. I still don't understand how you can do what you're telling me,' she said.

'Each one of us carries six million base pairs of genes. Of

these we all have eighty-five per cent of them in common. Nine per cent reflect differences among ethnic groups within any given race. Six per cent represent genetic differences between races. We just keep crunching the numbers on bigger and bigger computers looking for genetic comparisons. Take the Basques, for instance.'

'The Basques?' repeated Abene.

'They're an ethnic minority in northern Spain. They don't fit into the genetic map of Europe. They are as racially pure as the human comes.'

As Abene listened to Miller, things became clear for the first time. Her heart pounded.

'When you look at their genes you're unlocking the secrets of the past,' she said.

'You could say that,' said Miller.

3

Colonel Jackson took his jacket off the coat hanger behind the door of his office and put it on. He worked in the United States Defense Intelligence Agency in Virginia, the Pentagon's intelligence-gathering organisation. His agency had five times the budget of the CIA, an outfit he didn't trust because it was essentially a civilian operation. The DIA filtered all intelligence coming into the United States before forwarding necessary details to the CIA or the White House. Much of the material was so secret that it would never appear in the DIA daily newspaper, DINSUM, which landed on the desks of the President, the Secretary of State, and the few senators and congressmen who'd been security-cleared for it.

Jackson worked hard, eighteen hours a day, six and a half days a week, because knowledge was power. He didn't drink, bought fast food, could read a page in fifteen seconds, pick out the facts and give a critique on the style if necessary. He had developed a high-cholesterol look as the muscle turned to fat on his thickset body, and jogging twice a week with his dogs wasn't enough to keep things in shape. The once-angular face was softening. His hair was too short to hint at colour. Once an army man, always an army man. He exuded an air of authority and, even when out of uniform, strangers deferred to him. It had been a long time since anyone had posed him an awkward question or contradicted him. He had lived alone since his wife left him while he was on a secret mission because she couldn't take the months of separation.

Jackson was opening the door when the telephone rang. He hesitated, looked at his watch and then answered it.

'We have a development on that Spanish operation,' McFarlane said.

Jackson was annoyed. He'd thought Guttman was history. He'd seen to that. There had been one or two loose ends, a few enquiries by the Spanish police which he'd managed to silence. He'd talked to Karen Guttman and put her mind at rest.

'What now?' he snapped.

'I've had a visit from Leon Garrett.'

'What does he want?' Jackson growled. As he listened to McFarlane he recalled what he knew about Garrick. He'd pulled the file on him as soon as he heard he was involved in the Guttman negotiations. The only thing he didn't like was reading that Garrick's nickname was Trotsky. Why would someone put up with a name like that? He had some distant memory that Trotsky was the Communist who got an ice pick in his head down Mexico way. That was promising.

The file had been opened because Garrick had located one of the eight hundred surface-to-air Stinger missile launchers that the US had supplied to the Afghans to help them fight off the Russian invasion. Only half the Stingers were recovered and, when they started appearing on the black market, Congress was terrified they'd be bought by terrorists, so made their retrieval a top priority. After successfully repatriating the Stinger, Garrick worked on a few joint Anglo-American operations before being pensioned off with a wound he collected in South America.

Nothing was ever what it seemed with the British. That had been Jackson's first lesson when he joined Intelligence. The British were experts at reworking the truth. Always had been. Take Charles Darwin. Everyone thought the British Admiralty sent him to the Galapagos Islands so that he could write about the evolution of species, but that wasn't the reason. Darwin was a tiny cog in a massive operation to map the world so that Britain could control it. However, the British Empire was gone and there was no more red on the world map. America was doing the mapping now, making a blueprint of humanity's genes in the Human Genome Project. He wasn't going to let Garrick get in the way of that.

'I'll take care of it,' Jackson told McFarlane. His conversation with Karen Guttman evidently hadn't been sufficient. This time he'd come up with something better.

'You want me to take any other action?' asked McFarlane.

'Stay cool, hang loose and I'll be in touch.' Jackson put down the receiver and thought.

He considered hiring Garrick. The Secretary of State would pay half a million dollars for information leading to the prevention of terrorism or the apprehension of terrorists. That kind of money bought people like Garrick. Correction. Money bought everyone. Except patriots. But Jackson couldn't give Garrick that kind of freedom because there was too much at stake.

Garrick wasn't a problem. He could be dealt with. He could disappear. Coincidence was the problem. What others saw as an isolated coincidence masked the existence of something more sinister. Coincidence was the work of the Devil. It masked the true nature of events and seduced people into making false decisions.

At the beginning of the week McFarlane had reported that there were no records of the woman living with Paul Miller. No Social Security number. No bank account. No marriage certificate. Abene Pehrzon was Argentinian and had been married to an American citizen. When they checked, she had no history, and people without a past needed investigation. It hadn't seemed too important at the time, and there were plenty of explanations for her existence in America. Immigration were in the process of checking out her visa applications.

Now, all of a sudden, Garrick had turned up to talk to Paul Miller. Nothing coincidental about that. But it was definitely time to check out the girl.

He wondered whether to speak to the general, but decided against it. There was no point alarming him. If he knew, then the White House would know. If the President knew, then the whole world would know.

He looked at his watch, then called Karen Guttman. If she wanted to know who had killed her father, then he'd hand her the killer on a plate.

4

Michel spent four nights in the Mayflower Hotel in New York City before he found the SoHo apartment in the pages of the *Village Voice*. He gave a month's rent as deposit and a month's rent in advance. His landlord was an artist who made it clear that the sublet wasn't legal, but Michel wasn't interested in the intricacies of New York's housing regulations, and it suited him that no one would be advertising his presence. He paid an additional three hundred bucks deposit for the telephone calls he might make, and disappeared from view.

Michel was growing impatient, when Abene finally sent him an e-mail message telling him that she was coming to Manhattan. When he met her in Grand Central Station he realised how much he'd missed her. They barely spoke of what they'd done since they last saw each other, piling into a cab and going to his apartment. The urgency of their emotions took him by surprise. He forgot that he'd intended to keep his address from her. Once inside the apartment, they ripped off their clothes and fell on to the bed and made love as if it were for the last time in their lives. All thoughts of contraception or protection were abandoned, but neither of them cared and afterwards neither mentioned it.

Eventually Michel asked the question he'd been dreading. It was as if he wanted to spoil the moment, to withdraw from reality and deny what he felt.

'Are you sleeping with Miller?' he asked.

'Why do you ask?'

He didn't answer.

'Are you jealous?'

'I need to know on an operational basis,' he said.

'Would you please laugh when you say things like that,' said Abene, her fingers pulling at the corners of his lips.

Michel smiled. 'I'm serious.'

'So am I.'

'You're sleeping with him,' said Michel, and felt jealousy and betrayal. If she could sleep with Miller so easily it didn't say much for his relationship with her. He slipped out of bed and fetched a beer from the fridge.

'No,' said Abene. 'I haven't slept with him, and I don't intend to.'

Michel didn't know whether or not to believe her. He was angry with himself. Whatever she said made no difference anyway. If she had to sleep with him, she would.

'What have you found out?' he asked.

'Miller knows what went on in Bilbao.'

'He told you?'

'Not specifically. He told me that our genes are unique.'

'He knows you're Basque?' Michel was alarmed.

'No. He was talking about Basques in connection with his work. Guttman was right. There was some sort of experiment. Maybe it was something to do with a project Miller's working on for the Department of Defense.'

'Why would the Pentagon be interested in Spain?' wondered Michel.

Abene shrugged.

Historical reasons, thought Michel. President Truman made a pact with Franco so that America could have a foothold in Europe, and that ended any hope of toppling Franco's regime. Even when a plane carrying nuclear weapons went down off the south coast of Spain, Franco didn't object, thus proving that America had Spain in her pocket.

'I don't think it has anything to do with Spain. It was just expedient to do it there. It's part of a bigger project to develop genetically manipulated viruses as weapons for the future.'

'Then our own government was involved,' said Michel. 'Can you get samples of the virus?'

'I don't see how. First I'd have to get into the laboratory. I wouldn't know what to look for.' She stared at Michel. 'Are you thinking of using them?'

Michel didn't answer.

'Here? In America?'

'That wouldn't do any good,' said Michel. 'If there is a conspiracy, then we need the proof.'

'What do we do with proof?' Abene snapped. 'The world doesn't want to know about the truth. No one cares about that any more. Truth gets distorted. We know how Iraq bought chemical and biological weapons technology from Europe and America in the first place, but now America bombs Iraq for having it. It doesn't make sense.'

Michel nodded. She was right. America had refused to join the sixty-five other countries that signed the convention on chemical and biological weapons, arguing that compliance couldn't be verified and their manufacturers would be subject to unconstitutional searches by an international inspectorate. America didn't want to jeopardise her national security. There was one law for America and another for the rest of the world.

'We need those viruses, whatever they are,' said Michel.

'Either that, or we turn Miller. We need to get some details from him.'

In the evening Abene went back on the train to join Miller. Michel felt a pang of jealousy. He hated suggesting that she should try to get into the laboratories, because it would probably mean she'd have to sleep with Miller. It was the only way she'd be able to get in close. He was angry with himself for having such feelings and tried to put Abene out of his mind. If he had feelings, he could have regrets, and there wasn't room for them in his life any more.

During the following days he read about viruses and genetic manipulation at the New York Public Library. He was surprised to discover that if Abene obtained a virus sample it didn't require specialised equipment to store it. He could buy what he needed over the counter at any laboratory supplier.

On the fifth day, one of the librarians asked him what he was researching. It was an innocent question. She was pretty and plump. She had made a list of all the books he had consulted. 'You don't look like a scientist,' she said, 'but you must be because no one ever reads those books.' Michel was nervous. This was how people were caught. Whatever he did now, she would always remember him. If she read something in the news about viruses, nitrogen or cryogenics, she'd think of him.

'I'm a biologist,' he said quickly. 'I'm working on a theory. There is a *sapo*, a toad which hibernates under the ice. The whole body freezes, even the eyes and the heart, but in the spring it thaws without problems. It is interesting, because you or I, we would explode,' he said. 'I will buy you dinner and tell you of it. There is much money to be made in cryogenics.'

'I'm not fond of toads,' she said.

'Ahh! But have you thought about being frozen when you die? Maybe one day they will find a cure for what killed you.'

'Then a prince will come, kiss me and wake me up?'

'You're already a princess,' Michel flirted.

That's good, he thought. Now she would always associate

him with toads. After dinner they went to bed, and he made sad, fumbling love to her in an Upper West Side apartment. It made him feel better about Abene. He was breaking the bond between them. He was destroying the feelings that made him vulnerable. He slept with the librarian for three nights in a row, until he heard her talking on the telephone to a friend about the new man in her life, and he knew it was time to get out. He made an excuse about a research trip to Canada and promised to see her on his return.

People were always a danger. Trusting people took time. It was like establishing the provenance of guns before buying them, checking that they hadn't been used for a murder. People, like guns, carried baggage. The baggage was often dangerous.

5

Leon Garrick found Karen Guttman's gallery on Fifth Avenue. He stepped off the humid street into the cool interior. 'Can I help you?' asked a designer-dressed assistant. People like him obviously didn't drop in off the streets.

'I'm here to see Miss Guttman.'

'Can I ask what it is regarding?'

'It's personal,' said Leon.

The girl disappeared. A doorman kept an eye on him until the girl returned.

'Please. Follow me,' she said.

He was escorted up the stairs to a large office. Karen was on the telephone. She acknowledged his arrival with a wave. The assistant asked him if he wanted coffee and he declined.

Karen seemed to have changed. He wondered if it was because he was seeing her against a different background, surrounded by people. She was wearing a pastel-blue linen dress. He'd seen her only in dark colours before. He looked around, surprised that she employed so many people. He'd thought her business was more of a hobby.

'I don't have much time,' she said, putting down the phone, 'but I've booked a table for us down the block.'

She issued a stream of instructions to one of her employees, then they left the room. She seemed more cheerful than he remembered her. There was a spring in her step. He'd only known her to be thoughtful and reflective, moods occasionally interspersed with anger. She was altogether a more attractive person.

'They found the man who killed my father,' she said when they were outside. She turned to face him. He could see that she was relieved.

'How do you know?' he asked. He should have known there would be a reason for the change in her mood.

'I met the men who caught him.'

'Tell me about it,' said Leon.

'Over lunch,' she said, turning into a restaurant.

Leon barely noticed the attention the manager bestowed on Karen. He was distracted. He realised that his job was coming to an end. He'd grown fond of her and had begun to see himself as her protector.

'You remember I told you about Colonel Jackson,' she said, once they were seated. 'He called me on Saturday to make an appointment. He took me to the air force base at Annapolis to see the body on Monday.'

'Body?'

'The kidnapper's.'

'How do you know it was the kidnapper?'

'I spoke to the agents who arrested him. They'd planned to bring him back here to stand trial.'

'I thought it was a woman. We spoke to a woman on the phone.'

'This was the person who organised it. They arrested him and questioned him. He confessed. When they were leaving the house some ETA terrorists tried to rescue him.'

'You saw the body?'

'Yes.'

Leon nodded. 'You spoke to the agents?'

'Yes.'

'What were they like?'

'They apologised. They said they were late getting on to the kidnap.'

'Didn't they have problems with the Spanish police? If you remember, it wasn't exactly easy for us to repatriate your father's body.'

'What's wrong? You sound suspicious.'

He denied it. 'It's just a shock. I wasn't expecting such a quick result, and I haven't been in touch with Inspector Suarez.'

Karen continued. 'The man was an American. He'd planned my father's kidnap for a long time. As Colonel Jackson said, these things are sorted out behind the scenes.'

Leon nodded. 'Are you glad?'

'What do you mean?'

'Are you glad it's over now?' That had been the point of her hiring him, after all. She'd wanted to get even, and now apparently the slate was wiped clean.

'Yes,' she said. 'I've prepared a money order for you which should cover all your expenses. Thank you.' She looked in her handbag and removed an envelope. Leon took it. He didn't open it but put it in his jacket pocket.

'Did Colonel Jackson ever tell you who he worked for?'

Karen smiled. 'No. But I think it's obvious.'

Leon smiled. He nodded. It wasn't that obvious to him. He wanted to talk to Suarez. 'Did they give you any details?'

'Yes,' she said. 'Like you, I wasn't sure they had the right person at first. Then they told me he'd confessed. He knew the code words. He mentioned the opera *Les pêcheurs de perles*. He could only have got it from my father. It was his favourite. He knew the name of the puppy I had when I was a kid. You remember how I told them to ask my father that? No one else would have known I'd asked that question.'

Leon nodded. Not unless they'd listened in on the telephone conversations. These guys were organised and very good at their job. He ate his lunch and listened as Karen explained how her father's kidnap was a botched attempt by ETA to raise funds. 'They showed me the dossier which the FBI had on the man.' Leon didn't disillusion her. Karen had a right to believe that it was all over

Two hours later, in a well-worn room at the Gramercy Hotel, Garrick called Suarez. The phone rang for a long time before it was finally answered.

'Who is it?' asked Suarez, his voice muffled by sleep.

'Leon Garrick. I'm phoning from the States.'

'Yes?' responded Suarez.

'Karen Guttman tells me they found the person who killed her father.'

'Where?' Suarez suddenly sounded alert.

'In Bilbao.'

'I know nothing about this.'

'There was a shooting. They brought the body back to America.'

'There has been nothing like that. But we should not speak on the telephone,' said Suarez. 'We will arrange to meet.' He hung up.

Leon stared at the wall of the hotel room for a long time. Eventually the rattle of the air-conditioning disturbed him. The job was over. The reward had gone. Karen had paid him off. There wasn't anything left in it for him and he wouldn't be seeing Suarez again. He picked up the receiver and booked his flight back to London.

In the morning he got up, dressed and packed his bags. He'd slept badly. The trip to America had resolved nothing for him. He opened the envelope Karen had given him and looked at the money order. It was generous but it didn't remove the question marks which hovered over his handling of the negotiations in Spain. He was still suspended from work and it was unlikely that another insurance company would want him working on a case. He took out Colonel Jackson's number and dialled it. He had nothing to lose by talking to the man.

An answering machine cut in. The message was brief. 'Leave your name and I'll get back to you.'

'This is Leon Garrick with a message for Jackson. I'd be grateful if he'd contact me with the details he gave Miss Guttman. I'm anxious to close the book on her father's murder.'

He went downstairs, paid his bill and caught a cab to the airport. He realised he hadn't left a phone number for Jackson but reasoned that the colonel obviously had the resources to find out how to contact him.

Chapter Eight

I

Somehow, meeting Michel changed things for Abene. He opened a window. He provided a faith and gave her a sense of purpose. He restored a belief that individuals could make the world a better place. He wasn't discouraged by the indifference of others but was prepared to do something about injustice, and it made her more determined to prove herself. She waited impatiently for the opportunity to present itself so she could get into the laboratory.

She worked hard on Miller to gain his trust, but he sensed she was holding back. She suspected the only intimacy he recognised was sexual. 'Tell me what I'm doing wrong,' he said one morning, 'otherwise I'll never learn.'

'You're not doing anything wrong,' she tried to reassure him. 'You've been good to me. You're perfect the way you are.'

'But we don't get any closer. You're always pushing me away,' he complained. 'We don't do things together.'

'But we're so much closer now,' Abene said. 'Relationships take time.'

He grunted. A moment or two later he said, 'I have to go to work this afternoon.'

'Why?'

'To check on some cultures.'

'You promised we'd go skating,' complained Abene.

'I'm sorry,' said Miller. 'This is important.'

'We made a plan.' She pouted. 'If you'd told me before I could have arranged something else. Take me with you. I want to see where you work.'

'You'll be bored,' he said.

'No, I won't,' she insisted. 'I promise.'

'All right,' he said. 'But if you complain, just once ...' he teased.

'What?' she asked.

'You have to kiss me,' he said.

Abene laughed while cringing.

When they approached the laboratory Abene felt frightened. The enormity of what she was trying to do struck her for the first time. She looked at the innocuous building with apprehension. It was little more than a purpose-built warehouse, and only the stainless-steel pipes attached to the cladding hinted at what went on inside. The interior was as bleak as the exterior, divided into four compartments, each capable of being shut down and sealed off from the others and from the outside world. The air-conditioning hummed and the fluorescent lights pulsed. The humidity was controlled. The temperature was kept at a steady sixty-two degrees Fahrenheit. Everything was controlled. She listened carefully as Miller explained how the laboratory worked and noted the security procedures.

He'd told her what the inside looked like long before she saw it, and she'd drawn a blueprint of the layout in her mind, but being there was different. 'The original laboratories attempted to isolate everything in cabinets,' explained Miller. 'There were glove boxes and filters, and if you brought something into the lab you had to pass it through the autoclave first. If the object couldn't be subjected to heat it had to be dipped into Lysol and retrieved from a submerged opening inside. Those labs were impracticable, and finally this kind of environment was designed. Here, everything inside is considered to be contaminated and only the people need to be protected. That's why we call it a hot lab. This laboratory operates under negative air pressure, so if there's a leak then air gets sucked in. All the air is filtered as it leaves to protect the outside world from contamination.'

'Even the air's dangerous?'

'Especially the air,' said Miller.

Abene watched him run his checks on the systems, ticking them off on a list. A few moments later he opened a cabinet and removed a syringe. 'I have to take a blood sample from you,' he said.

'Why?' she asked, alarmed.

'In case you claim you caught something here and try suing us. We'd test the sample to see if you were already infected.'

Miller rolled up the sleeve of her blouse, pressed on a vein and pushed the needle home.

'I think this is the most sexual thing we've done,' he said, as her blood flowed into the syringe.

She shuddered at the thought. He labelled the sample, then went to the laboratory. Abene followed. She memorised the code he punched into the lock. She peered through the glass.

'You don't have to come inside if you're frightened,' he said. 'You can see everything from the outside. That's one of the safety features. If something happens to someone, if they collapse or get into trouble, then you want to be able to see them from the outside.'

'I've paid in blood,' Abene joked, following him through the door.

'This is the changing-room. Now we take off our clothes and put on a scrub suit. I try to encourage a buddy system here. That means there should always be two people in the lab at the same time. If something happens to one person, the other can help them out. It also means fewer lapses in safety and security because one person's always looking over the other one's shoulder.'

'What sort of lapses?'

'Let's say someone cut himself through his gloves, he might not admit it.'

'Why not?'

'Because he'd have to go into quarantine. We have isolation rooms in the building for personnel who are exposed to the biohazards. We have to monitor their blood to make sure that they haven't caught anything. You can't have them going out into the real world infecting people.'

'How long do you keep them?'

'It depends what they've been working on. Usually a week to ten days. Long enough for antibodies to show up. You can see why they'd be tempted not to report a minor accident and make their own assessment of the risk. Who wants to be locked up for a week? In some cases it only takes a needle stick to become infected.'

Miller opened the door into the next chamber, where he handed Abene a pair of thin surgeon's gloves and told her to put them on. He pulled down a suit and checked it for size. He looked carefully at the rubber gloves taped to the end of the arms before passing it to her. He pulled down his own suit and said, 'Copy me as I put this on.'

Abene watched as he put his legs and arms into the suit, careful not to trap the airlines which would keep the suit under positive pressure. 'Are you all right?' he asked, before pulling on the helmet.

Abene nodded. The preparations reminded her of a holiday when she went deep-sea diving. She was about to enter another world. Following Miller through the next door, she pulled down a hose and connected it. She heard air rushing into her suit and started breathing the pressurised oxygen mixture.

She was in the laboratory at last.

Abene looked up at the airline and realised that she could walk anywhere in the room without having to disconnect. The noise inside the suit was a constant roar. Miller was tapping her arm. She saw how he pinched the airline to stop the noise and heard him shout, 'It's difficult to talk, so I'll show you everything and explain later.' His voice was distorted by the sound of the pressurised air inside her suit.

He pointed to the liquid nitrogen storage vessels. He pulled on an asbestos glove and opened one. The air condensed and fog shrouded his hand. He took out a propylene test tube and held it in front of her. Abene looked at the cryo-tube and shivered. She had a sudden image of the virus. She was looking at the beginning of time and the end of time simultaneously. It was as if the virus in the cryo-tube had lived a long time ago but had killed everything it contacted, and so it, too, became extinct. She watched as he replaced the tube and closed the storage vessel. He removed the glove. She remembered once hearing that cold burned worse than fire. She could see him grinning behind his visor.

She walked past centrifuges, cabinets, fridges and computers. She peered at Petri dishes where cultures were growing. She noticed a difference in Miller here, even though he was disguised by his suit. He was in his own world, and he was in control. For the briefest second she felt attracted to him. She watched as he adjusted the settings on a bioreactor, memorising everything so she could ask him questions later.

Leaving the laboratory took longer than going in. First there was a shower to decontaminate their suits, and after they had removed the suits and their scrubs, another shower, before they changed back into their clothes.

'Were you frightened?' asked Miller when they were in the changing-room. He was drying himself slowly.

Abene shook her head. She dressed hurriedly, keeping the towel wrapped around her body. The room was uncomfortably intimate.

'Not many people ever want to go into a hot lab,' he said. 'Why would they want to take a chance? If we need an electrician or a plumber we have to bomb the place with formaldehyde to make it safe.'

'Huh?'

'Viruses are sensitive. They're easily destroyed by ultraviolet, heat or formaldehyde.'

Abene nodded. She pulled on her socks. Miller came up behind her and began caressing her breasts. She didn't want to make love to him, but she needed to gain his trust and keep it. She turned to face him. She let him kiss her.

She broke away. 'You stole that,' she said. 'You only get a kiss if I get bored.' She giggled.

He kissed her again.

'Not here. Not now,' she murmured. It was another promise she was going to break, but each time it was becoming harder to find an excuse.

She tried desperately to distract him. 'What was in the frozen test tubes?'

'We call them cryo-tubes,' he corrected her. 'Those were fusion viruses. Remember I told you about them?'

'You made them?'

He nodded.

The next day Abene left an e-mail message for Michel. They needed to find out about the security systems at Korbett Biotek. Michel had to ascertain who marketed them and how they worked, or they'd never get inside without Miller's help.

2

The telephone woke Leon Garrick. For a moment he wondered where he was before remembering he was in his flat in London. He rolled over and picked up the receiver. It was four in the morning. 'Who is it?'

'Is that you, Leon?' It was Karen Guttman. What the hell was she calling him for? The case was over. He'd been fired by Fraser, who'd found out from someone, Jackson probably, that he'd been hired by Karen. It was against company rules to accept independent investigations.

'Yes. It's me.'

'I was thinking about our meeting.'

That was history. 'Yes?'

'I've been thinking about it a lot.'

'Yes?'

'You showed a lot of attitude.' Her voice was harder.

'I'm sorry ...?' He didn't know what she was getting at.

'What was your problem?'

He wondered if she'd been drinking. He sat up. 'You want to know?' he asked, irritated.

'Yes.'

'Do you really want to know what happened?'

'What do you mean?' She was cautious.

'What happened to your father?'

'We know. They found his killer.'

'No, they didn't.' He wasn't going to dress up the truth.

'What do you want, Leon?' She allowed the briefest pause. 'More money? Didn't I pay you enough?'

'When someone calls me at four in the morning I guess they want the truth.'

'What kind of a sick person are you?'

'They never found the killer, Karen. There's been a cover-up.'

There was a long pause this time. They had to get this sorted out for once and for all. He didn't want to be receiving calls in the early hours every time Karen Guttman had a few doubts.

'Why are you saying this?' Her voice dropped in pitch.

'Because I think you knew it all along. You wanted to believe what you were told. I didn't contradict you at the time. I thought you had a right to peace at any price.'

'How do you know it isn't true?'

'Nothing like that happens in Bilbao without Inspector Suarez hearing about it. But the real clue was in the details. You asked the kidnapper to prove he had your father. You asked for the name of the puppy you had as a kid, but the kidnapper apparently knew the code which your father's life depended on. Your father would never have told him that until he was asked the right question.'

There was another long pause. The line crackled. 'You're a bastard.'

'I'm sorry,' he said. She wasn't the first person to make the accusation.

'Someone took me for a fool. I don't like that.'

'No one does.'

'Will you find out who's doing this to me?' she asked.

'Do you really want me to?'

'Yes.'

'All right.' He hesitated. 'Try and get some sleep, Karen. I'll be back in a week.'

'Thank you,' she said, and hung up.

Leon replaced the receiver, set his alarm clock and sank into a contented sleep. He'd hated the idea of leaving the job half done.

3

Antonio Suarez discovered that the files and personal notes in his office had been ransacked on the morning that Leon Garrick flew into town. It was easy enough to discover who was responsible. It was as hard to gain entry to the police station as it was to escape from it. He checked the log for the previous night and discovered that some agents from the Ministry of the Interior had arrived to transport a prisoner down to Madrid. They'd obviously made sure they had some extra time on their hands.

He was pleased. The Guttman investigation was starting to cause ripples. A little hint from the boys in black wasn't going to make him give up the investigation, though. Not yet, anyway. Not while it looked like being his passport out of the North. His marriage wouldn't last much longer if he didn't get out soon. His wife had admitted on their holiday that she'd had an affair, although she didn't reveal the man's name. A name didn't matter, of course. She said it was some businessman she'd met in a bar and claimed it was over. As a result Suarez had spent most of the holiday fishing off the rocks with his son, Lorenzo. In the evenings his wife, Carla, had disappeared into the casino in the basement of the hotel and gambled.

Guttman was going to save his marriage. He was going to get promoted or posted for this. He was out of there one way or another. Agustín Hernando had better believe it because there were still plenty of avenues to explore on this case. Although he'd expected an approach from the American Federal Bureau of Investigation, which was the department responsible for enquiring into the murders of American citizens overseas, none had been made. It looked as if there was dirt whichever way he turned, and Garrick would help him find out what was going on.

Suarez arranged the meeting in the Parque de Doña Casilda as opposed to the bar at the Parc Hotel. He did so because he wanted to know if Garrick was being followed, but in the event he didn't spot any unwelcome observers. Nevertheless, they moved on to a small restaurant where strangers would stick out. He listened patiently to Garrick's account of his trip to America. He was amused by the attempt to deceive Karen Guttman into believing that her father's killer had been found. There had been no rumours of any activity in Bilbao during the past month which would substantiate Jackson's charade. However, he was disappointed that Garrick hadn't spoken to Miller.

'You must speak to him on your return,' he insisted.

'Why?' asked Garrick.

'You remember I said I would visit Guttman-Tiche here to look at their records? When I did so, they could not find them. Later they said the records were in America, so it was impossible for me to see them.' Suarez stopped abruptly.

'Nothing too suspicious there,' remarked Garrick.

'OK. But some nights ago I was eating dinner with a friend.

The husband is a *médico* . . . a doctor. She is telling me how her father died in the—' He searched for the word. '—*gripe*.'

'Influenza.'

'*Sí*. She said it was strange how this *epidemia* never travelled outside the region. I, too, remember the influenza. Many people became sick by it. Like all influenza, the young survive but the old ones . . . often they die.

'My friend told me that each influenza has an origin. You can follow it like a fugitive. Each new one is called after the place it first explodes. Johannesburg, Victoria, Hong Kong . . . then the doctors follow it until it dies. The same as a serial killer. But this one had no history. There are no records. It came and it went. This is strange. My friend tells me how each influenza begins its life living inside the duck on Chinese farms. It jumps . . . *género* . . . *género*?'

'Species,' prompted Garrick.

'Your Spanish, it is very good now, Señor Garrick. Perhaps you will give me the name of your teacher.' He didn't wait for a reply. 'So, the influenza jumps species into a pig and then to the farmer. It goes to market with the farmer. It travels west across the land, and that is why they call it *la gripe asiática*. Now, of course, it comes by aeroplane to Europe and America. So last week I am in the hospital to visit a colleague. I ask the hospital administrator about this influenza. He shows me the records. What I discover makes no sense, but I will tell it to you in any case. I expect the influenza to affect all sections of the population, but there was a predomination of Basque family names. When I telephoned one person with a Castilian family name I discovered that the wife was Basque. So, what I am saying is that Pirineo influenza infected especially the Basque people, or those with Basque blood.

'So I go to another hospital. It is the same story. I ask the hospitals what they remember. They say Guttman-Tiche did much work on research. They took blood and were making some vaccine. Then suddenly the influenza was finished. It was gone.'

'Do you think there might have been a problem with the vaccine after all?'

'What do you think?' asked Suarez. 'The doctor said some of those with the vaccine are in hospital again with strange . . . *síntoma* . . .'

'Symptoms,' translated Garrick. 'But if that's the case, why did ETA kill Guttman? Better to have him alive than dead.'

'I think he knew something and someone thought it was better to silence him.'

'So it wasn't an ETA operation?'

'I'm not saying anything officially,' said Suarez.

'Have you made any progress at all on the kidnap?' asked Garrick.

'I have been checking the names we received from Wiesbaden. I have compared them to the associates of Bernal Lasturra. You will remember Lasturra was killed at the same time as Guttman, but his wife died during this influenza epidemic.' Suarez pulled a file from his briefcase. 'I have interviewed people, but it is the ones I cannot find who interest me. There are three names. The first is Ardanza, Michel Ardanza. For many years he has owned a business here. Fifteen years ago he was under surveillance. Nothing could be proved against him. Maybe he was in the wrong place at the wrong time or maybe he was just a subversive. But now he disappears when I want to talk to him.' He paused and passed the file to Garrick. 'The other two, you can read for yourself. There are photographs. Keep them. I have copies.'

Garrick flicked through the pages.

Suarez looked at his watch. 'We should go,' he said. Garrick was leaving on the last flight for Madrid to catch a connection for New York.

Suarez returned home from the airport, dropping into a bar for a beer and some *pintzoak* which served him for his dinner. Once again he found himself distracted by the football on the television screen in the corner of the bar. He enjoyed the anonymity of being among a group of people cheering when one team or another scored a goal. It was late by the time he reached his apartment, poured himself a nightcap and sipped it by the window. He liked living on the plaza named after Miguel Unamuno, who once said that when one Spaniard killed another then he killed Spain.

He remembered that he had meant to tell Garrick about rumours of an operation that was already nicknamed 'Mengele', in which intelligence agents were supposed to have experimented on vagrants with drugs intended for use against Basque separatist guerrillas.

He was impatient for Garrick to start asking questions in America. He wanted to see if word of Garrick's investigation filtered back to him through Agustín Hernando. If so, then the Minister of the Interior was at the heart of some kind of conspiracy, and he didn't for the life of him know what he would do with that information.

Suarez stared down at the deserted square below and saw movement in one of the corners. He turned out the lights in the room so he could see more clearly. It was a young student daubing graffiti on the walls. In Franco's day the kid would have got a year in prison.

In the morning he went to see what the boy had written. It was a quotation from Camus. 'I rebel – therefore we exist.'

4

The hotel lay on the Hudson River. Michel Ardanza looked out of the dining-room windows and watched a tug steaming upstream. Two women were watching him. He flashed a smile and then turned his attention back to the river. It was curious how women sensed danger and were attracted to it. They had a sixth sense.

He poured the maple syrup over his French toast, perched the *New York Times* against the coffee pot and tried to find out what was happening in the world. He looked at the five sections of the paper with irritation. Americans lived in a vacuum. They barely knew there were other countries beyond their shores. There were fifty pages of news in front of him and not one mention of the hundred or so wars being fought. The news was devoted to baseball results and drug-related murders.

Anger welled up inside him. The only political activists the country produced were paranoid right-wing militia groups who opposed the government because they thought it had been infiltrated by liberals. It was pathetic. Prejudice and racism were hardly a sound basis for a political agenda, but without education or decent news coverage there was little hope for anything else. If they were interested in terrorism they needed to take a look at their own government's activities in Chile, Nicaragua and El Salvador, which were all good examples of what a dedicated regime could achieve through terrorism.

An article on the defence budget caught his attention. 'Despite the cuts to keep the Pentagon budget at a stable $250 billion the US will still spend more than the next nine military powers combined. "We don't want to engage in a fair fight," commented the defense secretary. "We want to dominate across the full spectrum of conflict, so if we ever do have to fight we will win on our terms." The Chairman of the Joint Chiefs of Staff said, "We want to determine to the year 2010 and beyond what the environment will be out there, what America's interests are, and what the challenges to America's interests will be."'

'Was everything all right?' asked the waitress.

'Yes. Thank you,' replied Michel, grimly.

'Have a nice day,' she said.

Michel nodded irritably. He read the quote from the Defense Secretary again. 'We don't want to engage in a fair fight.' It was no wonder that America refused to sign a convention on chemical and biological weapons. Or even land-mines. They couldn't say it any plainer than that.

He stared out of the window and wondered if there was a message from Abene waiting for him. It was clear from his research that there was no way around the security systems at Korbett Biotek. He'd e-mailed Abene his findings without bothering to edit them. It was a pity they'd come so far and got so close, but the viruses would have to stay in their liquid nitrogen flasks at minus 170 degrees Celsius until someone else liberated them.

He looked forward to returning to Europe.

5

Abene watched the indicator on the pregnancy test turn blue and knew that her life had changed. She never had a moment's doubt about whether to keep Michel's baby. Simultaneously she knew she would never discover the exact nature of the virus behind the outbreak of the Pirineo epidemic, nor indeed what had been at stake during the court case. Miller wasn't going to volunteer that information, and she wasn't going to sleep with him now to elicit it. Suddenly life with him had become unbearable. She was impatient to leave America.

After she had visited the laboratory with Miller she had told Michel in an e-mail what they needed to bypass the security systems and waited impatiently for a reply. She heard nothing. She felt isolated and vulnerable. She wanted to communicate with Michel but her only means was through the Internet. In order to access her service provider she needed a public telephone and had to drive fifteen miles to the mall where she'd first met Miller. Sometimes she made the journey twice a day, desperate for some word from Michel. Once she used the phone outside the bar in the town but it was too conspicuous. She loathed the town. It had no centre. There was the bar near the rail track, a convenience store, a hardware store and a liquor store. There were two churches and a hall which was rented out to two other denominations. The place was a ghost town. There were no pedestrians because no one walked. She couldn't wait to get out of there.

Her first visit to the mall seemed so long ago. She didn't remember Michel ever congratulating her on engineering that meeting. He'd never asked her what it had been like watching Miller's movements for two weeks on her own. She grew resentful of him. It seemed she was taking all the chances while he lurked in the background.

After taking the pregnancy test that Friday she decided that if she hadn't heard from Michel she'd go to Manhattan at the weekend and surprise him. She connected her modem to one of the telephones. A minute later she found she had a message. She downloaded it, disconnected and went back to the car. The waiting was over.

Her heart pounded as she drove back to Miller's house. A voice inside urged her to pack her belongings, leave immediately before Miller returned, and meet Michel at the hotel he'd specified in the e-mail. But she was still standing at the kitchen table wondering what to do when Miller's car swept into the driveway. She looked at her watch. He was early. She had to pretend there was nothing wrong.

She'd have him take her out for a pizza or whatever else they could find in this gourmet's wilderness. Burgers or buffalo wings at the local bar. She gagged at the thought. Perhaps he'd know how many chickens were killed a year to keep all those bars in wings. It had to be over a billion. No wonder the animal rights activists were upset. Maybe the American people were going to come down with chicken wing virus or cluck-cluck fever, but that was Miller's department.

Miller walked through the kitchen and into his den. He didn't speak. Something was wrong. She frowned, then shrugged. Maybe he'd caught cluck-cluck fever from one of his viruses. He could lay an ostrich egg for all she cared. Fuck him! She went to the bar, grabbed a glass, poured some bourbon, held it under the ice-maker and counted the ice cubes splashing into the drink.

'You lied to me,' Miller hissed in her ear.

Abene reeled round, shocked. She hadn't heard him creep

up on her. He'd never spoken in that tone before. His thin face was taut, and his lips curled back from his teeth. 'What do you mean?' she asked. Something was very wrong.

'You were never married,' he said.

Abene looked away and wondered how he'd found out. She tried to work out where she'd made a mistake.

He hit her on the side of the head. Her ears rang. The glass of bourbon flew out of her hand and shattered on the tiles. She heard him, hollowly. 'Did he hit you like that? Did he?' She said nothing. 'Or did he hit you like this?' He punched her in the stomach, winding her.

Abene crumpled to the floor, thinking fast. 'I *was* married,' she said weakly. 'I was married in Mexico. Then he beat me and I ran away, like I told you.'

'You've been checked out, Abene,' he said. 'If you live with me you get positively vetted. The Investigative Service want to know about you. Your story doesn't hang together. That puts me on the line.' He put his hand into her hair, caught it in a fist and turned her face towards his.

She'd been complacent. She should have anticipated being vetted if Miller's project was part of the defence programme. Security had obviously asked him for her details and stupidly he'd told them what he knew without referring back to her.

'You're making a mistake,' Abene said. 'I can show you. Please——' She wondered who else knew. She'd find out. '——don't beat me, like he did,' she pleaded.

'Maybe you like it,' sneered Miller. 'You were the one who invented the husband who beat you.'

'No.' Abene shook her head and tried to shake his hand free, but he tightened his grip. 'You're like him now.'

Miller hesitated, and Abene sensed his confusion. He had sympathised with her over the descriptions of how her fictitious husband had behaved, but there was something more sinister beneath the hesitation. Suddenly she realised what it was. He liked this feeling of power. He was no longer angry. He enjoyed hitting her.

'No,' she screamed.

Miller let go of her hair and punched her. She doubled over, gasping for breath, and grabbed the counter to support herself. She caught sight of the knife block, but she was spinning to the floor as she reached towards it. He'd kicked her legs from under her. He reached down and ripped her shirt open and stared at her breasts. A shadow crossed his face. For a moment they looked at each other. His expression turned ugly. He looked away, looked back and slapped her again. And again.

She reached up, clawing at his face, fighting for her life. He punched her on the side of the head.

She closed her eyes.

She felt his hand on her mouth. He was on top of her, ripping at her skirt, his hot breath on her face. She struggled, but he crushed her windpipe with his forearm. He forced himself into her. She lay still.

Finally she felt Miller shudder and finish. The pressure on her neck relaxed. It was pathetic how a little power could get a man so excited. She looked away, staring at the floor. She'd get even for this.

Miller lifted himself on his arms and crawled off her. She heard him zip up his trousers. She turned on her side and began whimpering quietly, her breaths little convulsions.

Miller shook her gently. He called her. 'Abene.'

She ignored him.

'I don't know what happened to me, Abene.'

She didn't react.

'Abene ... Abene,' he pleaded.

He lay on the carpet beside her and put his arms around her to comfort her.

The stupid bastard! Someone had run a check on the Argentinian passport. If they dug any deeper she was in trouble.

'I want to leave,' she whimpered.

'We'll go away,' said Miller. 'This weekend, we'll go somewhere together. Just you and me.'

'No,' she said. 'I want to be on my own.'

'I didn't mean for that to happen. I was upset.'

Abene didn't reply.

'I want to make it up to you,' he said. 'I'll make it up to you. You'll see.'

Abene slithered out of his grasp and went to the bathroom. She locked the door, looked at herself in the mirror and saw bruises welling up on her face. She ran the bath, then saw the door handle turn.

'Abene,' he called. 'Unlock the door.'

She ignored him. Fuck his remorse. She got into the bath. Somehow she felt she'd never be clean again. She'd never have a moment's privacy again. The violation had struck at her core, and she wanted revenge for it.

Then the reality of the situation hit home. Miller was worried. Rape was a felony. He was wondering what she would do. He couldn't let her report it, he couldn't let her leave. No one knew she was there: after all, she'd made sure of that. He could kill her and no one would know. Her heart missed a beat. He would kill her to protect himself. She knew that much.

Chapter Nine

I

Miller was ashamed. He kept apologising, but Abene didn't care. It was too late for that. She had a feeling that he was more concerned about losing control of himself than about what he'd done. He glanced at her. The look said it all. He was deciding if she'd really forgiven him. He was wondering what to do.

She stared at him. He kept his eyes on the road. Yes, she thought. He was wondering how to get rid of her. He'd locked her door the previous night in case she left. He was terrified she'd report him to the cops. One look at the state of her face and they'd lock him up, no questions asked. It didn't matter any more that she'd lied about her past. It didn't give him the right to do what he'd done, and he knew it.

She knew why he wanted to get her out of the house. He didn't want to kill her in his precious home in case it left clues. That was why he suggested the weekend in the mountains. He was safe enough while they were driving behind the tinted windows of his car, but as soon as they mingled with people his problems would start again. He darted a glance at her. He was right to be wary. Right, but for the wrong reasons. She was going to get even.

She'd packed all she needed before they left the house. It was strange how Miller never questioned the number of things she was taking. He must have been glad she was taking so much. It left that much less for him to clear up when he returned. She was making it easy for him. She made sandwiches, even though she doubted either of them would have an appetite. She packed a cooler with some beers for the picnic. He'd be glad there was no excuse to stop at a diner. She filled a Thermos flask with ice.

Now they'd been driving in silence for almost an hour. Abene looked at her watch. Time to get it over with.

'Let's stop,' she said. 'Time for our picnic.'

Miller turned off the highway on to a road that disappeared into woods. The car bounced over ruts alongside a stream. A track forked off the road. Miller pulled on to it. The chassis grounded a couple of times.

'I think we should walk from here,' said Abene.

'OK.' Miller parked under a tree.

'Get the cooler,' ordered Abene, getting out of the car. She waited while he retrieved it along with a groundsheet.

'Let's go,' she said, marching in front of him. Now and then she looked behind. She walked a few yards ahead of him, but his hands were full and she knew he wouldn't try anything. Not yet. Not while she was leading them deeper into the woods. They scrambled over rocks until at last they were overlooking the Hudson. In the distance a sailing-boat drifted lazily upriver.

Miller laid the groundsheet over the undergrowth. 'There's a lot of poison ivy around this time of year,' he said.

He didn't need to explain the groundsheet. They both knew it was there to roll up the body.

Abene opened the cooler. It was strange how the ritual of a picnic kept the scene from slipping into anarchy. She handed Miller a can of beer. He opened it and drank.

'Tastes good,' he said.

'I'll bet it does.'

'You having one?'

Abene shook her head. She emptied the bread, cheese, meat and fruit on to the sheet. She stared across the river for a moment or two. A crow crossed the ravine to her right where the stream emptied into the river. She looked back at Miller. It was time to scatter his thoughts.

'You can fuck me now,' Abene said.

Miller winced. He looked at her, but unable to see her eyes he looked away.

'I want you now,' she said.

'Not here. Not now,' he said, alarmed. 'Someone might catch us.'

'Who would be here?'

'Let's wait until we get to the hotel.'

'No,' said Abene. 'What's wrong with here?'

Miller seemed to be considering the possibility. She pushed herself on top of him and pressed her lips to his mouth. His eyes were open. She pulled back so he could see her face. The purple bruises, the cut lip. His revulsion was tangible. The ugliness he'd inflicted was forcing itself on him. She slipped her hands down to his trousers and unzipped him. She wasn't surprised to find he was excited despite his protestations. He hadn't considered this possibility.

He grabbed her hair. 'No,' he said. His mood had changed. He looked at her. She recognised the look. His control was slipping, the way it had the previous night.

Abene reached out for the cheesewire on the plate. She leaned forward, put her arms around him and whispered, 'The picnic's over.'

She snapped the cheesewire around Miller's neck and pulled it tight. She slipped behind him. Miller struggled. She pulled the garrotte tighter, put her knees against his back and pulled.

Miller gasped for breath as his fingers clawed at the wire biting into his flesh. Blood flowed down his neck and over Abene's hands. Miller's heels rattled on the ground. He was stronger than Abene had expected. He flipped over. His body slammed up and down. Abene knelt on his back and pulled for all she was worth. Her muscles ached. She wondered if she had the strength to finish him off.

At last she realised he'd lost consciousness in a series of convulsions. The wire had cut deep into his neck. She pulled tighter now there was no resistance. She watched his muscles twitch. The spasms were the last signals his brain would ever make.

Eventually Abene released the cheesewire, dropped it on the ground and stared at Miller with curiosity, searching for signs of life. There was froth and bloodstaining around his nose and mouth. He was dead. She felt like laughing. She looked with disgust at where he had ejaculated. He sickened her, although the loss of seminal control interested her for a moment. Men were curious creatures. She felt no remorse. Not for Miller. This was payback time.

It was an appropriate death. The garrotte was the official means of execution in Spain.

Abene wiped her hands on his jacket, then put her hand into his pocket and withdrew the keys to the car. She took his wallet from his jacket. When he was found he'd be just another John Doe.

She reached for the Thermos flask and opened it. She took a knife from her pocket and turned to Miller's corpse. Now she was ready for the final cut. She could barely bring herself to touch him. She felt the still-warm flesh and began sawing. Blood dripped on to the ground. The blood made it hard to grip him, and the job was tougher than she expected.

Her bloody fingers slipped on the red handle of the blade.

2

It was early evening when Abene reached the hotel in Cold Spring. She was pleased that the drizzle which had begun falling as she left the woods had now turned to rain. People were less likely to stumble across Miller's body. It gave her more time. She drove past the hotel and parked the car a few streets away, then walked back. Michel was reading a book in the bar. She watched him for a few seconds, surprised that he looked so calm, before remembering that he didn't know what had happened. A moment later he caught sight of her and stood up. He walked over to her quickly, took her arm and led her past reception and up to his room.

'What's happened?' he asked.

She began to tell him, then she started crying. He put his arms around her, trying to calm her as the sobs racked her body.

'Tell me,' he said.

She wouldn't look at him. She hid her face in his chest and clung to him. 'Tell me,' he insisted.

Slowly he pieced together what had happened the previous night. He felt the rage against Miller rising inside him, but before he could articulate it Abene said, 'There's something else I have to tell you.'

'Yes?' He waited.

'I killed him.'

Michel nodded. 'I understand,' he said.

'I had to.'

'I know,' said Michel, misunderstanding her. He could understand how she felt. He could sympathise with her anger.

'He found out about me. He knew that I wasn't who I was pretending to be. He found out that I hadn't been married before.'

'How?'

'They ran a security check.'

'That didn't give him an excuse to rape you,' he said. He was thinking that they had to get away quickly. Everything was going wrong.

Abene shook her head. 'Killing him was the only way to get into the laboratories.'

He didn't understand her.

'They won't find his body for a while,' she continued. 'And when they do it'll take time to identify him. By then we'll have what we want.'

Michel shook his head. 'It's too dangerous now.'

'I've come this far and I don't intend to give up.'

He looked at her gravely. 'You're sure you want to do this?' he asked. She was in shock. He was worried that her judgment was impaired.

Abene nodded. 'Don't forget, we're doing this for Bernal and Theresa. We're not alone.'

'I know,' he said. 'But let's think about it. We need to assess the risks. Tell me about the laboratory. Describe what you saw when you were inside.'

She told him about her visit. He questioned her again and again until he knew what to expect as each door opened. He wanted to know where the closed-circuit cameras were situated. He made her repeat the security procedures. Abene assured him that she had left nothing out. He asked her what the exterior of the building looked like to check that her description concurred with what he'd seen when he staked it out.

'There aren't any internal checks. Once we're inside we have the run of the place.' She made it all sound easy.

'You're sure you want to do this?' he repeated. 'If we're caught we'll be looking at a death sentence one way or another.'

'What do you mean?' she frowned.

'The electric chair or a lethal injection.'

'You have a propensity for melodrama, Michel,' she said. 'But you're right about one thing. This is about lethal injections, one way or another.'

'Then let's do it tonight,' said Michel. 'We need as much time as possible to cover our tracks afterwards. It leaves us the whole of Sunday to get out of the country. On Monday, Miller will be reported as missing when he doesn't show up at work.'

'I thought the security system was going to be the problem, but you came up with the answer,' said Abene.

Michel frowned. 'I don't understand.'

'You sent me that e-mail.'

'I know, but that doesn't solve the problem.'

'Yes it does,' said Abene.

3

Michel drove Miller's car to the Korbett Biotek laboratory. The headlights cut through the darkness. He concentrated on the road. Beside him Abene dozed. They'd gone over the plan time and time again, but there was still a danger they might have overlooked something. He wished he had a gun.

The viruses scared him more than he expected. He hadn't really understood how recombinant viruses worked until Abene explained it to him. The basic structure of a virus was RNA, but bits could be snipped out or added. It was like a book. A chapter could be removed and one from another book pasted in. The book would still read like a story, with a beginning, middle and end. Except that the message would be changed.

The easiest way for a virus to enter a body was through an open cut or the lungs. When it penetrated a body's cell it would break open and replicate itself. The contaminated cell would finally burst and the virus would multiply, continuing with its simple strategy until the body could no longer sustain the viral load.

'We're here,' said Michel, as they approached the perimeter fence. Abene opened Miller's wallet and removed a card. Michel recognised the car in the parking lot. It belonged to the guard. He'd watched the laboratory for five nights, driving up from the city in a hired car and hiding out in the woods bordering one side of the compound. The guards changed shifts at eight in the evening and four in the morning. With any luck the guards on night duty wouldn't be familiar with all the personnel. His heart thumped in his chest and he psyched himself up. He knew he'd have to kill the guard if necessary.

Korbett Biotek didn't pose the same dangers as the Guttman-Tiche plant. By comparison, Korbett Biotek was small, low-profile and innocuous. There was nothing to arouse the suspicions of the inhabitants of this Connecticut town. Nothing suggested danger. The ventilation stack on the side of the building looked as if it belonged to the furnace and not a Level 4 biohazard laboratory. It was hard to believe that the cluster of offices lay at the heart of the Guttman-Tiche empire, and Michel guessed that if there was ever an investigation nothing would link the two.

He stopped the car at the gate and slipped the card Abene gave him into the machine. The gate opened and he drove through. He parked near the entrance of the building and sat for a moment as the rain lashed down. From here on he was entering the unknown. He only knew what happened beyond the doors from what Abene had told him. He looked at his watch. It was nine. Their timing was perfect. He'd never seen one of Miller's colleagues visit the plant as late as this. The latest anyone had visited was half-past eight.

Michel turned off the engine and grabbed the briefcase from the rear seat. Abene unscrewed the Thermos flask. Michel took a deep breath. 'Ready?' he asked.

Abene nodded.

They opened the car doors and stepped into the rain. Michel didn't bother to lock the car. They ran towards the building.

Abene slid Miller's card into the aperture beside the lock. The door opened. The guard inside gave them a cursory glance as they walked into the foyer before looking back at his miniature television. As they approached the reception desk, he swivelled towards them irritably, pushed a book across the desk and turned back to watch the baseball. A guard with an attitude problem suited Michel fine. He signed, noticing that no one else was in the building. The last person had signed out an hour before.

'Who's winning?' Michel asked.

'Patriots!' replied the guard. He didn't look away from the screen.

Abene took Michel's arm and led him to the only door in the foyer. Michel tensed. He expected the guard to challenge them at any moment, although there was no need for him to do so. Not yet. Heat-sensitive closed-circuit cameras followed their movements, recording them on hidden tapes. Abene fumbled with Miller's identity card, slid it into a recess in the door and this time punched a code. She took Miller's index finger from the flask, pressed it firmly on the scanner and a second later the door clicked. They were inside.

'This way,' Abene said, leading Michel along the corridor. 'That's Miller's office.' She pointed to a glass-enclosed cubicle containing books, a desk, computer and filing cabinet.

Michel followed her to the laboratory, eyeing with curiosity the microscopes and tools of an unfamiliar world. He'd read about them, but seeing them was different. At the end of the room was a door, the international biohazard symbol emblazoned on it.

Abene looked through the windows into the laboratory beyond. Michel looked over her shoulder. 'I didn't expect it to be so small,' he said.

'The smaller it is, the easier it is to contain,' she answered. 'It's also cheaper. Each person needs a minimum twenty-four cubic metres of space. Federal law. The whole laboratory must be visible through windows in case there's an accident inside.'

He didn't relish the thought of going into the room.

Abene looked at the register on the door which listed the people authorised to enter. She keyed the number she'd memorised when Miller had taken her there. She opened the door and immediately Michel felt a draught as air was sucked past him.

'The laboratory is kept under negative air pressure,' said Abene. 'Air always flows from the outside into here, before being cleaned through filters. Nothing from here escapes into the outside world.'

'Except for you,' whispered Michel.

Abene closed the door behind her.

Michel looked through the windows into the laboratory. He wandered around the offices, wishing he knew what to look for. When he looked back at the laboratory he saw Abene inside. The protective clothing she wore emphasised how dangerous the viruses were. She pulled on a pair of insulated gloves and lifted the lid of a stainless-steel storage vessel. He watched the nitrogen boil as the temperature rose. Abene pulled out the racks and looked for the tubes she wanted. She ran her hand down the racks. The gloves she wore were thick and her movements clumsy.

He imagined the virus being released from its frozen state and allowed into the real world. It would take a little while for it to acclimatise itself. It would have to avoid sunlight and find a host immediately. It needed the safety and shelter of a body so it could replicate. The virus was alive, but not alive; dead, but not dead. He couldn't get his head around the concept of something so small having so much power without consciousness of any sort.

A reflection in the glass caught Michel's eye. Someone was in the room behind him. He didn't turn. He waited for the person to get up close. The man stood beside him and looked into the lab. Michel turned and they looked at each other simultaneously. Surprise and confusion registered on the man's face. 'Who are you?' he asked.

'I'm here with Dr Miller,' said Michel, looking back towards Abene. The man followed his gaze. He'd know in an instant that the suited figure wasn't Miller. Abene was smaller.

The man moved just as the edge of Michel's hand hit the back of his neck. He catapulted forward and ricocheted off the reinforced glass in front of them. He sank to his knees, stunned. Michel knew he should have killed him, but he'd pulled back at the last moment. He'd lost the killing instinct.

He looked through the glass at Abene. She was facing him,

but he couldn't see her expression behind the visor of her helmet. He signalled for her to hurry, then bent down. 'Listen to me carefully,' he said. 'If you struggle I will kill you. Understand?'

'Yes,' grunted the man. He held his head between his hands. Michel guessed his neck had been damaged. A numbness was spreading up his own arm from the blow. He dragged the man across the floor to the nearest office and looked for something to tie him up with. He found a roll of yellow tape, leaned the man against the office wall and bound his wrists and ankles together. The tape ran out. He scrabbled through the drawers until he found another roll and wrapped more tape around the man's head, covering his eyes. He started on the man's mouth but he struggled. 'I can't breathe through my nose,' he said. 'I've got sinus problems.'

Some people never knew when they were ahead, thought Michel. He stretched the tape taut and pulled it across the man's mouth, pulling his lips back and winding the tape round. He could hear the rasping breaths. At least he wouldn't suffocate and gasping for air would keep him from making too much noise. He locked the door of the office as he left.

Abene emerged from the laboratory. 'Did you kill him?' she asked.

'No.'

'Why not?'

'There wasn't any point,' he said. He could have admitted that he'd tried and failed. But in reality there was little point in killing him. Their faces were already on the security-camera tapes. Dead or alive, the man's body would be found.

'Do you have everything?' he asked.

Abene nodded. She was looking through a bank of cabinets. She pulled out two boxes and gave them to him. 'We need these suits for handling the viruses.'

'Let's get out of here.'

Michel tried to open the door. It was locked.

Abene passed him Miller's bloody index finger. He pressed

it on the scanner. The door opened. He'd be glad to get rid of that finger. 'Don't forget to sign me out before we leave,' Abene said. Michel nodded.

He peered cautiously into the foyer. Now there were two security guards watching the television. He walked to the desk, turned the book towards him and signed it. 'Goodnight,' he said.

It was still raining outside. They were in enemy territory, and a long night stretched out ahead of them.

4

Antonio Suarez took the Metro a couple of stops from the Casco Viejo. He could have walked, but the humidity was high and it was cooler underground. He looked at the policeman on duty by the gates and wondered when they could stop guarding the subway. The ETA leaders might be talking about peace, but there had just been a successful strike against a terrorist cell in Vizcaya during which two members of ETA had been killed and explosives, grenades and rocket-launchers had been seized. Eight hundred people had been killed in the last twenty years, most of whom had been carefully targeted.

Suarez emerged from the Metro and was simultaneously assaulted by the humidity and the sunlight. He took his sunglasses out of his shirt pocket, slipped them on and walked to work. No sooner had he sat down in his office than there was a knock on the door. The policeman from the front desk said, 'Some old man wants to see you. He's been here for an hour. He's a bit agitated.'

'What's his name?'

'He won't say.'

'What's it about?'

'He won't say.'

'Better send him up.'

Suarez waited curiously, wondering what the man wanted

to see him about. He heard him approach down the corridor long before his arrival. There was the clack of a walking-stick, then a couple of shuffles, a retching cough, followed by a gasp. The shuffling continued.

Finally the man appeared. The policeman wasn't joking when he said the man was old. Suarez started forward to take his arm, irritated that no one had helped him up the stairs. He took him into his office and sat him down.

'So what do you want to see me about?' he asked.

'My wife told me not to come. She says it's not our business.' The man spoke in a high-pitched voice that crackled like an old scratched gramophone record.

'You can let me be the judge of that,' said Suarez.

'I don't want to get anyone into trouble. I kept thinking it wasn't right. I can't get this thing out of my head. It gives me a ... *buruko min.*' The man broke into Basque and rubbed his head. 'It happened a long time ago. I forgot until I read it in the *eguraldi.*'

'*Eguraldi?* Forgive me,' said Suarez, 'but I don't speak Basque.'

'Newspaper,' said the man. 'It must have been forty years ago.'

Oh no! thought Suarez. Not some confession from an old man whose conscience troubled him. 'Well, if it happened that long ago I should forget about it,' said Suarez helpfully.

'*¡Ez. Ez. Ez!*' objected the man. 'It was then they gave me the box to mend. I remembered it when I read the *eguraldi.* I was a carpenter. That's why my lungs are bad. Full of wood dust.' He pulled out a stained, sticky cloth and hawked into it. Suarez looked away. 'You wouldn't forget the box. Made of oak. Old. Maybe two centuries. It came from *Inglaterra* and had a good carving on the front which was damaged. I made it like new. The house is still there where I collected it. Up in Neguri. I took it with my old donkey, Ana, and the cart, before I invested in a van.'

'This is in connection with . . .' Suarez waited for the answer excitedly.

'The box that was advertised in the newspaper. You know, they found that man who was killed inside it. That man with the factory across the river.'

'Señor Guttman?'

'Was that his name? My wife says it was a good job they did on him.'

'And you could identify this piece of furniture?'

'Oh yes. Certainly. I leave a mark on all the pieces I make or repair. I'll show you.'

'And you can take me to the house where you delivered it?'

'Naturally.'

'Do you have time now?' asked Suarez.

'If you bring me to the bar afterwards where I play *mus*.'

'Of course I will,' said Suarez, and picked up the telephone to order the car.

Before going to Neguri, Suarez took the carpenter to the store in the basement and showed him the box in which Guttman's body had been found.

'What a state!' commented the carpenter on seeing it. A tremor seemed to shake his head. 'You think someone like me is commissioned to make this two hundred years ago, and they treat it like this. But that is the way. The worker lives. He works. He dies. All without dignity. Then he is forgotten.' The carpenter spat. 'Now, turn it over.'

Suarez wrestled with the box, trying to hold it together.

'See! There are four small chisel marks cut into the base. Do you see them?'

'Yes.'

'That is my mark. Sometimes you remember the work. Other times you forget. This job was not usual for me. It was a grand family. They had money and paid me well.'

'Let's go and look at the house,' said Suarez, taking the

man's arm and helping him up the stairs and into the car. He drove out to Neguri, with the old man muttering along the way about how things had changed. Finally he told Suarez to stop and pointed at a house. It looked run-down, although the garden had been tended.

'You're sure this is the place?' Suarez asked.

'Quite sure,' replied the carpenter.

'Thank you,' said Suarez. He drove away, not wanting anyone to catch sight of them.

He dropped the old man around the corner from the bar where he played cards at lunch-time. The man made it clear he didn't want to be seen emerging from an official vehicle.

Suarez had enjoyed the carpenter's company. He admired the old man for speaking Basque in the police station, where not long ago he'd probably have been imprisoned, beaten or fined for the offence. He enjoyed listening to the entrenched politics. There was no doubt where the man's sympathies lay. The carpenter didn't remember who owned the house in the past, but that didn't matter. It wouldn't take Suarez long to find out who owned it now.

5

Tod McFarlane woke at 5.30 on Sunday morning and eased himself out of the king-size bed. Once again he'd had a disturbed night's sleep, getting up twice to relieve himself. Switching from beer to whisky hadn't improved the performance of his bladder. The hunchback of premonition perched on his shoulder; his father had died after a prostate operation. He looked with irritation at his wife. The mound of bedclothes continued to rise and fall rhythmically as she slept. He'd heard that prostate problems could be caused by a lack of sex. These days the only way he could take Irene was from behind, and neither of them relished the idea.

He pottered into his exercise room and mounted the bicycle,

set the controls for twenty minutes, level two and rolling hills, then pedalled for all he was worth. Within minutes he was lathered in sweat and the room exuded an aroma of stale whisky. The telephone rang before he'd covered a mile. He looked at it suspiciously before answering. A call at six on a Sunday morning was bad news. He held the receiver to his ear cautiously and listened to the garbled account of a robbery from Dr Rampton at Korbett Biotek.

'Hold on to your horses. Don't go calling anybody else. I'll be right there,' he said.

A few minutes later an unshaved McFarlane was seated behind the wheel of his Chevrolet, a glass of milk perched on the dashboard, a doughnut gripped in his fist and the premonitions piling up. He angled the rear-view mirror to inspect himself, grimaced at his reflection, and looked back at the road. Rampton had sounded mighty upset. He prepared himself for defence. He'd never liked him. The man gave him the creeps. He had once watched him kill thirty laboratory mice. Picked each one up by the tail and cracked their heads against a marble slab, like screwing up pieces of paper and throwing them into the trash. Throwaway mice was what Rampton called them.

This was the first time there had been any kind of problem at the research laboratory. He'd reviewed security shortly after Guttman's death and concluded it was satisfactory. As he entered the building he took a quick statement from the guards. According to them, Miller had turned up with a woman and assaulted Rampton.

He went into Rampton's office and heard a very different story. However, he wasn't prepared to jump to any conclusions. First he was going to review the security tapes. 'You're wasting valuable time,' screamed Rampton. 'I've told you what happened.'

'Take it easy,' McFarlane responded calmly. 'I'll take this thing at my own speed, then I'll get back to you.'

'You're going to roast for this,' snapped Rampton.

'I wanted to install cameras in these offices, Dr Rampton. You refused because you didn't want Big Brother watching. Maybe you'd like to reconsider that now.'

McFarlane left Rampton, told the guards to prevent him from leaving, collected the tapes and shut himself in an office. Rampton's story was absurd. There was no way an intruder could have got into the building.

Other than blowing a hole through the side of the building or dropping in by helicopter, the only way in was through the main doors. Access from the reception area required the fingerprint of a person authorised to enter. The computerised fingerprint-recognition system was the first of its kind. A scanner took thirty images of the fingerprint, selected the best, reduced it to a digital description of whorls and loops, transmitted it to the computer, checked it against records and unlocked the door within a second. It was state-of-the-art, quick and secure. The door wouldn't have opened if Miller hadn't been there himself.

When he checked the tapes it didn't take McFarlane long to realise that Rampton was telling the truth. It took longer to work out how they'd done it but subconsciously he'd avoided considering it. The thought of sawing off Miller's index finger was too gruesome to contemplate. Even so, the first thing he did was telephone Miller's house, although he knew he wouldn't be there.

A thought struck him. He had to assume the building was contaminated. The intruders had made it into the laboratory. The whole place needed to be sectioned and bombed with formaldehyde. Then he remembered he'd been back there in the vicinity of the lab. He'd be sharing the isolation ward with Rampton. He decided to overlook standard procedures for the time being.

His hand shook as he dialled the number for Colonel Jackson. He was aware that he was setting in motion a series of events that would probably mean the end of his career.

6

It had been a slow escape from Manhattan up the West Side Highway. Traffic was jammed the whole way up. If nothing else, it had given Leon time to think, but now he was on the Parkway the traffic had thinned. He opened up Karen's BMW coupé and smiled at the absurdity of power steering and automatic transmission in a sports car. Karen liked her toys.

Lights flashed in the rear-view mirror, a siren wailed and a police car loomed. The siren gave another burst, Leon pulled over and the police car cruised past. The policeman in the passenger seat shook his head. Leon nodded, taking his foot off the gas, and dropped from sixty to fifty miles an hour. He was driving a two-hundred-mile-an-hour machine in a country that had a fifty-five-mile-an-hour speed limit and where petrol was cheaper than water. He set the cruise control, forgot about driving and thought about Miller.

Karen had telephoned Guttman-Tiche's lawyers in Bilbao to find out where Paul Miller worked. That way she hoped to avoid alerting McFarlane to her continuing interest in her father's death. She discovered that Miller worked for Korbett Biotek, a company she'd never heard of, but she found out where he lived and passed the information on to Leon.

Since he was acting on Karen's behalf, Leon expected Miller would be willing to answer his questions, looked forward to catching him off guard and for that reason hadn't telephoned to make an appointment. Karen had wanted to go with him, but he dissuaded her. He wouldn't be able to ask the questions he wanted about her father in her presence.

He had tried once more to contact Colonel Jackson. Once again there had been an answering machine and he had left a message explaining that he was still investigating Guttman's death and would like some answers. He didn't say where he could be contacted. He wasn't ready for that yet.

Ninety minutes after leaving Manhattan, Leon turned off the highway and entered the township of Danbury. He asked at a petrol station for directions and finally found Miller's house. He didn't see it at first because it was set back off the road. It looked empty. He rang the bell and peered through the windows. He thought of breaking in but decided against it – he'd come back later or speak to Miller in the morning at Korbett Biotek. He stepped off the porch and noticed someone in front of his car.

'Can I help you?' asked the man. He'd emerged from the side of the house.

Leon sized him up. He was stocky. Just twenty-five maybe. Only a kid. Short hair. Casual dress. Trousers, not denim. Nothing to go on there. Maybe it was Miller. 'I'm looking for Paul Miller,' said Leon.

'In connection with?'

'A personal matter.'

'May I ask your name?'

'Garrick, Leon Garrick.'

'I'm Paul Miller.' The kid smiled and extended his hand.

Leon leaned forward to shake hands, but the kid swivelled on the ball of his foot. Leon saw the kick coming and braced himself, but even so it lifted him into the air and back on to the porch. He tried to get up, and winced with pain. His ribs were cracked.

'You ask too many questions, Garrick.'

Leon stood up with difficulty.

'We've been expecting you,' said the kid, implying that he wasn't alone.

Leon looked around. The others had gone somewhere, but they'd be back. Leon knew that if he was going to get away he had to do it soon, while the two of them were alone.

The man pulled a gun from his shoulder holster. Leon knew one other thing for sure: he wasn't going to talk his way out of this one. He had a hunch he wasn't going to have a happy ending.

Like Guttman.

But this kid wasn't calling the shots. Decision-makers didn't waste their time staking out locations. The head honcho was elsewhere. Leon gambled. This kid wouldn't want to take the ultimate decision.

'Not so many questions now, huh, Garrick?'

'Just one. How come you were expecting me?'

'You wanted a meeting. We've set it up. No point wasting time.'

'Where's the colonel?'

'He's busy.'

Leon guessed that Colonel Jackson's answering machine was monitored all the time.

Leon took a step forward. The kid pointed the gun at his head, then at his chest. Not decisive enough.

'Hold it there,' he said.

If someone pulled a gun he had to be willing to use it; otherwise he was better off without it.

A bird chattered. A momentary distraction. Leon sprang, arms stretched out towards the kid's head. He snapped his arms apart and then the gun was pointing away from him. There was a shot as Leon's forehead crunched into his face. They fell to the ground.

Leon smashed his knee into the kid's groin. He heard the scream, then cut it off with a blow to the windpipe.

He picked up the gun and got to his feet. Every breath he took cut into him. He examined the body at his feet. It was motionless. Difficult to tell if the boy was going to die. Air bubbled through the blood welling from his mouth. Leon turned him on his side to give him a better chance.

It was time to make tracks. He got into the car and hit the road, grateful now for power steering and automatic transmission. Every time he moved, the pain made him wince.

It was clear that the people who were responsible for Raphael Guttman's death were way ahead of him. He had to warn Karen, then get out of the country.

Chapter Ten

━━━━◆◇◆◇◆━━━━

I

The sheriff parked the car. His deputy stepped out and slammed the door. He was chewing gum. He stared at the legend on the car door: Sheriff's Department. One day he'd be running the place. He watched the sheriff ease himself from behind the wheel, adjust his shades and look through the trees to the gorge where the stream flowed into the Hudson.

'Follow me,' said the sheriff, leading the way. The deputy walked behind the older man. They followed the path, then veered off and headed upstream, descending deeper into the gorge all the while. The light was dim beneath the canopy of trees that towered over them, and they removed their shades when they reached the two boys.

'Where is it?' asked the sheriff.

'Couple hundred yards up there,' said one of the boys, pointing across the stream and into the trees.

'How come you found it?' said the deputy.

Dumb question, thought the sheriff.

'We were hunting snapping turtles,' said the younger boy.

'Well, don't go nowhere,' said the deputy. 'We'll want to talk with you in a while.'

They continued their journey, sweating now in the humid air. They crossed the stream and started climbing the opposite bank. They approached the body cautiously, stopping ten yards away.

'He's dead,' said the sheriff unnecessarily. He looked at his watch and noted the time. 'Wait here,' he ordered. 'Don't touch anything!'

'Where are you going?'

'To call for assistance. Then I got to interview the boys.'

'Don't be gone too long,' said the deputy. The woods had taken on a malevolent feel. The sheriff ignored him and began retracing his steps.

The deputy looked at the corpse. This was his first John Doe. No way was he touching the body. A cloud of black flies covered the man's skin. It didn't seem right to let the flies just feed on the body. He crept closer, picked up a stick and waved it over the corpse's face. The flies buzzed furiously for a second, revealing the gash across the man's neck, then settled down again.

The deputy retreated, feeling nauseous. He knew the black-tops around these parts and puzzled how the man had got there. Where was his car? It wasn't back on the track. It was a long way over the hill to Route 9D. Maybe he didn't kill himself after all.

Finally the detectives, the medical technicians and the cor-oner beat a trail up from the stream. They wound scene-of-crime tape around the trees, isolating an area of thirty square yards, and went to work.

The deputy's natural tendency to laugh and joke was tempered by the grim faces of the professionals. For the next two hours he watched while they took photographs and searched for evidence. He was keen to learn. After a while there were piles of evidence bags. He was surprised to see Homicide using paper bags. 'I thought you used plastic bags,' he said to one of the detectives.

The detective looked at him with disdain. 'You put the moist evidence in paper to stop it rotting,' he explained. 'It sweats in plastic.' He returned his attention to the corpse, edging towards it in a low crouch as if it might attack him. He waved a hand over the face, disturbed the flies and took a guarded look at the features.

The deputy thought about all the uses there were for paper bags. There'd been a boy at school whose father received some kind of dues on paper bags because one of his ancestors patented them a hundred years ago.

The detective hawked and spat. 'OK, let's wind this up. We've got what we need,' he said abruptly. 'You can bag him up,' he said to the technicians who'd been waiting apprehensively.

Despite the heat, the medical technicians stepped into plastic suits and covered their faces with masks. They were already sweating profusely but they weren't taking any chances. The smell of death got into the hollow centres of their hair follicles and hung around for days. 'Looks like animals ate a finger,' wheezed one technician from behind a mask.

'I'm out of here,' said the medical officer. 'Don't forget, now. Make sure you tie a bag over his head. We want that evidence.'

2

Karen Guttman locked the door of her penthouse and waited for the elevator. She was irritated by Garrick's phone call. It was inconvenient going to the gallery late on a Sunday night. She stepped into the elevator. He'd told her it was too dangerous to visit her home and that she was probably being watched. When she put down the phone she realised that if she was being watched then the phone was probably bugged. Garrick had missed a trick there.

She stepped out of the elevator and nodded to the doorman as she walked out of the building. It had stopped raining. The lights changed at the end of the block and she held her hand out for a cab as one drew up in front of her. She waited for the passenger to get out.

'Karen!' someone called.

She looked into the cab and saw Garrick.

'Get in,' he said.

She opened the door and slid in beside him.

'The World Trade Center,' he told the driver.

'Where's my car?' asked Karen.

Garrick was looking over his shoulder at the traffic behind them. 'I parked it somewhere on Ninth. Here's the ticket.' He reached into his jacket pocket and she saw his face screw up with pain.

'What's wrong?' she asked.

'I ran into a little trouble,' he said.

'You didn't crash the car, did you?'

'Nothing like that,' he said. 'I'll tell you in a minute.'

The cab hit gridlock at Columbus Circle. 'We'll get out here,' said Garrick. Karen glanced at the meter. Big fare. He must have taken the cab all over town.

'Christ,' muttered Garrick as he got out. He was holding his arm close to his chest. 'It only hurts when I move,' he explained.

They wove through the cars to the sidewalk. 'What happened?' asked Karen.

'You've got to stop this investigation,' said Garrick.

Karen didn't know if she'd heard him right. A man collided with Garrick.

'Watch where you're walking,' said the man.

Garrick doubled up with pain.

'No,' snapped Karen. 'No, *you* watch where you're walking.'

'Fuck you,' said the man.

'No, you fuck you,' said Karen. A few people stopped to listen. 'Can't you see this man's hurt?' She put an arm around Garrick and guided him into a bar. They sat down. 'How bad is it?' she asked.

'I've cracked a few ribs.'

'I'll take you to my doctor.'

'There's nothing he can do. I'll strap them up.'

The waitress interrupted them. 'What can I get you?'

'Two beers, please,' said Karen.

'Coming up.'

'Your life's in danger, Karen,' Garrick said.

'Why do you say that?'

'When I went to see Miller they were waiting for me.'

'Who's they?'

'Colonel Jackson's people. At least that's who I think they were. I telephoned him this morning and they knew about the call.'

'So, what happened?'

'I didn't wait to find out what was going to happen. Some kid took a swing at me, pulled a gun and I acted in self-defence.'

'Why does that mean my life is in danger?'

'Because I'm working for you and they know that.'

The waitress returned with their drinks.

'There's a possibility that if I stop asking questions they'll leave you alone,' said Garrick.

'I want to know what happened to my father.'

'I don't think that Colonel Jackson will let you find out. There's too much at stake.' He held Karen's gaze. 'I think he's prepared to kill.'

'That's ridiculous. It's outrageous.'

'I'm serious.'

'I've got connections in the press and in politics. They wouldn't dare.'

'This goes all the way to Washington.'

Karen stared at him. He couldn't be serious. He was hinting at a conspiracy. Garrick had been spooked by something, and she wanted to know what. 'Are you telling me that you're backing out?'

'Yes.'

'But you wanted to know the truth as much as I did.'

'That's right, I did,' he said. 'But I consider that protecting you is the most important part of the job.'

'So what's the problem? Not enough money?' she asked.

'Money's not the issue. Money's no good when these guys come looking for you. The world's not big enough to hide in.'

'That's rubbish. The Nazis hid out in South America. No one found them.'

'People knew where they were. They chose to ignore it.'

'I'll let you into a secret. My father bought somewhere in Patagonia before he died. No one knows about it. If you need somewhere to hide, I've got it.'

'I don't think either of us would get that far. But more to the point, why did your father buy that place? Maybe he knew he needed somewhere to hide.'

'This sort of thing doesn't get swept under the carpet. Not in America. It might in England. But not here.'

'Look what happened to your father. Six months later and we're being stonewalled at every turn. I went down to speak to Miller and walked into a reception committee. As soon as they knew who I was they were going to kill me.'

'So you keep saying.'

'I got away. I may have killed someone in the process. I've got his gun here in my pocket.' Garrick paused. 'I came here to warn you to call it a day. Maybe it's too late. Maybe these guys are already working out some accident for you. Believe me, they never found your father's killers, but they had access to a corpse and took you to some military base to convince you they'd done the job. That means they're well connected. Inspector Suarez has his suspicions.'

'Which are?'

'Ask him.'

Karen rummaged in her handbag and pulled out her mobile phone. She handed it to Garrick. 'Call him,' she ordered.

'It's three in the morning there.'

'I want to hear it from the horse's mouth.'

Garrick pulled a notebook out of his pocket. He leafed through it, dialled a number and waited. A few seconds later he started talking. Karen listened to his side of the conversation. There was a lot about his failure to talk to Miller. For a moment Garrick seemed animated by something Suarez said.

'Sure, put out the notice. That'll make them sit up and think. Get everyone involved. They can't ignore it then.'

She waited impatiently until Garrick finally said, 'I want you to tell Karen Guttman what you've told me.' He passed her the phone.

'Inspector Suarez?' Karen said.

'Señor Garrick is telling you the truth. I think I will soon find who was responsible for the death of your father. It is better you ask no more questions where you are. Like I told him. You can hide, but maybe it is better you come here and accept my protection.'

'My father was kidnapped by a terrorist organisation. What have I got to be frightened of here? I can go to the police.'

'Those people did not kill your father. You must look at the people who worked with your father. You should take care.'

'What's going on?' she asked. 'I just want a simple answer.'

'This is not a simple thing. I can say no more.'

'That's not very helpful.'

'I am sorry.'

'Goodnight,' said Karen.

'¡Adiós!'

Karen snapped the mobile phone shut. She looked at Garrick. She thought for a moment, then came to a conclusion. 'We're taking a trip, Leon.'

Garrick looked puzzled. 'We'd better travel separately in that case,' he said. 'They're looking for me.'

'No. I'm going to book us both on a flight tomorrow morning. We'll travel together.'

'Don't use your phone,' he said.

She shook her head. 'I'm getting the hang of this. We want them to know what we're doing. I'm booking a couple of flights to London. As soon as I've done that we're taking a cab down to La Guardia Airport. We're going to take my father's Gulfstream to Mexico. Except we'll fill out a flight plan for Puerto Rico. When they realise we've gone they won't know where the hell we are.'

3

By noon on Monday Colonel Jackson felt he had things under control again. At the beginning of the day he'd been faced with chaos, but after careful analysis he realised there were only two issues that needed immediate attention. First, he had to find the couple who'd broken into the Korbett Biotek laboratory. Second, he had to silence Garrick and Guttman's daughter. The rest of the details would take care of themselves. He could plug up the cracks.

Garrick and the girl had disappeared temporarily. They'd never checked in for the flight they'd booked for London, but they weren't crossing any borders or taking any flights out of the country because every law enforcement agency had Garrick's picture and knew there was a young serviceman in a coma because of him. He was dangerous. They knew he'd taken a gun from the agent he'd half killed. With any luck he'd resist arrest and that would be the end of him.

Shortly after lunch Jackson discovered that Inspector Suarez had issued an Interpol notice stating that Miller was missing and was wanted for questioning in connection with Guttman's kidnap. He picked up the telephone and called Madrid. They'd make Suarez regret his action. Madrid would see to it because they had too much to lose if the truth ever saw the light of day. Unfortunately, the call didn't put an end to the complication. The Federal Bureau of Investigation was the official liaison route for Interpol, and when they started snooping there was no knowing what they'd find, especially now that Miller was presumed dead.

Jackson knew he had only a limited amount of time to wrap up the situation. He telephoned McFarlane and discovered he'd made progress. 'We traced the calls made from Miller's telephone. We got one to an Internet service provider. It was made by the woman we were checking out, Abene Pehrzon.'

'Yes?' said Jackson.

'The service provider automatically keeps a record of the telephone numbers that access it. It also keeps mail and files on disk, although users think they're deleted. From there on in, it was easy. Turns out the woman's contact was called Landow. Carl Landow.'

'What do you have on him?'

'Dead end. The real Landow's a sick puppy in some mental institution out west. We're working on that. Someone stole his identity maybe twenty years ago.'

'Anything else?'

'Pehrzon and Landow got out of the country. Through Canada. Landow sent a file to a *Washington Post* reporter from Vancouver telling him to check out Guttman-Tiche and Korbett Biotek. He mentioned the robbery, the dengue fever outbreak in Havana and the Pirineo epidemic in Spain.'

'Has Dr Rampton checked the inventory? Did they steal any sensitive material?'

'He checked as soon as the lab was safe. They took viruses.'

'I'll need briefing as soon as possible about their effects.'

'Yes, sir.'

'Anything else?'

'We could have a lead on this woman, Pehrzon. Dr Rampton looked through the records and found that Miller brought her into the laboratory a while back. Turned out he took a sample of her blood.'

'Why did he do that?'

'It's a routine procedure.'

'That sample might be more significant than you think,' observed Jackson. 'And what about the reporter? No way we want this to break. Especially not the Havana story.'

'Your people here say they can handle it.'

'Let me talk to them,' said Jackson.

As he approved the various steps being taken, Jackson thought about the dengue virus, and how the epidemic had cost the Cuban government over a billion dollars to contain. It had almost bankrupt the country. In 1989 Castro finally caught on to what had happened, and shortly afterwards the Russians started engineering the D7 virus. It sounded as if Miller had talked to the girl.

He wondered who Landow really was and for whom he worked. It wasn't the Russians: they were out of the game. The girl had made too many mistakes. She wasn't up to their calibre. She used the telephone and that led straight to her messages. A good agent would know that messages weren't ever deleted. He'd find out who they worked for soon enough.

4

Antonio Suarez was completing his reports for the week when there was a knock on the door. He grunted in response. The door opened and a policeman saluted him. 'Sir! The chief wishes to see you immediately.'

'Very well,' responded Suarez. 'You can go now,' he added, when the man made no move to depart. 'I'll be there in a few minutes. Shut the door behind you.'

The policeman closed the door reluctantly.

Suarez raised his eyebrows. He wondered what the chief was up to, sending a messenger instead of picking up the phone to summon him. The gesture irritated him. He completed the report he was writing, then put on his jacket and went to find out what was going on. He didn't often see the *jefe*.

They kept their distance. The chief didn't like to get his hands dirty.

The chief's office lay on the other side of the building, which meant returning to the ground floor, crossing the foyer and climbing the other staircase. The carpet started on the first floor. Not too much traffic along these corridors. No bloodstains, no paintwork gouged from the walls by visitors' fingernails. No dents and bumps in the skirting boards.

The police stations were one of Franco's most enduring contributions. The buildings reflected bureaucracy. Even the minions were crisply dressed, their ranks carefully delineated with buttons, stripes and hats. The concept of power was reinforced as a person passed through room after room until reaching what seemed to be the central seat of power.

Suarez was kept waiting in the secretary's office.

Some ten minutes later the telephone rang on the secretary's desk, and Suarez was summoned. He stood up, opened the polished door and closed it behind him respectfully.

The chief blotted his signature carefully, put the paper to one side of his desk, and screwed the cap on his pen. He looked up. He'd put on weight since they'd last met. Nearly five kilos. Soon he'd need a new uniform. 'Did you have anything to do with this report?' The chief flipped open the copy of a newspaper on his desk with a silver letter-opener. It was *El Mundo*.

Suarez leaned forward. 'Which article?'

The chief stabbed the letter-opener at an article. 'Operation Mengele,' he snapped. 'It claims intelligence agents experimented on vagrants with drugs intended for use against Basques.'

Suarez read the article quickly. When he had finished it he said cheerfully, 'Nothing to do with me, sir. Of course, rumours have been floating around and it was only a matter of time before they reached the newspapers.'

The chief glared at him.

'I didn't know a judge had been appointed to investigate the allegations. When should we expect him?' Suarez asked.

'I haven't heard anything,' growled the chief. 'They want to know what you're up to in Madrid. They're not pleased with you.'

'I can't imagine why.'

'Your enquiries have been causing problems.'

'What enquiries?' asked Suarez blankly.

'What the hell do you think you're doing putting out Interpol notices without reference to your superior?'

'I don't know what you're talking about, sir,' replied Suarez innocently.

The chief looked down at a sheet of paper in front of him. 'Dr Miller.'

'Perhaps you remember that small matter of Raphael Guttman?' said Suarez.

'That was nearly six months ago.'

'Since when do we close the books?'

'We don't, Suarez. But the Ministry of the Interior is handling the investigation. When they find the culprits, they'll deal with them.'

'That's not the usual procedure.'

'That's the way Madrid wants it,' the chief said firmly. They sat in silence for a few moments. 'And you can honestly tell me that you had nothing to do with this article in *El Mundo*?'

'Yes.'

'God help you if you're lying.'

'As a matter of interest, sir, what do you make of the article? Do you think there's any truth in it?' asked Suarez.

'I wouldn't give a damn if they wiped out all the Basques.'

'The idea's stupidly conceived. But it's just the sort of thing they'd come up with in Madrid. Don't shoot them, inject them. Do you think there's any truth in it?'

The chief's eyes darted to a corner of the room before focusing on Suarez again. 'All I know is they picked up some Basques, gave them some tranquillisers and one of them died. No big deal.'

'Is that what they said in Madrid?'

'Yes,' answered the chief irritably.

'If they were just injecting tranquillisers there's nothing to worry about, then.'

The chief pulled a sheet of paper from the tray in front of him. He picked up his fountain pen. 'Is that all?' he asked Suarez.

'You may remember I sent you a memo about that safe house up in Neguri. I want to know who controls it. I'd like a list of people authorised to use it.'

'You didn't get my reply?'

'No, sir.'

'It's not under our control. It used to be, but it was reallocated to the Ministry of the Interior five years ago.'

'Who do I speak to, in that case?'

'You don't.'

'You mean Agustín Hernando?' It was too much of a coincidence that the only forensic evidence he had from the Guttman case now seemed to be linked to the Ministry of the Interior, which had been cropping up in his investigation from the very beginning.

The chief glared at him. 'I mean, Suarez, that we don't get our lines crossed.'

'I'd like to inspect the house. I want forensics to take a look at it.'

'What are you suggesting?'

'I don't know if you're aware that Señor Guttman's daughter is returning here. She might find it strange that we haven't completed essential parts of the investigation. My report is thin, to say the least.'

'She has no right to information in a case still under investigation.'

'I'll tell that to her lawyers when they contact me.'

'Is she being persistent?'

'She has a point.'

'I'll make the necessary enquiries on your behalf.'

'Thank you, sir,' said Suarez.

'Now, is that all?'

'Yes, sir.' Suarez left the room.

Back in his office, Suarez considered what he knew about Agustín Hernando. He was a right-wing hardliner who'd survived a lifetime in politics. He'd encouraged Spain to join NATO and opposed the nuclear moratorium. He continued to oppose the granting of any autonomy to the various regional governments. He opposed the conversion of the half-built Lemoiz nuclear power station into a gas-fed electricity plant on the basis that it would encourage the Basques to demand full autonomy, and anything that encouraged that was a danger to the state's security. He was a smooth operator. He had the politician's touch of making everyone he spoke to feel that they were important.

Suarez leaned back in his chair and lit a cigarette. It was definitely time to take a close look at Agustín Hernando, Minister of the Interior, who was taking a sudden keen interest in what was happening. Suarez remembered how his wife, Carla, had gone weak at the knees when she was introduced to Hernando, and he'd turned on that charm and asked her what it was like being married to Spain's most important investigator. Hernando had praised her for not abandoning their home after the organised crime syndicates had made the death threats.

Suarez stubbed out the cigarette angrily. Bilbao had turned out to be his reward.

With a jolt he remembered that he'd promised to protect Garrick if he came to Bilbao. He wasn't sure how easy it would be now that he suspected a conspiracy at the highest levels. He couldn't allow Garrick and Karen Guttman to stay in a hotel or assign a policeman to them because he couldn't trust his men. He toyed with the idea of accommodating them in his apartment but decided against it. He would ask Felipe at the Parc Hotel if he knew of some suitable self-contained apartment. Felipe would be happy to oblige, especially if he thought he was helping a state witness. He'd love the intrigue and it would make him feel important.

5

Forty-eight hours after the viruses had been stolen from Korbett Biotek, Colonel Jackson was talking to an FBI pathologist. Ever since Suarez had put out the Interpol notice Jackson had expected FBI involvement, but he had never expected it to come under these circumstances. Miller's body had been found in New York State, but because he lived in Connecticut, and might have been abducted there, the investigation crossed state lines, which meant it fell under FBI jurisdiction. Jackson knew he could shut down the investigation by insisting that it was a matter of national security, but he would only do that as a last resort.

Jackson listened patiently as the pathologist told him how Miller had been killed with a length of cheesewire. Apparently he had entered the woods alive and probably voluntarily. He trusted the person, or persons, accompanying him. Unfortunately, careless activity at the scene of the crime by the sheriff's department, as well as the medical technicians, made further study of the ground unfeasible. It was possible that he had been killed by a third party while indulging in sexual activity with a second party, in which case another body might turn up. The right index finger had been removed shortly after death occurred, and the penis was exposed. The pathologist had forwarded the report to the psychological profilers in case the latter two details were connected in some way. Jackson didn't enlighten him as to the significance of the severed finger.

Jackson then produced the blood sample which Dr Miller had taken from the woman when she visited the Korbett Biotek laboratory on some previous occasion. 'Can you check this out for me?' he asked. 'Tell me what sort of a person it came from.'

'You don't realise what that entails,' said the pathologist. 'We'll need some kind of a control. All we can do is match it to a suspect. Everyone expects miracles these days.'

'You can tell more than that,' said Jackson. 'I have a hunch.'

'We all have hunches.'

Jackson's eyes narrowed. He didn't like the man's tone. He tried to ignore it. 'I think I know who these people are, but I need confirmation. I'd like you to confirm race.'

'Listen, Colonel, forget everything you've read about genetic testing. We're all different, but we're all the same. We're all made up of the same DNA. Our personal codes are less than point two per cent different from a stranger's. The difference is less between family members and more between those whose ancestors haven't intermingled in recent history. All the same, a random selection of people from Alaska to Cape Horn provides eighty-five per cent of the whole genetic variation of *Homo sapiens*. I can run a test for you, and all I'm going to prove is that the blood doesn't come from a chicken or a cow. I might even have some difficulty proving it didn't come from a chimpanzee.'

'Thanks for the lecture,' said Jackson coldly. 'But you don't understand how important this is, buddy. We need to find out where the blood comes from.'

'You still don't get it, Colonel. Genes aren't like that. You don't have a white gene or a black gene. You don't have a gene which says you're American or Venezuelan or Indian. You can't run a test like that. You're asking too much. We have databases for comparative studies, but they are for Caucasian, Afro-American and Hispanic. The kind of test you want takes ten weeks. And before I'd be willing to start I'd need interdepartmental authorisation so I know who to bill. When we get the same budget as the military, we'll be more generous. So, you better come up with something more specific, or forget it.'

Jackson stared at the pathologist. There was another way to

get the answer he wanted. The trouble with federal agents was they thought they were too damn smart, and to cap it all they weren't part of the National Security Decision Directive which imposed a lifetime censorship. 'I won't forget this,' Jackson threatened venomously. He stormed back to his helicopter.

The Armed Forces Institute of Pathology was famous for identifying the remains of soldiers missing in action for over twenty years. Its DNA specimen repository stored frozen samples of every member of the armed forces.

Lieutenant-Colonel Schroeder, the chief pathologist, listened sympathetically to Jackson's problem. 'You seem well informed on the subject,' he said.

'I've done a little research,' said Jackson evasively. 'Although we're much the same, about fifteen per cent of our genetic material differs widely from one person to another. I understand that material isn't randomly distributed. It's that fifteen per cent I'm interested in and whether it can help to pinpoint the origin of this blood.' He was picking up the lingo.

'Maybe,' said Schroeder. 'The genetic variation is predominantly geographic. It reflects the migrations and movements of the person's ancestors. It tells us who and what they contacted. Only a very small part of it is racial, probably only a quarter.'

'But if you knew what you were looking for, could it be done? If I supplied you with a control specimen, could you sort out some sort of—' Jackson's knowledge of the terminology petered out. '—test?'

'A gene probe.'

'That's the thing.'

'Yes. In principle,' said Schroeder. 'In practice things are a little different. I don't know where you'd get your control. That's a whole research project in itself. You'll need to know exactly what you're looking for.'

'I do,' said Jackson. 'I need confirmation of race type. How quickly could you give me a result?'

'That depends how well the control has been mapped. Let's say two weeks, and that's pushing it some.'

Jackson winced. 'How about a week?'

'I'll try.'

'I'll get the control,' said Jackson.

He knew where to find it. Running alongside the Human Genome Project was the Human Genetic Diversity Project. It recorded the dwindling diversity of *Homo sapiens* by taking DNA samples from several hundred distinct human populations and stored the samples in gene banks. Researchers examined the DNA to trace the evolution of the populations and ascertain their resistance or susceptibility to particular diseases. The Diversity Project would be more than helpful. They wouldn't want a formal request from the army because they were already accused of being pawns in a conspiracy to develop biological weapons that targeted ethnic groups. It would be easy to compromise them. Indian tribes in Brazil who objected to deforestation had already caught a nasty flu and anthropologists were looking for someone to blame.

By the end of the day Jackson had his control. He waited patiently. In a week he would know a lot more about the woman who called herself Abene Pehrzon. Her blood would tell him where she came from.

Chapter Eleven

I

Michel woke. He felt clammy and exhausted. It was night. It took him a while to work out that he was back in the apartment in Paris. He remembered slowly what had happened in America and how he and Abene had escaped through Canada. It seemed like a dream. He sat up and saw Abene sleeping on the couch. He looked at his watch and discovered that he'd lost two days. He'd developed a fever during the flight back from Vancouver. For a moment he wondered if he could have caught something in the Korbett Biotek laboratory, then discarded the idea.

He got up and went to the kitchen. He removed the flask from the freezer and opened it. The nitrogen had boiled away, but the cryo-tubes were still frosted. He worked fast. The viruses were delicate, and they would deteriorate soon. He picked up the fire extinguisher he'd bought before the fever incapacitated him, took a kitchen towel and slowly fired the carbon dioxide through the material. Dry ice formed. He filled the flask, screwed on the top and returned it to the freezer.

An image had kept returning again and again during his fever. It was a picture of children covered in blisters, with blowflies emerging from their open mouths. At first he thought it was the same old nightmare, his subconscious reacting to the horror of his involvement in the Barcelona bombing. But the images weren't the result of the bomb that had haunted him for so many years. They were the victims of biological weapons. He'd seen the photographs more recently, when Iraq attacked the Kurds.

Certain crimes couldn't be justified. He'd long ago given up any attempt to exonerate himself for his own actions. Burying adults was about burying the past, but to bury children was to bury the future, with its promises and dreams. Without children there could never be any hope for a future. Ever since the bomb in Barcelona he'd known he was living on borrowed time, but now he had a chance to make amends.

As soon as the shops were open he went out with Abene, made the necessary purchases and returned to the apartment. He sealed the top of the aquarium he had bought with a pane of glass that had five holes in it: two large ones for his hands, and two smaller ones in the corners. He sealed a small electric fan and an air filter with silicone rubber in the final hole. He welded industrial rubber gloves to the inside of the glass. He led electric cables through the two small holes and sealed them. One cable was for a kettle, the other to power a compressor pump. When he had finished packaging the virus he would bomb the tank with the formaldehyde crystals which he placed in the kettle. He'd turned the aquarium into a makeshift glove box.

He placed everything he needed inside the aquarium and practised manoeuvring the bottles and jars. His first efforts were clumsy because of the gloves, so he revised some of the procedures. He experimented with water the first time. He removed the valve from the nebuliser he'd bought in the medical supply shop and poured the water into it. He replaced the valve and connected the compressor, timing it carefully in case the nebuliser exploded and shattered the glove box.

At last he removed the prototype, depressed the plunger and watched a fine mist spray from the nozzle. It worked. He told Abene to leave the apartment. There was no point in both of them taking a risk. Then he put on one of the protective suits Abene had taken from the laboratory. He placed the helmet over his head. He took the viruses out of the freezer and put them into the aquarium. He was ready to start work in earnest.

An hour later he pulled the helmet off his head and gulped at the air. He felt faint. He looked back at his primitive laboratory and knew he didn't have the energy to charge another aerosol. One was enough. He switched on the kettle and the formaldehyde destroyed everything inside the aquarium.

He stripped off the protective suit and dropped it on the ground. He adjusted a small cramp he had modified so it gripped the aerosol and taped a solenoid to it. He connected the nozzle to the solenoid and wired up the battery through a clockwork timer. At the right time the electric current would activate the solenoid, which would contract and depress the nozzle, and the virus would be disseminated. His bomb was ready. He was exhausted. He placed the aerosol on the table in front of the glove box and took a photograph of it with a digital camera to demonstrate that he had a method of deployment.

That evening he composed a message for Peter Busby at the *Washington Post*. The journalist would be waiting to hear from him again. By now he'd have tried to find out what had happened at the Korbett Biotek laboratory and would be helping the authorities. He would be the messenger. Michel had to make sure he was waiting for the message when it came. There wouldn't be any time for mistakes.

2

Colonel Jackson brushed a few imaginary specks off his uniform, licked his lips, took a deep breath and opened the door.

General Franklin Tyler looked big, although he was only five feet ten inches. He was a three-star general in the Defense Intelligence Agency, nerve centre of America's military machine and the largest and most discreet agency in the world. It employed fifty-seven thousand people operating out of Arlington Hall in Virginia and Bolling Air Force Base in Washington, DC.

Presidents came and went, but he stayed, curator of America's secrets and hidden policies. He believed he was more important than the President.

His office was sparsely decorated. There were no photographs, because he didn't like being photographed. He was seldom seen with politicians and counted none as his friends because he didn't trust them. He'd known three Presidents and held them in low esteem: he thought they were unprincipled and prepared to do anything for power. He remembered how Ronald Reagan had become a creationist to get a few more votes by saying 'evolution is a theory which is not believed in the scientific community to be as infallible as it once was'. Reagan had been easy to handle, though.

'What's the problem, Colonel?' Tyler asked.

'Terrorism,' replied Jackson. 'Research samples from the Guttman-Tiche programme have fallen into the wrong hands.'

Tyler nodded. A muscle on his jaw twitched. He had been responsible for implementing the various research stations ten years ago. He'd nurtured the idea since 1972. He'd been a major then, serving in Germany. He had organised the C-141 transfer jet and an Apollo space capsule to medevac two people suspected of contracting Lassa fever in West Africa. The patients sat in the seats designed for astronauts, insulated from the rest of the world. The doctors and nurses who attended them wore protective gloves, masks, gowns and footwear. He'd never seen anything like it, except in the chemical warfare units where the precautions they took were chickenshit in comparison.

In those days Lassa fever was the most contagious virus known to man. It killed three days after infection. It started with ulcers lining the pharynx, followed by fever, acute dehydration, skin haemorrhaging, convulsions and finally death. Tyler had followed developments with interest as doctors and scientists tried to isolate the vector through which the fever spread. At first they thought it was a mosquito. Later they discovered there were different strains, but when one patient developed antibodies it was possible to manufacture a vaccine. Tyler realised its potential in the warfare arena.

In due course President Nixon signed a convention that prohibited the development and stockpiling of biological weapons except for defensive purposes. However, his National Security Adviser, Henry Kissinger, explained that the treaty didn't preclude research into the offensive aspects of biological agents because it was necessary in order to determine what defensive measures were required. 'Look at it this way: if you're testing a bulletproof jacket you need to develop the bullet.'

Tyler set up his research stations, and Kissinger won a Nobel Peace Prize.

'One of our research scientists has been killed. It appears he was seduced by a woman,' said Colonel Jackson.

'Typical swallow operation?' Tyler asked.

'That's how it looks.'

Tyler shook his head. He dreaded swallow operations. He thought anyone working on classified projects ought to be castrated as a precaution. 'Have you located the girl yet?' he asked.

'No, sir,' replied Jackson. 'We're checking it out.'

'What sort of samples did they obtain?'

'Hot agents,' said Jackson.

Tyler pursed his lips. There were no antidotes to hot agents.

'An inventory is under way,' said Jackson. 'I thought you should be advised of the situation immediately.'

'Who's responsible? Our friend Saddam?'

'We don't have a clear picture at the moment.'

'Fill me in from the beginning,' said Tyler.

When Jackson had finished, Tyler said nothing. He was considering how to limit the damage. It might mean he'd have to speak to the President. He hated speaking to politicians. They hated him, too, but they didn't cross him. They'd learned. Memories were long in the White House. He remembered the senator from the Midwest who tried to block his budget. Big mistake. The senator should never have visited a psychotherapist when his first marriage disintegrated because he appeared to be no more than a repentant rapist when Tyler leaked the story.

Tyler looked at Jackson, surprised to find he was still in the room. He'd been lost in his thoughts. 'So who are these terrorists?'

'The woman's Basque, sir. We got the results of a DNA test on her.'

'Who does she work for?'

'We don't know.'

'Is everything else secure?'

'At present. We may have to put pressure on the FBI to back off. I don't know about Madrid but they're aware of the situation.'

'Who else knows what you told me?'

'Limited to a few people at the moment, sir. We need to distance ourselves.'

'What do you have in mind?'

'Intelligence reports about biological weapons missing from Russian laboratories.'

'I already anticipated that, Colonel. I think we'll find that the public's perception of the international situation will work in our favour.'

'Sir, our best hope is these guys make some mistake. Maybe we'll hear about someone with symptoms suggesting contamination by one of the viruses. We're looking for hospital reports. We're on to the manufacturers of biohazard suits, especially battery-operated ones. They need specialised equipment to use the viruses. We're checking it out.'

Tyler frowned. He didn't like details. Sounded like Jackson was nervous. When people talked details they weren't in control. 'Good,' he said without enthusiasm.

3

Leon Garrick stretched his legs out in Guttman's Gulfstream. It would be his first flight in a private jet. He watched Karen walk down the aisle of the plane. She sat next to him. 'I had a problem with the pilot,' she said. 'He wasn't happy about submitting a flight plan for Puerto Rico and then going to Mexico. He said it would put his licence on the line.'

'Did you sort it out?'

'Money,' she said. 'It works every time.' Then she smiled.

When they were in the air, Karen stood up. 'Come back here,' she ordered, and led him to one of the two sofas that faced each other at the back of the plane. 'Let's take a look at you.'

She hunted through the emergency medical kit and found a bandage. She helped him take off his jacket and shirt, felt in the jacket pocket, took out the gun and looked at it.

'So what happened?' she asked, putting the gun to one side.

'This kid pulled that gun and I acted in self-defence. I hope he's all right.'

'Why are you concerned about someone who might have killed you?'

'I don't enjoy doing things like that. The kid would probably be on my side if he knew the whole story. If he dies life will get difficult for me. I'll be facing a murder charge.'

'You acted in self-defence,' Karen pointed out.

'Small difference,' said Leon.

Karen began strapping his ribs. 'Tell me if I hurt you,' she said.

'The tighter the better,' Leon told her.

'You've been in the wars,' she said, commenting on the scars that marked his back. 'How did you get them?' She ran her fingers across his skin.

Her touch sent a shiver up his spine. He hoped she didn't notice. 'You don't want to know.'

'Did it hurt?'

'At the time. But pain's a relative thing. You remember the pain of losing your first girlfriend more vividly than you remember the arm you broke as a child.'

'Where did it happen?'

'On a dance-floor in a place called Guildford.'

'I was referring to the visible scars.'

Leon smiled. 'I'd rather talk about you.'

'No scars here,' she said, taping the end of the bandage.

She put on a tough face, but Leon knew that her father's death hurt her more than she showed. He knew she'd bring up the subject sooner or later, but was surprised when she did.

'I want you to know I'm grateful, Leon, for what you've done so far. I didn't expect you to get hurt or find yourself in a dangerous situation.'

He tried to make light of it. 'I'd like to say it's an occupational hazard. It used to be, but it's not any more.'

'I had no idea that my father was involved in anything dangerous.'

'It's possible that he didn't know.'

'He was secretive. I never knew his friends. He was always having meetings with people, but I never knew who they were. My mother seldom saw him. I think that's why they didn't have any more children. In six years of boarding-school he visited me only twice. My mother moved to Switzerland so she could be close to me, and then she died in a car crash in one of those tunnels through the mountains. She was on her way to pick me up for a holiday. I used to think it was my fault. I mean, she wouldn't have been driving in that place at that time if it hadn't been for me.'

'Sometimes taking responsibility for things that go wrong can make sense out of random, meaningless events like car crashes,' said Leon.

'I think I've warned you before about that psychotherapy thing, Leon,' she joked. 'But that wasn't what I wanted to say to you.' She hesitated. 'I want to know the truth about my father. I want to know what happened to him and why no one is telling us the truth. I don't want you to hide anything from me.'

Leon nodded. He could understand that.

Then she spoiled it all. 'I don't want you pulling any punches on my account. Look after my interests, Leon, and I'll look after you.' She was referring to their financial relationship.

'I'm not doing this for the money, Karen,' he said. 'I'm doing this to put things right.'

When they reached Mexico, Karen booked the seats to Madrid. While they waited for the flight she spent the time on the telephone. Leon noticed she'd stopped using her mobile. She was learning fast. 'Who were you calling?' he asked as they boarded the plane.

'A couple of people I thought might help us if we get into trouble. My lawyer and a congressman.'

'What did you tell them?'

'I told them what's happened so far.'

'Did you tell them where we were?'

'No.'

Garrick nodded and closed his eyes. He was asleep before the plane took off.

In Madrid, Karen hired a Mercedes at the airport. 'Normally I'd hire a smaller car,' she said, 'but I think you need something comfortable.' As she drove they talked, and for the first time Leon felt there was something special about her. They travelled north, past fields still being ploughed by oxen, not tractors. 'This country's so full of contradictions,' she said, stopping the car and taking photographs.

All of a sudden she was in no hurry to reach Bilbao. The pace of their journey slowed. She took detours through villages, and endless photographs of storks nesting on church steeples and clock towers. She walked him around churches, looking at statues and pictures. 'They'd be worth a fortune in Manhattan,' she said, pointing at the carvings. 'It's hard to reconcile the spiritual side of Catholicism with all this idolatry,' she commented in one church. In another she was almost moved to tears by the tin imprints of parts of the body which had been hung under the pictures of saints by the afflicted, who hoped for a miracle. 'The simple, sad piety gets to me every time. People here believe in religion more than doctors,' she said. 'Is it because they're just poor?'

Leon turned over one of the pieces of tin. There was a date on the back. 'A lot's changed in forty years,' he observed.

'Trust you to spoil it,' she said.

A journey that should have taken half a day took three days, and Leon wondered whether she was frightened of finding out the truth and wanted to put off the moment. He hoped he didn't have to protect her from it.

4

It was a beautiful spring morning without a cloud in the sky. There had been a chill in the early hours, but now the sun was warming the air. A gentle breeze played with the flags. The President of the United States looked over the lectern at the rows of people stretching into the distance, where they merged with the white crosses of the military graves. They were gathered to honour the dead.

The President imagined how he appeared on the television screens, framed by the memorial behind him. In the distance people were moving closer so they could hear his speech. America would always honour those who had fallen in the name of freedom.

He turned to the autocue on his right and continued his speech.

We must be alert.
On our guard.
Eternally vigilant.
The enemies of freedom never sleep and neither must we.

Eight years ago our intelligence services learned that Iraq held enough
biological and chemical weapons to wipe out the entire population of
the world.
Several times over.
We were able to end that threat but there are other threats.

The President's brow furrowed for a moment. On the
television screens it would resemble passion. He didn't remember
this from when he had approved the speech, but it had been a
busy week. Maybe he'd been distracted when he was reading
the draft.

Since the collapse of the Soviet empire,
terrorism has gained access
to these chemical and biological weapons.
These weapons are cheap and readily available
on the black markets of the world.
They will become the first choice
of emergent nations in the weapons field.

The President glanced up and focused on the faces in the
front row. They were riveted to every word. The disadvantage
of the autocue was that the words spilled across the screen. He
had no idea what he would be saying next. He was certain he
had never seen this part of the speech.

Such weapons are only safe and acceptable
when held by a nation which is
free, strong and responsible.
A nation such as ours.

Heads were going to roll for this. The speech was intended
to emphasise NATO's effectiveness at maintaining peace.
Nothing more.
He turned back to the autocue, reluctantly.

The United States is the only NATO country
which admits to active research in this field.
We are not ashamed.
Not ashamed of taking steps to protect democracy
from the dark forces of fundamentalism and fanaticism.
New technologies and developments in genetic engineering
will mean the invention of new weapons.

The President turned involuntarily to the other autocue,
hoping that the words would tell a different story.

These new bio-weapons have capabilities
beyond our darkest imaginings
against which there is no known defence.
That is why the United States of America
will take the strongest measures
against any regime with such weapons.
Our armed forces have always defended freedom.
Now they have a new and even more lofty role.
The defence of the human race itself
against those who threaten it with disease, pestilence and famine.
Biological weapons recognise no frontiers.
For the first time in history
a weapon used in a minor conflict
may threaten the very survival of the American people.
This nation reserves the right
to strike out this new evil
wherever and whenever it is necessary.
As your President, I can do no less.
Let the faceless cowards who threaten
our country with terrorism know:
There
Will
Be
No hiding-place.

The audience rose. They were clapping.

'God bless America,' said the President. His words were lost in the ovation.

The President smiled grimly. The speech had struck a chord with the people, but he'd wait until the press had commented before making any judgments.

5

As soon as Carl Landow accessed the Internet service provider his computer was interrogated by powerful software which downloaded all the information on his hard drive in the short time it took him to send the e-mail. Within a few minutes the serial numbers of his application programmes would tell Jackson where they'd been bought. The credit cards would tell him by whom. Even the deleted files on the hard disk would be resurrected, and Landow would be none the wiser. With any luck Jackson would know Landow's real name by the end of the day. Computers were more dangerous than the written word.

The e-mail Jackson had intercepted was destined for Peter Busby at the *Washington Post*, but it wouldn't be forwarded and he'd never receive it. The message had been sent from a telephone at Heathrow Airport, which meant the target was on the move. His last message had been sent from Bombay. The one before from Paris. Landow was on the move but they were tracking him now. Soon they'd be anticipating his next move.

Any feelings of triumph Jackson experienced at having intercepted the e-mail evaporated as he read the downloaded message.

URGENT

Dear Mr Busby
I did not find a report concerning the removal of biological agents from the Korbett Biotek laboratory in the newspapers

and I am disappointed. I assume you are compromised. I chose you because I have enjoyed your articles in the *Washington Post*. This business I am telling you about . . . who knows . . . maybe you can win a Pulitzer Prize. No, I think not. It is too radical.

I offer you a second chance to tell the truth to the world. I have put a virus on flight UA049 departing from Heathrow Airport, London, which arrives at JFK, New York, today. I also include a photograph which shows the method of deployment.

I will communicate with you after the plane has landed and been placed in quarantine. You will see that the authorities have no option. They must place the passengers in quarantine. You will see that in this case they cannot afford to gamble with lives.

You should tell the airport, the police and the FBI as soon as you receive this message. When the plane is in quarantine I will tell you whether there was or wasn't a virus on board.

A picture file was attached.

Jackson opened the file. It was a photograph of an aerosol. In the background there was a primitive laboratory. Beside the aerosol was the familiar shape of a cryo-tube. He zoomed in on the image until he could read the batch number on the tube and made a note of it.

A few minutes later Jackson was told that the United Airlines flight that originated in Bombay had left Heathrow an hour ago. He concluded that Landow must have left the virus on board when he got off the plane in London.

Chapter Twelve

━━━━━◆◆◆◆◆━━━━━

I

The United Airlines plane climbed steeply from Heathrow on the final leg of its journey from Bombay to New York City. A young Japanese woman put her hands to her ears and tried to stop them popping. She didn't like flying. When the plane levelled off she noticed an object rolling on the floor near her feet. She paid it no attention. The plane was less crowded now that so many people had disembarked in London, and she pulled up the armrests and stretched out on the seats. She closed her eyes and tried to sleep.

She was looking forward to visiting America. Her parents had paid for the flight, and she'd be staying with family friends in New York. Later she would travel to Memphis, Tennessee. She wanted to visit Graceland. She was an Elvis Presley fan. Some of her friends had seen his ghost crossing the road, and she wondered if she'd be as lucky.

When she woke up she looked at her watch and found she'd been asleep for three hours. She wasn't sure if the cylinder on the floor had made a noise, but it seemed to be spraying something. She sat up quickly and drew her feet up under her. She pressed the button for the stewardess. She looked down uncertainly at the object on the floor and wondered if it might be something to do with the life jacket under the seat.

The object stopped spraying its contents as the stewardess

arrived. The Japanese girl pointed at the object and the stewardess picked it up without thinking. Her eyes widened. 'Does this belong to you?' she asked the girl sternly.

The girl shook her head. 'It was under the seat.'

The stewardess read the instructions on the label and said hurriedly, 'It's something the cleaners left behind.' She walked forward briskly. There were a few minutes before lunch was due to be served. She hurried towards the cockpit to speak to the captain. Her heart was racing. The contraption obviously didn't belong on a plane. It was crudely made and had a small timer mechanism attached to it.

The captain examined the object and passed it to the navigator and co-pilot. The captain was irritated that the thing had found its way into the cockpit. He didn't like surprises on planes. However, he was reassured that it had so far caused no harmful effects. It was light, so it probably wasn't explosive.

A small sticker on the canister bore the legend *Biohazard*. There was a handwritten code number, followed by the message *Property of Korbett Biotek*.

The captain told the stewardess to reassure the passenger who had found it, and to examine her closely to see if she was betraying any ill effects.

He looked at his instruments. He was five hours from JFK Airport. He adjusted the throttles, feeling uneasy. If he made a quick passage he might be given an earlier landing slot. There was precious little else he could do. The last thing he wanted was to have to radio ahead and tell them he had some kind of a biohazard on board. They'd have him rerouted to some military base where everyone would be placed in quarantine, and it could be weeks before they were released. His wife was expecting a baby, and he wanted to be home for the birth.

He talked to his co-pilot at length and reluctantly concluded that he had to do something. If word ever leaked out that he had taken no action, they'd lose their jobs. However, he decided not to mention it until they were an hour from JFK. They'd have little fuel left so there would be less chance of being diverted to some other airfield.

2

Colonel Jackson and Dr Rampton sat opposite General Franklin Tyler in his office. Only these three men knew the full extent of the danger threatening the United States. They had to make a decision in less than an hour, and no one would leave the room until it had been made. They'd been in session for half an hour.

'The question is,' said Tyler, 'do we play their game?'

'We've learned from history that the only way forward is to take a firm line with terrorists,' said Jackson.

'So, is there a virus on that plane?' asked Tyler.

'There could be,' said Rampton. His head perched above the neck brace he'd been forced to wear after his ordeal in the laboratory. He was thin and grey. He suffered from eczema, and the steroids with which he treated the condition gave his skin a shiny appearance. Nervously, his tongue darted out to lick his lips. He looked at the sheet of paper in front of him. 'I've examined the photograph, and as far as I can tell there's no reason to doubt that a virus has been nebulised. The batch number is authentic.' He hesitated. 'Personally, I wouldn't care to experiment with the virus under the conditions in that photograph.'

'Do you think the terrorist is infected?' asked Tyler.

Rampton shook his head. 'Impossible to say.'

'What evidence do we have that the virus is on the plane?'

Jackson fielded the question. 'We have evidence that the virus can be deployed. We have evidence that it could be on the plane. Let's consider it from a more traditional viewpoint. If we receive a bomb warning through recognised channels, we evacuate a building. We have to assume a bomb has been placed there, even if subsequently we find it hasn't.'

'So you're suggesting we play their game, Colonel. We assume the virus is on the plane and we put it in quarantine,' said Tyler.

'A bomb is a known risk,' said Rampton. 'It has a limited effect. It goes off. It destroys a few buildings. In this case, if people are infected by this virus they become bombs themselves. Each person becomes a time bomb and will infect others in due course. The situations are not comparable.'

'Tell us about the virus,' said Tyler.

'There are no antidotes or vaccines.'

'What are the effects?'

'They are not known, but I can tell you what it was designed to do. It is expected that forty-eight hours after exposure the victim will suffer flu-like symptoms and conjunctivitis. After approximately seventy-two hours the symptoms will disappear. However, the virus will mutate in the optic nerve and cause damage to the brain. Initially there will be sensory deprivation followed by rapid loss of all motor function.'

'Then what?' asked the general.

Rampton hesitated, confused by the naïvety of the question. 'The victim dies, or more likely becomes paralysed.'

'The obvious solution is to divert the flight to one of our bases and place the crew and passengers in quarantine,' said Tyler.

Jackson wondered when the general would finally get the full picture. 'It's not a viable option, sir. There are one hundred and eighty people on that plane. They all have friends and relations who will be asking questions. We can't afford that. This virus is hot. We can't quarantine people without explanation any more than we can imprison them. We don't have the facilities to contain that many people. Each encounter with the virus, even taking precautions, poses a threat.'

'General!' snapped Rampton, catching Tyler's attention. 'Imagine how it would be if AIDS became airborne. Then imagine the virus was one hundred per cent more efficient.'

The general blinked and looked away. There was silence in the room. Outside they could hear the whup-whup of a helicopter landing. It was hard to tell whether or not Tyler was in the process of imagining the effects of the virus.

'What's the estimated casualty rate?'

Rampton glanced at Jackson. Tyler seemed to be on the wrong track. 'It's airborne. It's a recombinant virus. It was engineered for efficiency. We expect that a very high percentage of people who come into contact with the virus will become casualties. Probably in the region of seventy per cent, with thirty per cent mortality.'

'What's the profile on these terrorists?'

'We don't have much information, but there's no reason to doubt their threat. So far they've proved to be ruthless and capable.' Jackson paused. 'Sir, time is running out.' He wanted to focus attention on the decision to be made. 'The plane is now less than three hours from the American coast.'

'I'm aware of that, Colonel.'

'If the virus reaches these shores it will be only a matter of time before the American population is under siege. We're talking about fifty million body-bags.'

'I'm aware of the scale of things.'

'The virus must be stopped before it reaches our shores,' said Jackson. 'We have been challenged with an act of unspeakable evil, and the only solution is to consider how it can be limited. We have to consider the greater good: that is, the defence of the people of this country.' He couldn't put it more plainly than that.

General Tyler dodged the question again. 'What do the terrorists want?'

'They appear to be demanding that we publish our research in the press. It's an irrelevant demand and at this stage it's immaterial. They've made a first strike. The virus is on the plane and we have no option but to believe that they have unleashed it.'

'We need proof?'

'If we radio the plane then we publicise the existence of the virus.'

'Who are the terrorists?'

'We're operating on the assumption they are Basques.' Jackson rapped his fingers on the table irritably.

'How did they get on to this thing?' asked Tyler, reluctant to address the central issue.

'We don't know yet.'

'The Spanish connection?'

'I'm making enquiries.'

'What kills the virus?' asked Tyler suddenly.

'Extreme heat,' snapped Rampton. 'If you want absolute certainty, we're talking about a nuclear explosion. The virus won't survive long-term exposure to the elements and ultraviolet light. If that plane was to explode over the sea I think it would probably destroy the virus.'

General Tyler looked at Rampton. He flinched. He was reacting as if this were the first time he had considered the solution. 'Are you suggesting the deliberate downing of a civilian aircraft over American waters?' He added unnecessarily: 'It would involve the killing of American citizens on that plane.'

'It's the only solution,' said Rampton. 'It's a small sacrifice which has to be made. If that virus has been disseminated we can't allow the passengers to land.'

'You said an explosion would probably kill the virus. Probably? Considering such a drastic solution, I want certainty,' said Tyler. He knew he would ultimately be held responsible.

Rampton sighed. It sounded like exasperation. 'There's always the danger the virus could find its way into marine life. There might be warm-blooded creatures in the vicinity of the accident. Dolphins or whales. Who knows? A genetically altered virus may affect marine life or interact with related viruses with uncertain consequences. However, time is running out. I suggest we agree that there is no alternative.'

'We must consider the greatest good of the greatest number. That virus is capable of wreaking havoc,' added Jackson.

They sat in silence.

Jackson imagined the plane exploding.

Tyler imagined the body-bags.

Rampton thought about the impossible option. One hundred and eighty-odd guinea-pigs in quarantine.

Jackson broke the silence. 'I propose we dispatch a fighter to shoot down the plane. For the purposes of national security we will also have to do a wet job on the fighter's pilot and navigator.'

'Wet job?' repeated Tyler. It wasn't clear whether he didn't understand, was objecting, or was simply repeating the words.

'They'll have to disappear. They'll be a weak link for us, but we can deal with that later. The plane will be blown up over the sea. At that altitude there is no possibility of any survivors. Any wreckage will be spread over the open ocean. There will be little danger of rescue teams coming into contact with the virus. The explosion on the plane will be attributed to a terrorist organisation. No black box will be found. I will see to that.'

There was another silence.

'I will brief the President as soon as the plane is downed,' said Tyler. 'Before we eliminate the civilian airliner, I think we should establish contact to find out whether there is any evidence that the virus has been deployed. Is that understood?'

Colonel Jackson understood. The general was covering himself. 'Yes, sir,' he said. The implied compliance was a lie. Any contact with the airliner posed a security risk. He couldn't carry out Tyler's instructions.

General Tyler pushed back his chair and stood up. 'You have work to do, gentlemen,' he said, dismissing them.

Jackson exchanged a glance with Rampton. The general had given permission for the operation to proceed.

3

When Michel planted the aerosol on the United Airlines flight an hour before it landed at Heathrow, he envisaged no problems. Everything was going according to plan. He spent fifteen minutes in the lavatory preparing the various pieces. He peeled off the medication label he'd attached to the aerosol in case airport security inspected it. He connected the battery and the timer and ran the wires to the solenoid. He set the watch to complete the circuit five hours later. He took the aerosol back to his seat and, under the guise of searching for something, taped it to the life jacket beneath him.

When the plane landed at Heathrow he disembarked and cleared Customs. Under a different name, he checked in for a connection to Basle ninety minutes later. He would be in Switzerland long before the United Airlines flight was due to land in America.

He waited until his flight was announced before connecting his modem to a telephone in the departure lounge and sending the e-mail to Peter Busby at the *Washington Post*.

He walked to the departure gate. Ten minutes later he was sitting in the plane. The plane taxied on to the runway – then stopped. Minutes passed. Michel looked at his watch. The passengers became restless.

The pilot made an announcement. 'I regret to inform you there's a heavy backlog of traffic over Basle because of the French air traffic controllers' strike. We are returning to the terminal while we wait for further instructions. We anticipate that the delay will only be half an hour, so we won't be disembarking. I apologise for the inconvenience.'

Michel didn't believe the pilot. They never told passengers when there was something wrong. He suspected they'd found a problem with the aircraft. He looked at his watch. He still had plenty of time in hand. He needed to be in Switzerland within two hours, but it was only a forty-five-minute flight. The plane taxied back to the terminal.

Fifty minutes later the plane was still on the tarmac and Michel was anxious. He was beginning to wonder if the Americans had traced his call back to Heathrow. If so, they'd know he'd made it from a departure lounge. If they were checking all the flights, it would bring the airport to a standstill. He peered out of the window. There was no sign of mechanics feverishly attending to the landing gear. Other planes were taking off. His flight seemed to have been singled out.

Michel felt nauseous. Black spots danced in front of his eyes. He tried to breathe normally and the nausea disappeared, but seconds later his stomach was racked by pain. He doubled up in agony. Perspiration trickled down his forehead. He wiped it away with the sleeve of his shirt. Anxiety had never caught him like this before. He waited for the pain to subside.

The pilot made another inscrutable announcement. The mood in the cabin grew angry, and the stewardesses tried to pacify the passengers. The aircraft taxied out again, then stopped. The activity subdued the passengers for a few moments, but they weren't fooled. The pilot announced they had been given a landing time and were preparing for takeoff.

Michel listened to a passenger arguing with a stewardess. The man wanted to disembark because he'd missed the function he was supposed to attend. If he got his way, Michel decided to leave the flight with him.

The plane began moving again. Michel peered out and saw it was held in a queue. He counted eight planes in line. He waited impatiently. The time he had allocated for this part of his operation was disappearing rapidly.

Finally, the plane took off and forty-five minutes later was put in a holding pattern over Basle. By now the United Airlines flight would be in quarantine.

4

The Japanese girl pushed up the window shade and looked out at the dusk. The clouds below her tumbled across the sky like giant snowdrifts. She imagined lying on them and gazing up at the blue sky retreating into the loneliness of space. She put on her earphones and listened to a tape of Elvis Presley hits. She pulled the blanket around her thin body and listened to the words she barely understood. On the screen in front of her she watched the plane's progress across the world. It was heading towards a place called Gander in Newfoundland. She guessed it would turn south there, but now they were still over the sea. She wished she could go back to sleep but the incident with the canister had upset her.

The Japanese girl saw the clouds parting under the plane. She saw a strange black thing. It looked as if it had emerged from a comic. She couldn't tell in which direction it was travelling. It looked like something from another world. She couldn't explain its shape. At one moment it was box-like, a kite with wings; then it turned and looked like something else, a paper dart. It wasn't really black. It was a silhouette. The sky and the clouds had been cut away. It was like a piece of origami fluttering in the sky. Two red streaks flashed angrily against the clouds. It didn't make sense. It frightened her. Then the plane juddered. A ball of fire roared through the aisle. The girl closed her eyes.

5

Ray McCormick was more alone than he'd ever felt before and only wished they'd chosen some other pilot. He didn't discuss the mission with his navigator. He knew that if he mentioned it he'd voice his doubts.

The navigator looked at his radar screen. The fighter had stopped being interrogated by the US shore-based radar stations. Soon the airliner would be visible to the naked eye. He listened to his radio. He could hear the civilian planes calling into Gander, announcing their positions, and receiving their onward flight information. Radios were his hobby. As a child he had dreamed of picking up some radio message from another world hidden in the clutter out there. Now he didn't believe there was intelligent life in space. There was little enough intelligence on earth.

In the cockpit Ray McCormick armed the missiles. He saw sunlight reflecting off the airliner's body. He ignored the doubts, concentrated on the target and fired the missiles. The fighter recoiled. He shuddered against the seat.

He peeled the plane to port and put some distance between himself and the target. The seat thumped him in the back as the fighter accelerated. He banked and looked down at the towering explosion. The flaming debris of the airliner took on a surreal quality. The pieces tumbled through the clouds and fell into the sea far below.

For the briefest moment McCormick felt the excitement of a kill, then turned for home, his mission over.

6

Michel disembarked from the plane in Basle and took a taxi into the city. He changed cabs to cover his tracks, then joined Abene at the hotel where he had begun his journey two days before. By travelling through Switzerland he'd made it difficult for his movements to be traced. Swissair didn't keep passenger lists because they might compromise people delivering cash to the country's bank vaults.

He had used up all his false identities. He'd said goodbye to Pepe Fernandez on the United Airlines flight. Soon he'd have to consider plastic surgery in one of the Swiss clinics. He didn't like the idea of that. He wondered what it would be like to see a stranger in the mirror every morning.

At the hotel he asked for the key to his room and the receptionist told him his wife was upstairs. He checked in the lounge to see if there were any signs of surveillance. A family was playing some card game. Three kids under ten years old. No warning signs. If the police were around and expected trouble they cleared children out of the firing line. He went upstairs and knocked on the door.

Abene opened it. He was expecting her to look happy when she saw him, but instead she looked worried. 'It's on the news now,' she said. 'They blew up the plane.'

Michel closed the door behind him. What she said didn't make sense at first. He looked at the television screen.

There was a picture of the White House, with a reporter superimposed on it. It took Michel a few seconds to register what the reporter was saying. A plane had exploded over the Atlantic. It was a terrorist bombing. No one had accepted responsibility. There were interviews and the picture of a United Airlines plane.

Michel closed his eyes. When he opened them he realised that he was shaking. It had happened again. He was responsible for killing innocent people. The plane had been shot down.

Abene put her arms around him. 'We should have expected that,' she said. 'They claim Iraq has the biological capability to kill everyone in the world, but that didn't stop America from bombing the biological weapons factories and releasing deadly substances into the environment. Killing a hundred and eighty people doesn't register on their scale.'

Michel shook his head. 'The virus wasn't on the plane,' he said. 'I used the aerosol we filled with water.' He'd never have killed all those people in cold blood.

'It's not your responsibility,' said Abene, trying to calm him.

It was clear that however ruthless he was prepared to be, the state would be more ruthless in its own defence. But one thing was certain. He had the five-star virus. He had something that frightened the people who had invented it. They would stop at nothing in order to find him and retrieve the virus he had stolen.

He listened to the voice of the President of the United States. 'Once again innocent people have been subjected to the cowardice of terrorism. The people of America join with me in condemning this violence, and in offering our sympathy to the families of the victims. If I have a mission, it is this. The perpetrators of this evil deed will not escape. We will find out who they are. Our agents will bring them to justice. There is no country in the world which can keep them from us. Whatever it takes, we will bring them to stand trial in America for the deaths of innocent people.'

Michel wondered whether the President knew the truth and whether he had given the orders for the plane to be destroyed. He switched off the television angrily. The room was suddenly quiet.

He stood up and looked out of the window at a barge on the Rhine, and knew that if he was ever caught no one would believe his story. No one would take the word of a terrorist against that of the authorities. They would never believe that he hadn't intended to take innocent lives. But he still possessed the virus. He could still negotiate. He still had the evidence.

He drew the curtains and took off his clothes. He crawled into the king-size bed. He felt like a child in the vast expanse of linen.

Abene put her arms around him.

It could have been five minutes, it could have been an hour later when he made the decision. Only one course was open to him. In the morning he would call Rodriguez Cristobál, the ETA lawyer in Bilbao, and make the arrangements. 'I've decided to become *arrepentido*,' he said.

Abene froze. Michel was going to turn himself over to the police and repent his actions. He would be expected to give them the names of his accomplices and tell them about the actions he had carried out. He would tell them about her, about Guttman and what they had done in America.

In Abene's eyes he didn't have the right to do that.

Chapter Thirteen

I

Leon telephoned Suarez at home to tell him they would be arriving in Bilbao. When he said they'd be arriving by road, Suarez arranged to meet them outside the restaurant where they had eaten the last time. 'You remember where it is?' he asked. It was clear he didn't want to mention the name over the phone.

Suarez was waiting when Leon and Karen pulled up at the kerb. He got into the rear seat. 'Turn the car round,' he ordered. He looked behind them a couple of times.

'What's the problem?' asked Leon.

Suarez didn't answer directly. 'I have arranged for you to stay in a place close to where I live. When we spoke I said that I could offer you protection, but it is better that no one knows where you are. I do not know who we can trust any more.'

He issued a series of directions to Karen, finally telling her to pull into a small courtyard and park in a corner. They got out and followed him into an apartment. He turned on the lights. The place was dark, with minimal furnishings. Bookcases lined the walls. 'It belongs to the brother of a friend,' said Suarez. 'He is a professor, but he is in South America at the moment. I think you will find it comfortable.'

'You promised to tell me what happened to my father,' said Karen bluntly.

Suarez looked uncomfortable. He darted a look at Leon.

'I want to know the truth,' said Karen. 'If you don't tell me I'm going to make life difficult for everyone concerned. I'll have every lawyer in this town working on the case and asking questions. That's just for starters.' She had Suarez's attention. 'I'll cause problems for your precious Guggenheim. There won't be a newspaper in the world that doesn't cover my story. I'm not joking. Donating a Goya gave my father certain rights and I'll exercise them on his behalf. That's before I talk to my political connections and tell them what I think's going on here.'

'I understand you,' said Suarez, 'but I have not completed my investigation.'

'I'm entitled to some answers,' insisted Karen.

Suarez nodded.

'Your father was kidnapped, but they released him like they told you on the telephone. I do not have the tape of this conversation, but I have heard the copy which Señor Garrick supplied. When you went to find your father, you arrived too late. If you had told me perhaps I could have reached him before the others.' He shrugged. 'They took him to another location where they killed him.'

'Who were they?' asked Leon.

'I do not know for certain,' replied Suarez.

'Does that mean you can't say, or that you won't say?' asked Karen.

Suarez shrugged.

'Any suspicions?' asked Leon.

Suarez didn't reply.

'I didn't expect a simple answer, Inspector Suarez,' said Karen. 'Obviously there isn't one. But it seems my father made enemies here. I want to know who they were.'

'When you have trouble in a case,' said Suarez, 'you have to go back to the beginning and build it again, piece by piece. You arrange the rocks in a different order. But the problem is knowing where something begins. When a man kills a woman, maybe we start when he argues and picks up the knife. Or maybe we return to the time when he finds her with another man two years before. It makes a difference. Is it a crime of passion or is it premeditation?'

Karen shook her head. 'Right now I'm not interested in subtleties, Inspector Suarez. I've come three thousand miles for some answers which you've got and I want.'

'So, I find your father in a box. Then I find the house where this box belongs. I send the forensic experts to look at the house. They tell me this is the house where your father was killed.'

'So who owns the house?'

'The person who owns a house is not necessarily the person who uses it.'

'What do you mean?' snapped Karen.

'You see the problem now?' said Suarez. 'When you ask questions from officials, they do not answer.'

There was a long silence. Karen stared at Suarez. 'Are you screwing me around?'

Suarez shook his head. 'I will find out why your father was killed. Please be patient.'

'I'm not a patient person,' warned Karen.

'Maybe I will have some answers for you in one or two days. I must go now. I will speak to you in the morning. Please do not tell anyone where you are staying.'

When Suarez had left, Leon said, 'Take it easy on him. He's helping us. He's the only chance we've got.'

'I noticed you didn't exactly push for information.'

Leon shrugged.

'All he gives us is some lousy metaphor about building a case.'

'He seems to be making some progress.'

'You want metaphors?' asked Karen, irritably.

'Huh?' Leon didn't know what she meant.

'I'll give you one,' she said. 'You ever been to Acapulco?'

'No.'

'There are sharks in Acapulco, but they don't come in to shore. They don't bother the guys who dive from the cliffs. They've got nothing to do with the action. Except everyone thinks they do.'

'I don't understand what you're getting at.'

'The divers start their dives when the waves are out and there's nothing but rocks below them. They hurtle down, but they have faith in nature's clockwork, and the waves roll back just on time and break their fall. But that's not enough for the tourists. The divers have to work at night, lighting fires on the beaches to see when the waves are out. They have to hold burning torches so you can see them flying through the air as you drink your martinis.'

'What's that got to do with us?' he asked.

'Nothing yet.' She had his attention. 'The divers retire, racked by migraines, nursing skeletons shattered by a thousand impacts with the sea. They spend their days begging pesos outside the marble hotels where the tourists stay, until like all of us they're kissed by death.'

'That's not much of an ending,' said Leon. 'Why did you tell me that?'

'The tourists think that if the diver makes a mistake the shark gets dinner.'

'I don't get it.'

'If the diver makes a mistake, he's dead. No one cares less about the sharks.'

'So what's the point of the story?'

'Exactly. You like metaphors, so I give you a pretty story.' She paused. 'I want facts, Leon.'

'Am I missing something?'

'I'm tired of being strung along. I wanted to give you something to think about because I don't like metaphors,' Karen said. 'And I once went to Acapulco with my father.'

Just when Leon thought he was getting to know Karen he found he didn't understand her at all.

2

'You're clear about what this involves?' asked Cristobál. 'The terms for repentance are absolute. You can't withhold anything, otherwise they won't accept you into the protection programme.'

'I know what it involves,' Michel snapped into the telephone.

'If they find that you're lying then you're in a worse situation than before, and it's not one that I'll be able to extricate you from.'

'Just start the ball rolling. I know what I'm doing.' Michel replaced the receiver and turned to Abene. He smiled weakly. 'I know that's what repentance is supposed to involve,' he said. 'But I don't intend to repent as such. I plan to do a deal. I'll tell them about some actions in which I was involved, but only those which incriminate no one else.'

'They won't accept that.'

'I think they will. I'm a catch for them. They can wrap up a lot of cases if I talk. I go back twenty years.'

'I don't like it.'

'I don't see any other option. If I can get to a judge then I can tell him what we know. The Justice Department is independent of the government under the Constitution. If we put what we know on record there's a chance of it becoming public. I can tell them what happened to the plane and I still have the virus.'

'You could call the newspapers and tell them.'

'They won't believe me. They'd think it was just another rumour floating around the bars.'

Abene knew that the witness protection programme was flawed. The system was so corrupt that the new identities and whereabouts of those who had been accepted by it were often leaked. Michel was committing suicide.

The loneliness she had always dreaded was knocking on the

door again. Just when she'd found someone she could love, he was abandoning her. They'd been through so much together and now it was over.

'Cristobál told me something else,' Michel said. 'People have been asking about me.'

'How did they find out?'

'I don't know. But I won't stay alive for long out here. By involving the lawyers I'm taking the initiative. The judicial process is the only way of publicising what's happened.'

'I wish I knew how we came to find ourselves in this position. It all seems like a waste of time now.'

Michel put his arms around her. 'Don't think like that. We've come a long way. We've uncovered a lot. It was never going to be easy. You must have known that. If we give up now it really will have been a waste of time.'

'I know.'

'We have more important responsibilities. We're talking about saving lives in the event of some future conflict. The concept of these weapons is obscene. It's bigger than you or me – or Basque independence, for that matter. People have to know what's going on. They have to be made aware that governments condone the development of viruses like these.'

Abene nodded.

'When I've gone I want you to go away somewhere. Take a cottage in Tuscany for a few months. Maybe somewhere more exotic. There's money here in my bag. I have a safety deposit box at Crédit Suisse in Geneva. Here's the key.' He gave it to her. 'Don't try to contact me or anyone else. I need to know you're out of the picture. If the police ever catch you it will be the worst thing for me. Will you promise me that?'

Abene didn't want to agree but felt herself nodding. She wondered whether to tell him that she was pregnant. Somehow it didn't seem appropriate. She didn't know how he'd react. She felt a tremendous surge of love for him and wanted to lose herself in the courage of his convictions.

'How will you find me again?' she asked.

'When I have a new identity and I'm sure it's safe I'll look for you. Sign up again under your real name for our Internet service.'

She pulled him on to the bed. 'Let's take the rest of the day off and pretend none of this has happened. We'll have dinner at the best restaurant in town. Maybe tomorrow things will be different.'

Michel smiled. 'OK,' he said. 'But wait a minute.' He went to the door and opened it. He slipped on the 'Do Not Disturb' notice.

They made love to each other slowly. It was the first time there had been any tenderness between them. At different times they felt it was both the first time and the last time they were making love.

As the darkness began to fall Abene said, 'I never spent all day in bed with my lover before.'

'You didn't have to say that. What happened will always belong to us,' responded Michel.

'How come we achieved all that without rehearsal?' she asked.

'I don't know.'

'You should know. You're older than me.'

'The years only help you forget,' said Michel softly.

Abene stared at him with her big eyes.

'I got the feeling you thought I was a tart when you first met me,' she said suddenly.

Michel looked at her face turned towards him in the half-light. 'No,' he said, and shook his head.

'My first act of rebellion was against my background. I took a job as a topless waitress in a bar in Barcelona,' Abene confessed. 'I was paid a commission on every drink the customers bought. Sometimes they used to proposition me. You may think I'm hard, but you should have seen them.'

Michel imagined men with features like quarry pits and

muscles of granite, splintering notes from their wallets in exchange for smiles and soft drinks. He'd been in places like that in the past.

'There was once a man who offered me ten thousand pesetas to go with him. I got fed up with his propositions. I told him I wouldn't spit on him for that. He was really serious. He increased the price. Finally he offered me two hundred thousand pesetas. I told him to forget it.'

Michel stretched his arm down to pull her towards him. 'He didn't deserve you.' Then he asked, 'Did you ever accept money?'

'No. But I thought about it sometimes.'

'I'm glad you didn't,' he said.

They made love again before going out for dinner.

In the morning Abene woke to find Michel standing by the bed. He was ready to leave. 'I can't think of anything to say,' he said.

Abene nodded.

He leaned over and kissed her gently. 'Goodbye.'

'There's one more thing,' she said.

'What's that?'

'I love you.'

He smiled. She felt something breaking inside. 'I love you too,' he said quietly. 'Remember that.'

Then he was gone. She felt the tears rolling down her cheeks and found herself singing a song she thought she'd forgotten long ago.

'*Hegoak ebaki banizkion, nerea izngo zen . . .*' she sang.

> 'If I'd cut its wings
> it would have been mine,
> and wouldn't have flown away.
> It wouldn't have been
> a bird any more,
> and it was the bird that I loved.'

3

Antonio Suarez emerged from Rodriguez Cristobál's offices on to Calle de Los Héroes. He looked back at the building. The law firm owned the whole thing. They were the best in Bilbao and wanted everyone to know it. He'd never done business with them before. The kind of lawyers he usually dealt with operated out of one-room back-street offices near Calle de San Francisco and had shiny seats on their pants. He'd never in a million years have guessed why Cristobál called him for a meeting that morning, and was dumbstruck when he was told that Michel Ardanza wanted to turn himself in. He wasn't about to object, though.

Suarez opened the door of the car, got in the back and shivered. 'Julio,' he said to the driver, 'do me a favour. Don't keep the air-conditioning on when you're parked up. Turn off the engine. I've told you before. It's bad news burning up gas and polluting the planet, not to mention the city.'

Julio nodded. Suarez caught the long-suffering expression in the rear-view mirror.

'Where to?' asked Julio.

'The office,' replied Suarez.

The car pulled into the traffic, then ground to a halt.

'What's going on?' asked Suarez.

'Water services,' replied Julio curtly. He was peeved at having been reproved.

'Does the name Ardanza mean anything to you?' asked Suarez.

Julio was silent. Suarez looked in the mirror. The driver was frowning: maybe deep in thought, maybe wondering whether to answer at all, maybe something wrong with his hormones. 'I've heard the name,' he answered eventually.

'When?'

'Some days ago.'

'You didn't tell me.'

Julio shrugged. 'He owns two bars. One is Deusto. You know, where everyone hangs out. The other is that student place, Txistu. He also has some theatre place where you have to be Basque to go. It's a hangout for the wives and kids of ETA activists.'

Julio had done his research. 'So how come you know so much about him?'

'The word's out on him. People are looking for him.'

'Who?'

Julio shrugged again. Suarez couldn't bring himself to continue the conversation. The whole thing irritated him. The idea of the law was a joke out here. People just took it into their own hands. He glanced in the mirror and thought he detected a smirk on Julio's face.

'Fuck this traffic!' he said angrily. He opened the door, got out and slammed it closed. He walked back to the police station.

As soon as he reached his office, Suarez dialled the number in Madrid. He'd planned the call carefully. He wanted de Souza to make all the connections himself. He'd pretend to be innocent. Pretend he wanted to talk to the minister, Hernando himself. He needed to get de Souza on his side.

Suarez gripped the telephone. 'Who?' he asked in a surprised voice.

'Baltazar de Souza,' came the reply.

'I'm sorry. I asked to speak to the minister,' he lied, 'but they have put me through to you, sir. I will call again.'

'And to whom do I have the pleasure of speaking?' asked de Souza.

'Inspector Suarez from Bilbao.' He hesitated. 'About Plan Zen,' he said, referring to the operation aimed at repressing Basque dissidents.

'Ah, yes. How are things up there these days?' asked de Souza, his tone warming.

This was promising, thought Suarez. He was pleased with

his little ruse. The switchboard could quite easily have made the mistake of connecting him to de Souza. After all, his office was probably just down the corridor from that of the minister. 'I've got a terrorist who wants to repent.'

'That's always good.'

'There's a problem. He wants to do a deal.'

'We don't do deals. The law's quite clear on that. In return for absolute repentance they get a clean bill of health.'

'I know, sir. The thing about Ardanza is that he claims to have something important to trade.'

'Who?'

'No, sir. He has *something* he wants to trade. Not a person.'

'No. What's the man's name?'

'Michel Ardanza.'

'Ardanza?' De Souza repeated the name. 'No. I don't think I've ever heard of him.'

'I believe he has a variety of aliases.'

'Well, what does he have to say for himself?'

'He says he knows about the Guttman business. He says there's some kind of conspiracy.'

There was a silence. 'I thought you'd cleared that up long ago,' de Souza said at last.

'Not exactly. We had to reopen the case when the Americans contacted us. Now Guttman's daughter is here asking questions.'

'His daughter is here?'

'Yes.'

'It's all very embarrassing. What do you want from me?' growled de Souza defensively.

'Nothing, sir. I was attempting to contact the minister and was connected to you. I wanted clearance to arrange a meeting and hold preliminary discussions with Ardanza.'

'Leave it with me. Go ahead and interview the man, then report to me. I'll brief Agustín Hernando.'

'Thank you . . .'

'What's the name of the lawyer?' interrupted de Souza.

'Rodriguez Cristobál.'

'Play it tough. There are no deals with terrorists. They give themselves up unconditionally and we decide if they get an amnesty.'

'One other thing, sir. I made a request for information concerning a safe house up here which is used from time to time by the ministry. I'd be grateful if you could expedite a response.'

'Fax me the details. I'll see what I can do.'

'Thank you.'

'I don't have to tell you there are delicate negotiations taking place between the government and ETA at the moment. It would be better not to advertise that you have this witness. Keep it quiet for the moment.'

'Of course. And you'll tell the minister . . .'

'I'll tell him as soon as he returns.'

The dialling tone cut in. De Souza had ended the conversation.

Suarez smiled. At least he'd covered himself. Agustín Hernando would have to start being careful.

He picked up the telephone to tell the lawyer Cristobál to confirm a meeting with Ardanza.

Suarez looked forward to meeting Ardanza and seeing what he had to say for himself. He wanted to discuss the bombing in Barcelona all those years ago. Ardanza had probably forgotten about it; but Suarez would make sure he wasn't accepted for the witness protection programme if he didn't confess to it.

4

Colonel Jackson flipped through the reports that had been logged on the computer network overnight. Eventually he found what he wanted. A fighter plane had crashed. A pilot and navigator failed to eject. Thirty million bucks had gone up in smoke, and that didn't include the cost of two highly trained officers.

Accidents!

There had been too many of those recently, but no one expected anything else when defence budgets were cut. Planes were grounded so they could be cannibalised for spares to keep others operational. Cuts in defence put lives at risk. They were a false economy. The White House never learned. Unfortunately the two officers were now statistics which testified to that.

Jackson stroked the leather of his desk with his palms. Not a piece of paper in sight. Nothing linked him to the United Airlines flight. That's how he liked it. He kept paperwork to a minimum. Paper was patient. It left a trail and came back to haunt people.

He stood up and walked to the map of the world pinned on the wall. He looked at the Iberian peninsula and stared at Bilbao. Everything was ending back where it began. Garrick and Guttman's daughter were there again. So was the terrorist Landow, whose real name he knew to be Michel Ardanza, and who was now negotiating with Suarez.

At the beginning of the year he'd wanted a last operation in the field. He'd got his wish now. He turned away from the map and made the phone call to Arnault Lafitte, who'd recruited the members of GAL last time. They were going to do what Madrid had found impossible ever since the experiment in Bilbao had run into difficulties. They were going to remove all the evidence, once and for all.

Jackson slipped a video into the player and looked at the television screen. He watched Michel Ardanza as he entered the laboratory. The screen flickered. He watched Ardanza passing through La Guardia Airport. He was a cool customer, that was for sure. There in the background was the woman they knew as Pehrzon, keeping a distance from Ardanza, as if they weren't travelling together. It was hard to get a sense of Ardanza from the hazy pictures, but it was enough. There was a shot of the Bombay Airport departure lounge. A stream of faces surged towards the camera and passed underneath. Jackson froze the frame on a boy holding his younger sister's hand. It was strange to think those kids were dead because of Ardanza.

Later in the day, before he caught the plane to Spain, Jackson spent a few hours at the small-arms range. Guns are like golf, he thought: the more you practise the luckier you get. However, he didn't expect any close-range activity. Arnault Lafitte preferred to work half a mile from his target.

5

It was dusk when Michel reached Iparraldea. He stopped the bike for fuel then crossed the border into Hegoaldea, the southern Basque region. He was nearly home. It was as if he were playing the movie of his escape with Abene in reverse. Night fell and his speed dropped. The beam of his headlight searched out the barriers on the side of the long sweeping bends. He was tired and cautious. Increasingly he found himself braking and pulling the bike upright on the bends only to crank it over again. He had rolled the virus in his sleeping-bag, but he hadn't thought about what would happen if he wiped out. Some unsuspecting policeman looking through his belongings for identification might find the canister. He'd attach a warning to it as soon as he could.

It was past midnight when Michel turned off the *autobia*. He decided against staying in a hotel. He drove down the country roads until he came to a small track on the side of a mountain, then killed the engine and pushed the bike out of sight. He pulled the sleeping-bag out of the pannier and clambered over rocks. It took him a few moments to find the cave he'd used as a hideout long ago. In those days he couldn't drive to the spot, but now there was a road. Times were changing. In the past, members of his group had kept hostages there. He crawled into the opening, threw the sleeping-bag on the ground and fell on top of it.

He woke with bright sunlight streaming on to his face. It took him a moment to realise where he was. He looked at his watch. Nine in the morning. He crawled to the opening of the cave, lay on his stomach and peered into the valley. He saw a falcon hovering. Everything seemed more poignant now. The colours were vibrant and the sounds were distinct. For the first time he felt frightened of dying. He wanted to live. But he had to finish what he'd started. The falcon swooped and struck at some hapless creature in the bracken below. Michel felt uncomfortable to find himself identifying with the quarry.

He rolled up the sleeping-bag, pushed his motorbike out of the trees and rode down the hill. He stopped where the road levelled before it swept down to the ravine and crossed the stream. He stared across at the mountains and valleys. He usually looked forward to stopping there and walking into the forest where he would be cocooned by the silence, but all that had changed.

There was nowhere left for him to hide now. They'd never give him a trial for fear of what he might say. Either they did a deal or they killed him. It was a novel sensation. Out there, looking over Euskadi, it didn't really feel like he was on Death Row. Never once, as a child when he roamed these mountains, did he have an inkling of how it would end. He'd imagined the hail of bullets, but not this. It seemed like an anticlimax.

He started the bike and rode down the steep incline, past the Monasterio Bekoa. At the end he had the choice of turning to Lumo, and climbing back up the mountain again and changing his mind, or turning left to Gernika and entering the town on Allendesalazar Etorbidea, past Chillida and Moore's sculptures of peace.

Michel turned into Gernika.

Chapter Fourteen

I

Suarez was irritated that Michel Ardanza had chosen the Casa de Juntas in Gernika for their preliminary meeting. He guessed Ardanza thought it symbolic because it was where the ancient laws which governed the province were once passed. Gernika was a City of Peace now, after the Germans destroyed it, and it was inappropriate that a terrorist should demean its image with his miserable attempt to rejoin society.

Of course, the venue had its merits from Ardanza's point of view. There were various vantage points so he could see whether the place was staked out. Suarez entered the gates and wondered where Ardanza would reveal himself. He hadn't been there since he had first arrived in the North and felt obliged to soak up the local colour. He looked at the blackened stump of the original sacred oak tree where the assemblies had been held, under the shade of its leaves, before they were transferred to the chapel.

He went into the Assembly House and looked in the reception room. There was no one there. He glanced at the huge stained-glass window and the painted triptych. It wasn't his style. He went into the chapel with its tiered seats, altar and domed ceiling. He checked his watch. Apart from the woman in the office by the entrance no one else was in the building. He walked outside again and stood on the path. He became conscious of a figure standing under the oak tree watching him.

He realised with a shock that Ardanza was almost the same age as he. The photographs he had had been taken some time ago. He walked towards him.

'Inspector Suarez?' Ardanza's eyes flickered over his face and uniform.

Suarez nodded. 'And you are . . . ?'

'Michel Ardanza.' He held out his hand.

Suarez looked at the hand and decided against shaking it. Ardanza shrugged.

'Before we start, Inspector Suarez, I should tell you that I have a partner who will take action if anything happens to me.'

Suarez nodded. They all said that, but then they only gave themselves up when they'd exhausted all other possibilities and they didn't have anyone else. 'I also have something to say,' he said. 'First of all you should understand that I am a policeman. I do not make the policies and I do not interpret the law. My job is to protect people. The law is for the protection of the innocent.'

'Listen to what I have to say,' snapped Ardanza.

'No,' said Suarez. 'I'll ask the questions first.' He expected Ardanza to interrupt. 'Ten years ago there was a bombing in Barcelona. I think you were involved.'

'Yes, that's correct,' replied Ardanza. 'It was a mistake. At least the person who placed the bomb made the mistake. Hardly a day passes when I don't think of that. I've tried to make amends.'

Suarez shook his head. Those were fine words, but they didn't impress him. 'How do you make amends for the deaths of those children?' he asked.

Ardanza looked angry. 'Listen, Suarez! The terrorist always has this quandary. To be politically effective requires sacrificing means to ends. Unfortunately that sometimes contradicts moral principles. And there are bound to be mistakes at times.'

Suarez was used to this intellectual justification by terrorists for their actions. 'And that justifies killing children?'

'That isn't what I implied, Inspector Suarez.'

'Since when did kidnap and murder become virtues?'

'My actions are insignificant when you compare them to state terrorism and the deliberate dissemination of viruses that target ethnic groups,' said Ardanza.

Suarez wondered what he was talking about. He had a feeling he didn't want to hear this.

'That's right, Suarez,' said Ardanza. 'You're going to be shocked when you hear what I have to say.'

Suarez listened as Ardanza told him why Raphael Guttman had been kidnapped, and how he had been released when GAL abducted Bernal Lasturra. He heard Ardanza's suspicions that the taking of the hostage was an attempt to force Guttman's execution. He heard about Guttman-Tiche's research into genetic weapons. It was a story he wouldn't have believed if it weren't for his own investigation into the Pirineo influenza epidemic and the report of the Ministry of the Interior's Operation Mengele that he'd read in *El Mundo*. The story Ardanza told dovetailed into his own findings and made a kind of horrible sense. He heard how attempts to publicise the creation of the genetically manipulated viruses resulted in the destruction of the United Airlines flight.

'You said it was your duty to protect the innocent,' said Ardanza at last. 'What do you propose doing?'

'I'll make sure you go into the witness protection programme,' said Suarez. They could work things through from there.

Ardanza laughed cynically. 'That's not what I meant. I want a guarantee that some action will be taken over this.'

'I realise that,' said Suarez, irritated by his own inability to offer a guarantee. It wasn't his responsibility. He didn't make decisions of that nature. Normally all he was required to do was pass things along the chain of command.

'I have samples of the virus I took from the research laboratory in America. They haven't been kept in ideal conditions, but they can still be analysed.'

'Of course,' said Suarez. He was preoccupied. He knew that if he told Agustín Hernando about this meeting then Ardanza would be eliminated. Fortunately de Souza knew, and the more people who did know about Ardanza the better. For a moment Suarez was struck by the irony that he was concerned for a terrorist's life.

'I'll make arrangements to take you into custody. I won't need more than a couple of days,' Suarez said. 'I'll also approach the appropriate channels to instigate an inquiry into your discovery. I need the right judge to hear your case.'

'Do it quickly, before I change my mind,' said Ardanza.

They watched a group of tourists file past the oak.

'I'll let your lawyer know about the arrangements,' Suarez said.

Ardanza stretched out his hand. Suarez looked at it. This time he shook it.

As he walked away he felt older. He was angered by what he'd heard. He was disgusted by the conspiracy that had permeated his government. It would be a sad day for Spain when this history was made public, as he knew it inevitably would. The truth had a long and dangerous journey to make before it surfaced, but he would help it.

2

Despite promising Leon and Karen that he would visit them every day, Suarez had telephoned the previous night to apologise and say that he had been too busy. Leon had managed to persuade Karen not to instruct her lawyers and start the proceedings with which she'd threatened Suarez. Their survival depended on finding out as much as possible about her father's death and keeping a low profile.

'I am sorry I am so late,' said Suarez when he finally arrived on the second evening. Karen smelled alcohol. He'd been drinking, though not enough to affect his movements. She hadn't expected him to be a drinker. He didn't give that impression. He paid too much attention to his appearance, although she wondered whether his over-groomed exterior might be a compensation. She offered him a drink and he chose a whisky. She poured a stiff measure and noted that he didn't object. She took a beer to keep him company.

'I spoke to the man who kidnapped your father,' said Suarez. 'He confirms what I thought. He did not kill your father. I am accepting him into the witness protection programme. There has been much to arrange and that is why I was unable to see you yesterday.'

'Does that mean he's excused from prosecution?' asked Karen.

'Yes,' said Suarez.

'I won't accept that,' said Karen angrily.

'It is necessary.'

'Where I come from kidnap is a felony.'

'You don't understand,' said Suarez. 'He has more information but we must give him immunity.'

'He should stand trial for what he did.'

Suarez looked at Leon, appealing for help.

'If this goes ahead I'll put in a complaint,' she threatened.

'Let's hear what Inspector Suarez has to say, Karen,' suggested Leon.

'I am sorry you do not approve of this,' Suarez said. 'I understand that you feel betrayed. If we accept Ardanza's repentance there is a possibility of catching the people who killed your father.'

'Who were they?'

'People acting for someone who thought your father was going to tell secrets.'

'What kind of secrets?' snapped Karen. Suarez looked at Leon again. He gulped the whisky. 'You promised me the truth,' she said.

'Biological weapons,' responded Suarez.

Karen shook her head. 'I don't believe it.' There was a silence. 'My father wouldn't have been involved in them.'

'He might not have known about them,' said Leon gently. 'The company might have been involved, though.'

Karen accepted the possibility. 'OK. So who killed him?'

'I don't know yet,' said Suarez.

'Why did they kill him?'

'He knew about an experiment that went wrong,' said Suarez. 'I also heard something about this experiment four weeks ago, but I did not know how it was connected until I spoke to Ardanza today.'

'What experiment?'

'*Una gripe* – an influenza virus which would attack only the Basque people was released here in Bilbao. Something went wrong and people died before it could be controlled. That is why there was a court case and your father was kidnapped. He was killed because his knowledge was too dangerous, but he told it to Michel Ardanza.'

'Do you have evidence?'

'We have a virus for analysis.'

There was a long silence before Leon broke it. 'You're sure about this?'

Suarez nodded.

Leon felt angry and betrayed. If he'd known that Guttman was implicated in manufacturing biological weapons he would never have become involved. People like that deserved everything that was thrown at them. 'It's sick,' he said. 'Everyone's concerned with exacting reparations for Hitler's holocaust and the evil continues in another form.'

Suarez and Karen looked at him. It took them a moment to understand what he was saying. 'Are you telling me that these weapons can differentiate between different nationalities?' asked Karen.

'That is what I was told,' answered Suarez.

'Let me get this right,' said Karen. She stood up, then picked up the bottle of whisky. 'By the way, would you like another shot?'

Suarez held up his glass.

Karen filled it, then continued with her train of thought. 'You want me to believe that my father was making biological weapons? Who was he making them for? Iraq? Libya?'

'No, Karen,' said Leon, quietly. 'I think he was making them for America. They tried to stop you from finding out by pretending that they'd found your father's killer. When I kept asking questions it was clear that we'd stepped over a line.'

'When I came here this evening I did not want to tell you about this,' said Suarez. 'Now I think it is better that I tell you. The more people who know the better. It makes things more clear to talk about it. Spain was not alone in this. Perhaps the bad things come to Europe from the New World, like Columbus returned with syphilis.'

Karen stared at Suarez. He'd finished his drink and it was clear that he'd drunk a lot more than they thought when he arrived. 'I'm sick of you guys always blaming America for anything bad that happens in the world.'

'It is not just America. I love my country too. I love Spain. I love her history but I also hate it. This country has so much pain. A stranger cannot understand it. The Civil War. The failure of her empire. We destroy ourselves. We turn in on ourselves like a cancer. Our greatest book is *Don Quixote*. We make the wrong people into our heroes. Ignacio Loyola. Francisco Franco.'

'So what happens to Ardanza now? You can't just hand him over,' said Leon.

'It's out of my hands. The Ministry of the Interior has control,' said Suarez. 'You don't understand anything. There is so much ... *mierda* under the carpet that when they lift it we will all be covered in it.'

'You realise that they can't afford to let this come out,' commented Leon.

'I know,' said Suarez. 'But in the end it will emerge. Piece by piece. Not at first. It will take time. We will hear of it because it is the Spanish nature. It will destroy our democracy. Unfortunately it is no longer in my hands. We can't change things. It is no more a world we care about.'

'They'll have to silence Ardanza,' said Leon. 'You know that.'

Suarez shrugged. 'It does not matter. But afterwards the truth will come out. This country cannot keep secrets. It is Catholic. We need to confess.'

'What's the name of Ardanza's lawyer?' asked Karen.

'Rodriguez Cristobál,' answered Suarez. 'He knows everything.' He finished his drink and stared at the floor. Karen glanced at Leon.

Suarez started speaking again. 'What a job! I'm just a collector of the—' He flailed around for the word. '—*basuro*.'

'Garbage,' said Leon.

'You know what we do on the streets of Madrid every night?' Suarez didn't wait for an answer. 'We collect Africans. If they have no papers in their pockets there are no questions, no trial. We take them to the military airport, put them on a plane and take them back to Africa. Every night. Some here, some there. To Morocco. Liberia. What kind of work is that?' He stood up suddenly. 'It is time for me to go,' he said. 'Excuse me for my talking. This was a bad day for me. I will speak to you again tomorrow when I have more news.'

'Are you driving?' asked Leon.

'No. I like to walk,' said Suarez, picking up his hat. 'It is safer,' he added, closing the door behind him.

When Suarez had left, Leon took out a folder, withdrew the list of terrorists and the photographs which Suarez had given him and spread them on the table. 'That's Michel Ardanza,' he said.

Karen studied the photographs. 'I want to speak to him,' she said. 'If he spoke to my father I want to speak to him.'

'It won't be easy. Someone will be trying to shut him up.'

'If he knows the truth I've got a right to speak to him,' said Karen.

'It'll be dangerous if they're trying to kill him.'

'Who do you think wants him dead?'

'Either the Spanish government or your government.'

'That's state terrorism. I don't believe my government would do that.'

'I'm not saying it comes from the President,' said Leon. 'Somewhere in a bureaucracy like the Pentagon there's always someone who abuses his power.'

'Suarez should do something.'

'He's just a tool of the state.' Leon looked at Ardanza's photograph and tried to understand the man. He had a presence; he filled the picture. He was concentrating on something out of the shot, but there was an intensity about him. Instinctively Leon liked him, but perhaps it was because he admired him for risking his life to expose what he'd discovered.

'We should warn him,' said Karen.

'I think he knows the risks,' responded Leon.

Karen stood up and looked in the bookcase. 'He still has rights.' She pulled out the telephone directories and flipped through them. She found Cristobál's office address, looked through the residential listings and found his home number. She looked at her watch. It was midnight. She handed Leon the phone. 'Call him,' she said.

Leon did as she told him. There was a naïvety to Karen that he found attractive. She was a product of her country. She reflected the best things in it, believing that the world could be changed. He admired her enthusiasm and her optimism. He knew that if she decided to take on the Spanish government, then she would, and nothing he could say would stop her.

3

Suarez left Leon and Karen and wandered through the city streets, thinking about the day's events. He finally found himself leaning on the wall by the canal. The tide was going out, slowly revealing car tyres, concrete blocks and a supermarket trolley in its slimy wake. He could smell the oil which the water sloughed as it retreated. People's indifference to pollution reflected their acceptance of all the other things that governed their lives.

He took out a cigarette and discovered he'd used his last match. He'd smoked almost a packet since the early evening. He had a lot to think about. When he'd talked to de Souza during the course of making the necessary arrangements for Ardanza's surrender, he had emphasised the fact that Hernando had continually ignored the phone calls and reports he'd sent when he'd first arrived in Bilbao.

'You know why that was?' asked de Souza.

'No.'

'I thought you knew,' said de Souza.

'What do you mean?'

'I'll get no thanks for this,' de Souza said wearily. 'About Agustín and your wife.'

'What do you mean?' asked Suarez, understanding full well what de Souza was suggesting.

'I am sorry I had to tell you, but under the circumstances I think you have a right to know.'

'Thank you,' said Suarez, before putting down the phone. He felt he was a child again, thanking the Jesuit priest for beating him.

Now things made sense. He'd been blind. At last he knew why he'd been sent to the North. Hernando wanted him out of the way. He remembered the way his wife simpered when the minister took her hand at the reception and wondered whether that had been the beginning of the affair or whether it was an unexpected bonus for the two of them to meet like that in public. He'd never know the answer because he wasn't going to ask.

Suarez had had a few drinks to digest the news. When he saw Leon and Karen he somehow felt detached from his investigation. He wanted to explain the intricacies of the story, but he knew they wouldn't be interested. Whatever he did now to draw attention to Hernando's complicity in the murder of Raphael Guttman would be coloured by their relationship. He could imagine Hernando dismissing his accusations as the pathetic attempt of a cuckold to embarrass him. He had to trust de Souza with the information that could bring down Hernando.

He thought about calling Carla to tell her that he knew everything, but decided against it. She'd told him about an affair during the holiday. They'd discussed it and agreed that Lorenzo was the priority in their lives and that they'd make every effort to keep the family intact. He was sure that she wasn't involved in the decision to post him away from Madrid. That was something Hernando had thought up on his own.

4

Karen dropped Leon outside Rodriguez Cristóbal's offices at eight and parked the car across the street. Leon went into the building and told the receptionist to tell Cristóbal that he was waiting. Although he was fifteen minutes early for the appointment he'd been given the previous night, he was shown into the lawyer's office immediately.

Cristóbal was younger than he had expected. He was tanned and had thick dark hair. A picture of his wife with his two young boys sat on his desk. On the walls there were photographs of him at the helm of a yacht. He listened carefully to what Leon told him.

'I've handled a number of cases in which activists have given themselves up. I accept that this one differs in a number of aspects. However, I don't think there's any cause for alarm. I'm in contact with the Ministry of the Interior, and the negotiations don't suggest that my client is in any danger. As soon as he is safely hidden I shall be making the application to the Department of Justice.'

'Don't you find it odd that Inspector Suarez isn't involved any more?'

'Not at all.'

'Is Ardanza aware of the risks?'

'Of course. For him risk has always been an occupational hazard,' said Cristobál. 'But I'm going to be present when he gives himself up.'

'When?'

Cristobál looked at his watch. 'I have to meet him in an hour.'

'Would he be willing to meet my client, Karen Guttman?'

Cristobál shrugged. 'Possibly. I can understand your client's desire to meet him but I have no idea whether he'll be willing to talk to her.'

'Once he's in custody there's little chance of her meeting him.'

'That's for sure.'

'Where's the meeting?'

'In Gernika. It's not far from here. He wants to meet at the Assembly House there. It's a public place. We usually choose somewhere neutral. Do you have transport?'

'Yes.'

'You can follow me. I'll have a word with Michel. He may be willing to talk. It'll have to be brief, though.'

'Thank you,' said Leon.

Cristobál led the way down to the street. He jabbed a remote-control device towards a metallic-silver Mercedes-Benz. The lights flashed and the horn emitted a beep.

Leon spotted Karen in the rented car on the opposite side of the road. 'That's our car beyond the junction,' he said.

'Don't bother to turn round,' said Cristobál. 'We can go that way. Just follow me.'

Leon crossed the road, jogging the last few yards to clear a passing car. For a moment he thought he'd misjudged the car's speed as a blast of air swept him off his feet, hurtling him into a plate-glass window which shattered around him. He lay on the ground, stunned. An explosion echoed. For a few seconds he lost consciousness.

When he opened his eyes it took a moment to piece together what had happened. There was mayhem. He lay there taking in the scene. The road was covered in broken glass. A car was burning. Other cars lay strewn at strange angles. Policemen were rapidly converging on the scene. He looked around. People were watching from a safe distance, uncertain what to do. Everything was suddenly quiet. He saw blood staining the tarmac and followed its trail to the body of a man lying in the gutter.

It wasn't quiet after all. He could hear someone screaming. He tried to stand, but his body wouldn't obey the instructions. He wondered if he'd been set up by Suarez but shook his head. No. That was absurd. At last he struggled to his feet, unsteadily. He took a step and winced. He felt a pain in his cheek, put up his hand and felt a piece of glass. He pulled it out, and stanched the blood with a handkerchief. He looked down at the ground. There was the ubiquitous shoe that lost its owner in every bomb blast. He thanked God there wasn't a foot inside it.

He looked for Cristobál's car and saw it burning. The lawyer was dead. That was for sure. Suddenly the sun was very hot and he limped away in search of shade, finding it in a nearby bar. A policeman approached and asked if he was all right. 'Sure,' he said.

A cacophony of sirens built up. He was aware that whoever had done this was probably watching. They'd know he'd escaped.

He pulled a chair to its feet and sat down. His ribs were killing him. They'd taken another battering in the explosion. He patted his pockets, looking for a cigarette, and realised he'd given up smoking five years before. Jesus! He was in shock.

He looked up. A waiter was watching him curiously.

'Are you all right?' he asked.

It took Leon a moment to translate his requests into Spanish. 'Bring me a drink,' he said. 'A brandy and a cigarette.'

The waiter immediately rushed forward and offered him the cigarette. Leon went to take it and realised that his hand was covered in blood. 'Light it for me,' he ordered. The waiter lit it and stuck it between his lips. Leon took a long drag. The cigarette hung from the corner of his mouth. Ash fell on his trousers. The waiter returned with the brandy and a glass of water, which he placed on a table.

Leon felt that things were returning to normal. 'How do I look?' he asked the man.

'Not bad. You were lucky.'

Leon laughed. He was still in shock.

'Shit!' he said. The cigarette dropped out of his mouth. He watched it burn on the ground. The waiter didn't pick it up. Leon leaned forward and removed the napkin from the waiter's arm, poured the glass of water over it and started cleaning blood from his hands and face. He downed the brandy.

He heard a familiar voice. 'Are you all right?'

He turned. 'Karen!'

'I couldn't find you.'

'I forgot,' he said. 'I thought you were still ...' He didn't finish what he was saying. He'd been concussed by the blast and had thought she was still at the apartment. It would sound stupid.

'What did Cristobál say to you?'

His mind seemed a blank. It would come to him. 'Let's get out of here,' he said.

5

Arnault Lafitte lay under a tree. The town was coming alive. He was in position before dawn while everyone was sleeping. He waited until the sun had burned off the moisture in the air before unpacking the rifle. He was just under a thousand metres from where he expected Michel Ardanza to be standing when he squeezed the trigger.

Any distance up to two hundred metres was point of aim. More than that and he had to allow for the wind, humidity and temperature. People thought he just put telescopic sights on the rifle and did the job, but it was more complex than that. This wasn't any old rifle. He knew it intimately. He'd had it for the past five years, and except for a few times a year it lived in its case, nestled in foam and felt. He took care of the case, never knocking or jarring it. The rifle's tolerances were easily upset.

The stock was made of laminated wood so it wouldn't respond to heat or change shape. Once the gun was out of the case and assembled, he placed the barrel on a bipod. It never touched the ground where one side could be cooled by the earth while the other was heated by warm air and the barrel imperceptibly warped out of true. A microscopic imbalance was magnified as the bullet travelled a thousand metres. A few centimetres one way or the other was the difference between success and failure.

Lafitte looked down at the cartridges which lay in the box. He chose six of the 7.62 NATO cartridges which he'd loaded himself, each one slightly different, some with more explosive than others. He slipped them into the magazine.

He looked through the sights, picked out the stained-glass window in the Assembly House, moved on to the sacred oak of Gernika, and then to the pavilion where the old oak had died a hundred years ago. He thought about sending a bullet into the blackened stump to check that the rifle was lined up but resisted the temptation. He'd tested it the previous day on the mountain.

He looked at his watch, picked up his binoculars and studied the road again. Not long to wait.

The back-up team was positioned down in the town waiting for his call. They'd signal the two policemen to go find Ardanza's body, secure the scene and pick up the evidence. By then he'd be in the car that had just pulled into the farm track and returning to Bilbao, where he'd report to Colonel Jackson. The colonel was treating this operation as if it were the assassination of a head of state. The money had been paid up front, and Lafitte had got the American passport he wanted along with asset status, which would grant him immunity from court proceedings if an operation went wrong. He'd made it to the top in the six years since he'd bought himself out of the French Foreign Legion. Fuck up an operation like this, get caught, and the Americans would fly him home now, no questions asked. He had a licence to kill.

He was lying on the edge of the park where the land climbed the mountain behind. He had a view of the entrance to the Assembly House. Things were in his favour. It was a grey day and there wouldn't be many tourists looking at sculptures in the park. If things went according to plan there would be only the one target.

He heard a motorcycle decelerating as it entered the town. It sounded like a worn twin-cylinder, out of tune, pistons slapping as the rider cruised down the hill. He caught sight of the bike for a second, before it disappeared behind a building.

6

Michel paid for his coffee in the café, slung his bag over his shoulder, then slowly walked up the steps that led to the chapel of Santa Maria la Antigua. No one recognised him. No one stopped him. Children on their way to school were shouting and crowding past him. He watched them go. He looked back at the modern buildings and tried to imagine it sixty years before.

His grandmother said it had been a beautiful market day. All the same, she'd had a premonition and was on her way home when the church bells started sounding the alarm. The first planes arrived and circled the town. The people watched. Then the planes started dropping their bombs on the marketplace. For three hours the Heinkels and Junkers dropped bombs on Gernika. The pilots strafed the streets. His grandmother remembered seeing the goggles on the pilots' faces. The town was reduced to rubble. It was the first aerial bombardment the world had known. There had been no defences.

Michel wondered what his grandmother would think of genetically targeted weapons. There was no defence against them either. He turned away, walked into the grounds of the Assembly House and looked at his watch. He was a few minutes early for the meeting. He leaned against a corner of the wall and closed his eyes, feeling the sun's rays. When the caretaker unlocked the door of the Assembly House he went inside.

He entered the chapel and sat in a seat beside the door. It was a long time since he'd been to church. They'd be wrong to think it was appropriate finding him there, as if seeking repentance. The whole nature of the confessional was anathema to him. The Christian God was too judgmental for him. Good people were excluded from rising again on the Day of Judgment unless they believed. Bad people could be saved just because they had faith. He looked at his watch again, stood up and went outside. He walked down to the gate.

Michel looked up and down the road. Empty. Rodriguez Cristóbal and the officials were late. It didn't make sense. They'd pushed the time of his surrender forward because they were so keen to debrief him.

The truth dawned on him slowly.

He couldn't see the enemy but they could still see him.

He looked around nervously and slipped the bag off his shoulder, reached inside and gripped the gun. As he retreated towards the church he saw a car hurtling up the hill with its headlights on.

Chapter Fifteen

I

Karen started the engine and was about to pull away when a policeman appeared at Leon's window. The waiter from the café stood beside him.

'Sir!' said the policeman. 'You were in the accident. We need to take a statement from you.'

'*No comprendo,*' said Leon. 'I'm English.'

The policeman looked baffled. The waiter's expression turned to indignation. Leon turned to Karen. 'Let's go,' he said. 'Before they block the road.'

The policeman put a hand on the car door. Leon locked it. 'Go!' he shouted.

Karen pulled out. She wove between two police vehicles and sped away.

'There's a meeting,' said Leon, remembering something of his conversation with Cristobál. 'He said there's a meeting in Gernika. We have to get there. Fast.' He scrabbled in the glove compartment for the map, then found it on the rear seat. He longed to take a deep breath but shards of pain sliced through his ribcage every time he inhaled.

They crossed the river and looped on to the main road out of Bilbao. Traffic in the opposite direction was building up. Karen put her foot down. Leon turned the pages of a guidebook, desperately trying to identify the rendezvous that Cristobál had told him about.

As they entered Gernika, Leon recognised the name in the guidebook. It had been staring at him. Casa de Juntas. The Assembly House. He snatched the map. 'Slow down,' he said, peering out of the window at the street names. 'We're on Juan Calzada Kaleo,' he noted, looking back at the small inset map of Gernika. 'Turn up that road there. See? Where it forks. It's up there on the left.'

Karen stopped the car in front of the Assembly House. There was a lawn, railings and a small gate.

A man was standing in the path, looking back at them, about to run for the shelter of the building. Leon recognised the tall silhouette from the photographs Suarez had given him.

Leon opened the door. 'Ardanza!' he shouted.

Karen was out of the car and running towards him. 'Get in the car, Michel! They're going to kill you,' she shouted.

Ardanza looked back at the building. He looked at Karen and the car. He was in two minds. Karen's urgency persuaded him, and he ran towards them.

Ardanza stumbled into Leon as he opened the rear door. Leon grabbed him and tried to break his fall. Ardanza was half in, half out of the car, his arms moving, scrabbling at the seat. For a moment Leon thought he was having a fit, then realised the seat was covered with blood.

'Help!' Leon groaned, trying to manoeuvre Ardanza into the car.

Karen pulled Ardanza's arms from the other side. The window in the door exploded as Karen clambered in on top of his body.

'Let's go!' yelled Leon. He was covered with Ardanza's blood. He slithered into the driver's seat and turned the key.

The windscreen shattered. A bullet thudded into the passenger seat. The engine cranked, then fired. Leon slipped the car into gear and pressed his foot to the floor. The rear doors slammed. Ahead, children ran out of the primary school. He kept his hand on the horn, and the children scattered to either side.

The car skidded as he turned right and bounced on the kerb. When he reached the main road he veered left. He put his foot to the floor and sounded the horn. The road ran straight, through the town and out the other side, following the line of the valley.

'How is he?' Leon asked. His chest was on fire. He didn't know whether or not he'd been hit as well.

Karen held Michel's head steady against her shoulder. She felt the warmth of his blood seeping through her shirt. He was staring at her. His eyes were wide open and he looked shocked, his face white. His pupils were almost as big as the irises. They contracted. His mouth opened and closed. His lips moved. He struggled.

'Take it easy,' said Karen. 'Relax.'

Michel struggled harder. Karen realised he was trying to do something. His hand was caught in the strap of the bag he was carrying. He jerked it off the floor on to his legs, looked down and tried to open it. His fingers scrabbled at the buckle. He took her hand and put it on the bag. They rocked from side to side violently as the car took a hairpin bend. He squeezed her hand, so hard it began to hurt. Then suddenly the pressure was gone. His head lolled. The car skidded on the verge. Michel was slipping away. Karen eased to one side, trying to lay him down on the seat. She looked at him.

'He's dead,' she said.

'Are you sure?'

'Of course I'm sure,' she snapped.

Leon looked in the rear-view mirror. In the distance he saw a car take the corner wide, skid off the road and raise a plume of dust. It snaked back in pursuit.

'They're behind us,' said Leon. 'Get the map. Work out where we are.'

'It's fucked,' she said a moment later.

'What do you mean?'

'It's covered in blood.'

'Jesus!'

Leon concentrated as he overtook a gas tanker. The road began twisting and turning. Now he could smell the blood in the car.

'I want to get out,' said Karen.

'You're not the only one.'

'I feel sick.'

She retched. He concentrated on the road.

'There's a gun in his bag,' Karen said a moment later.

'Show me.'

Karen leaned over the passenger seat and held the gun carefully. Leon looked. It was a Beretta semi-automatic. Good for close work but not much use in a car chase.

'Anything else?' he asked.

'I think the viruses are in here.' She held out a metal container for his inspection.

'Put it back,' he said.

The road straightened out. The car behind gained on them. Karen scrambled into the passenger seat as Leon swung the Mercedes on to a narrow road that climbed the side of the mountain.

'You're going to bale out in a minute,' he said. 'Take the bag and leave the gun. You're going to get out and hide. You'll have no more than five seconds.'

Karen looked at the side of the road. It fell away in stages, ending in a sheer cliff. A few bushes and trees clung to any soil that hadn't been washed away. She snatched the gun out of Ardanza's bag and stuck it between their seats. She stuffed her wallet and phone into the bag.

'Stay put. I'll be back,' said Leon. 'Open the door.'

He accelerated into a right-hand bend then braked hard. The door flew open as he accelerated away, the momentum spilling Karen out of the car. The tyres screamed. Karen was gone.

Leon looked at the gun. He had to do it now. He couldn't put too much distance between himself and Karen. He braked for a corner, held the steering wheel straight, opened the door and hurled himself out.

He'd misjudged his speed. As he hit the road his legs were torn away. He curled up, flipped over and tucked his head in. He landed on his back, found his feet and threw himself into a gully on the other side of the road. The Mercedes was still moving, slipping off the road and rolling down the bank. It disappeared from view. There was a groan and a crack. A treetop shook. The engine cut out.

Leon slipped the magazine out of the gun and checked it was full. He heard a car change gear, decelerating at the corner. They'd missed Karen. He cocked the gun. He lay on his back in the gully, looking at a rock face towering over him. Beyond that was the sky. The car skidded, then stopped and rolled back. He wondered how many people were in it. He'd seen two figures in the front seats. They'd be checking out the terrain.

The engine stopped. A car door opened.

2

Antonio Suarez picked up the phone and dialled Madrid. 'Agustín Hernando,' he snapped.

'He's in a meeting. Can I take a message?'

'No. Tell him it's urgent.'

'Give me your name and number and I'll have him call you back.'

'Not good enough,' snarled Suarez. 'Get him on the phone right now or you're dead meat. This is Inspector Suarez and I'm talking about a conspiracy at the highest levels.'

There was the briefest hesitation. 'Please hold the line.'

Suarez jammed the receiver to his ear with a shoulder and lit a cigarette. He'd smoked half of it when Hernando came on the line.

'Inspector Suarez? This is Agustín Hernando. What's the problem?'

'You tell me what's going on ...'

'What do you mean?'

'This morning we had arrangements to take Michel Ardanza into custody. Instead there's been mayhem up here.'

The line crackled. There was silence.

'I don't know what you're talking about,' said Hernando.

'Don't come the innocent with me,' hissed Suarez.

'Watch yourself, Inspector Suarez.'

'I think we can dispense with the formalities,' said Suarez. 'And you know why.' He paused to let that sink in. 'I briefed Baltazar de Souza about this because I knew you were intent on covering it up. But things have gone too far. You can't blow up a lawyer, kill innocent civilians and expect to get away with it. I don't care what sort of a neo-Fascist conspiracy you've got going but ...'

'Stop right there,' ordered Hernando. 'Start at the beginning and tell me what you told de Souza.'

'Why don't you ask him yourself?'

'I intend to. But I want to hear it from you first. All this is news to me. I've never heard of this man Ardanza.'

Suarez didn't reply.

'Antonio? This is important.'

'If you're telling me the truth, and you don't know anything about it, we've got one hell of a problem on our hands.'

'Tell me what's going on,' said Agustín Hernando. 'Let's see if we can sort this out.'

'I may have jumped to the wrong conclusion,' said Suarez.

He saw it clearly now. It was Baltazar de Souza who'd been covering things up all along.

3

Leon heard footsteps on gravel. The gully was shallower than he had thought. If they took a few steps in his direction, they'd see him.

'There's someone in the car.'

A car door opened. 'Check it out,' ordered a second voice. 'Cover me.'

Leon sat up, arm stretched out, gun held steady, and looked for the targets. Two men stood with their backs to him. The first in his line of vision wore a black jacket. He squeezed the trigger twice and caught him in the shoulder. The man turned and ducked. The third shot hit the side of his head and he dropped.

The second man turned and looked at Leon but was already jumping from the road. His hands were busy with a machine-pistol.

Leon fired again. The shot missed. He glanced at their car – no one else there. He scrambled to his feet and ran. His chest screamed. Pain paralysed his left side. He slumped against the front wing of the car. It was the only available cover.

He lay on the ground and peered under the chassis. Ahead of him lay a natural parapet. To the left his line of sight was obscured. That was where the man would be. He glanced at the body on the road. Blood pooled on the tarmac. He was dead.

He waited. Watched.

A pigeon swooped, then shied away and betrayed the man's position. He was in line with the Mercedes. Leon rolled to the rear of the car, taking cover behind a tyre. He thought about Ardanza and felt a sudden bond with him, gratitude for the gun: although it was small, it worked.

Leon guessed the man would be crawling away beneath the parapet. There was a creak of metal. He glanced at the Mercedes. He guessed it was setting against the tree. The rear door swung open. He saw someone move. There was a groan, followed by a burst of gunfire. Bullets thumped into the car.

Leon sprang to his feet. The man was crouching under the parapet a few yards away and was swinging the machine-pistol to aim at him. Leon fired. He scored. He pumped the trigger until the gun emptied then vaulted the parapet and landed on the man. He ripped the machine-pistol from his hands and fired a burst into the body. He backed away cautiously.

He could see what had happened. Ardanza hadn't been dead. Karen was no doctor. He had returned to consciousness and had managed to open the rear door. He'd got out and then been hit by the hail of bullets. He probably had no idea of what was going on.

Leon walked over to Ardanza and looked at him. He knelt down and felt for a pulse, even though he knew there wouldn't be one. This time Ardanza was dead. For a few seconds he looked at the person he'd never known but who'd saved his life. 'Thanks, mate,' he said under his breath.

He climbed gingerly over the parapet, dragged the body off the road and went to the car. He looked in the small flight case on the rear seat. There was a high-velocity rifle with a scope and the works. He closed the case and got into the car. He started the engine, turned around and coasted down the hill to find Karen.

He stopped on the bend and sounded the horn. There was no sign of her. He turned off the engine and wearily got out of the car. 'Karen,' he shouted. 'Let's go.'

She emerged from behind some rocks. Her jeans were torn across the knee.

'Are you all right?' he asked.

'Yes,' she said. Ardanza's blood had dried on her shirt. 'I thought they'd got you when I saw the car.'

'Huh?'

'That's their car.'

'It was,' acknowledged Leon. 'It's ours now. You drive.'

They got in. 'Where are we going?' Karen asked.

'It makes no difference.' He looked for a map but couldn't find one. 'It's Spain in every direction for a hundred miles.'

Karen pulled away, and they drove in silence until they reached the main road. She turned left, away from Gernika. 'Take the next right. We have to get off the main roads,' said

Leon. 'We still have some options,' he added a few moments later. 'We have something they want. We have the virus.'

'We'll always have something they want. We know what happened.'

'If we give them the evidence, maybe they'll call it a day.'

'They won't buy that,' said Karen.

'We have to try.'

'What about justice?' asked Karen.

Leon looked at her. That was what had got them into this in the first place. Her wanting to know what had happened. He guessed it wasn't the time to remind her. 'We're talking about saving our lives.'

'I know. I just want to know how you feel about it.'

'It's a shitty world,' said Leon. 'Let's think about justice later.'

Karen nodded slowly. He had a feeling that she didn't agree.

'We have to negotiate,' said Leon.

'Where do we start? Inspector Suarez?'

'Let's try Colonel Jackson, as he was so keen to prove he'd killed your father's kidnapper,' said Leon. 'Let's have your phone.'

'It's in the bag.'

Leon pulled it out. 'Do you still have his card?'

'His number's in the memory.'

He handed her the phone. 'Call it. You'll get an answering machine. Say we're willing to deal. Give him this number.'

'It could be days before he picks up his voice mail.'

'No it won't. Trust me. His machine is monitored every minute of the day.'

Karen pulled over. She scrolled through the phone's memory. 'I hope you know what you're doing,' she said.

'Negotiation is one of my specialities,' said Leon.

Karen looked at him.

'I'm sorry,' he said. He could have bitten off his tongue.

'Don't be,' she said. 'I don't hold you responsible for what happened to my father any more. I know it wasn't your fault.'

4

Colonel Jackson leaned over the balcony of his hotel room and stared across the city. His eye was drawn to the Guggenheim Museum which dominated the view, but it didn't register on his horizon. He was shaken by Baltazar de Souza's phone call. It was unbelievable how this whole business had got out of control. It had started off as a small trial to see if a virus could pick out an ethnic group from the background population. All of a sudden de Souza was running scared; but this would never turn into some drugs-for-arms fiasco. It would never get that far.

De Souza was worried that Ardanza's death would complicate negotiations with ETA, but he seemed to have forgotten that the terrorists had been an important factor in the decision to carry out the experiment here in the first place. With Ardanza and his lawyer dead it would merely look as if ETA had taken them out, and could only enhance the government's negotiating position. The spin was there.

In a few minutes everything would be over. Even if Baltazar's worst fears came true and his superiors contacted Washington they'd get nothing. No one knew about the trial. There was nothing to find out. They could exhume the bodies of the Basques who'd died but a virus didn't leave fingerprints.

Jackson looked at his watch. Siesta time. He wouldn't hear anything from de Souza for a while. In Washington it was after six and the offices would be empty. Soon Arnault Lafitte would call to say he'd killed Ardanza and got the virus and then he'd be out of Spain. This whole business would be a memory by the time he was back home.

Jackson picked up the phone on the second ring and listened to a message being relayed. It had been left for him by Guttman's daughter. 'If you want the evidence you have to meet us yourself.' Something had gone wrong. He jotted down the telephone number she left.

His eyes glazed over. Lafitte had fucked up, and now he'd have to meet Garrick and the girl. He looked forward to that. He needed the evidence and he'd give them the illusion of having done a deal. They could sail off into the sunset thinking it was over, but when he was back in Washington he'd decide what action to take. He'd decide whether they lived or died. Right now, without Lafitte, his hands were tied. He'd lost contact with the troops, and Baltazar, who might have been able to help, was running scared.

Jackson looked at the phone. His inclination was to play Karen Guttman against the clock. Keep her waiting until he'd re-established contact with Lafitte or called for some support. All of a sudden he was anxious. Karen Guttman was more resourceful than he'd expected. Her congressman was asking questions and here he was in Bilbao without any idea of what was happening in Washington.

He picked up the phone and dialled the number. This thing needed sorting out quickly.

'Hello.' It was a man's voice. Garrick's.

'This is Jackson.' He cut out the pleasantries. 'Where do we make the transaction?'

'There's a fishing village north-east of Bilbao called Bermeo. There's a quay. Your representative will meet Karen Guttman at the eastern end of the quay. He'll come alone. He'll wait there thirty minutes after the transaction is complete. Do you understand?'

'Seems clear.'

'You've got two hours to get someone there.'

'No problem,' said Jackson.

'How do we recognise him?'

'I'll come in person. Karen Guttman will remember me.'

'The time is now fifteen twenty-three. The meeting will be at seventeen thirty hours.'

'OK,' said Jackson. He put the phone down.

He was picking up his jacket when there was a knock on the door.

He went to open it. Three policemen were standing outside. He smiled. Baltazar de Souza had produced the goods. This changed things.

'Are you Colonel Jackson?'

'That's correct.'

'I am Inspector Suarez.'

Jackson recognised the name immediately. He looked at Suarez curiously. He hadn't expected him to look so insubstantial. He'd expected a bumbling policeman with jowls who filled his uniform.

'You are under arrest.'

'There's some mistake. I suggest you speak to Baltazar de Souza at the Ministry of the Interior.' Jackson pointed to the telephone.

'There's no mistake, Colonel. Señor de Souza has been relieved of his post.'

'I don't think you understand the situation, Inspector Suarez.'

'It is not necessary for me to understand,' said Suarez. 'It's only necessary for me to do my job.'

'Your job is to assist me, Suarez. What we have here is a delicate situation. I have made arrangements to retrieve something of importance to both your country and mine. I suggest you get on the telephone and speak to someone in authority. Try speaking to the minister. Try speaking to the Prime Minister. If he's in contact with Washington they'll give you the necessary instructions.'

'I can telephone them from the police station.'

Jackson looked at his watch. 'Time is running out, Inspector Suarez.'

5

Karen sat on the rocks at the end of the quay. She could taste spray from the breaking waves in the air. A warm wind blew off the land. She watched a fishing-boat steaming into the Bay of Biscay. The rusty trawlers reminded her of Maine. Same fish, different waters, she guessed. All along the quay kids were hauling out mullet on lines. They obviously raced back after school to start fishing.

She wondered what she'd say to Colonel Jackson when they met. Part of her wanted to know the details of her father's involvement, but she also wanted to keep the memories of him intact. In any event, what Jackson told her would be only what it was expedient to tell her.

She glanced down at the clothes she was wearing which Leon had bought to replace the bloodstained ones. He didn't have such bad taste, considering what was probably available in the shop. She looked across the harbour at the buildings lining the square. She could see the hotel from where she was sitting. Somewhere in the darkness of a third-floor window Leon was watching her through binoculars. She smiled and lifted her hand to wave at him. They'd come a long way together since they'd first met. It no longer seemed strange to be sharing a room with him. She'd never expected that they'd become so intimate when they first met, and she was beginning to find him attractive.

She'd lain on the bed and watched him set up the sniper's rifle which he found in the car. He explained what he was doing as he carefully adjusted the telescopic sights and screwed on the silencer. When it was balanced on the bipod she looked through it.

'Not much chance of missing,' she said. It made her feel sick when the crosshairs picked out a man on the quay. The definition was so high that she'd have been able to shoot the cigarette from his mouth, but with her naked eye she couldn't make out his features at all. 'I don't know much about guns,' she said quickly.

Leon smiled. 'I'll tell you all you need to know.'

'Do I want to know this?'

'You've heard of a Colt .45?'

'The gun that won the West?'

'That's right. The typewriter was a direct result of the precision tooling that Mr Colt used to manufacture guns.' Leon grinned. 'But unfortunately typewriters didn't catch on in the same way.'

'I guess modern history would read differently.'

'Yeah. Mr Colt died of syphilis, but I don't think it had anything to do with the Colt 45.'

'Or typewriters?' she asked.

'And just for the record that wasn't a metaphor,' said Leon. 'It was a fable.'

He was growing on her.

Karen saw Jackson at the far end of the quay. She identified him by the way he walked. The wind whipped up some dust, stinging her eyes, and she looked away for a moment. She stood up, leaving the bag on the rocks, and walked a few feet towards him. Jackson looked different out of uniform. He was smaller and less significant. Lousy taste in clothes. Mail-order leisurewear. She'd never noticed how his eyes were sunken in their sockets before. She couldn't tell what colour they were, let alone what he was thinking.

'Stop there, Colonel Jackson,' she said. 'There's a gun pointed at you. If anything happens to me you'll be the first casualty.'

Jackson smiled. 'In that case you'd better take good care of yourself,' he said. He frowned. 'Where's the virus?'

Karen pointed behind her. 'In the bag on the rocks.'

Jackson nodded. 'And how do I know it's in there?' he asked. 'Perhaps you brought me here so your friend could shoot me.'

'He could have done that by now, Colonel, but it's not our style.'

'That's reassuring.' Jackson pushed past her and clambered

unsteadily over the rocks. The wind tugged at his jacket. He put a hand to his hat to hold it in place, then bent down and opened the bag. He felt inside and pulled out a plastic bag. He opened it cautiously.

Karen had double-bagged the aerosol and the cryo-tube for safety. He opened the second bag and looked inside, took out the cryo-tube and glanced at it, checking the batch number. He nodded at her. The wind rattled the plastic bags.

'Wait here for thirty minutes,' she ordered. 'There's a sniper's rifle aimed at you. He won't hesitate to shoot if anything happens to me.'

Jackson shrugged. He sat down on the rocks.

Karen turned away from him and walked down the quay. She resisted the temptation to run. She'd done it and got away with it. The ordeal was nearly over. She thought about a future which contained Leon. She sensed there was unfinished business between them. They'd come from different worlds but been brought together by chance. She couldn't imagine them just shaking hands and saying goodbye when this was over.

She reached the square but didn't notice the police car until it pulled out in front of her. The doors opened and she recognised Suarez as he stepped out. She shook her head, backed away, then looked at Colonel Jackson. He was still sitting at the end of the quay silhouetted against the sky. If the bastard thought he was going to win this round he had another thought coming.

She turned to Suarez. She should have guessed he would never be anything more than a puppet of the state. 'You're making a mistake,' she said.

'What do you mean?' asked Suarez.

'Get away from me. Leave me alone,' she said.

'What's wrong? I only need to ask you some questions.'

'You don't understand,' said Karen. She looked up at the hotel window and shook her head, hoping that Leon wouldn't jump to the wrong conclusions, assume that Jackson had lied to them, and shoot him as she'd threatened if anything happened to her.

The two policemen grabbed Karen's arms and held her.

'Believe me,' said Suarez earnestly, 'it's just a matter of a few formalities and then you are free to go.'

Karen was only a short distance from the hotel. Leon would hear her. 'Stop!' she shouted. 'Don't shoot him. It's OK!' Leon didn't know she'd taken care of Colonel Jackson, whatever happened now.

Her voice echoed round the harbour.

Inspector Suarez frowned. He looked up at the open hotel window where a curtain flapped in the wind.

'Don't shoot,' shouted Karen. 'Please don't shoot.'

6

Leon looked through the scope of the rifle and aimed at Jackson's head. He watched and waited. He saw Jackson take the plastic bag from Karen and open it, watched Karen walk down the quay towards him and kept the rifle trained on Jackson. He stood up and stretched, watching Jackson with his naked eye.

Leon hadn't told Karen that he intended to shoot Jackson. He doubted that she would have agreed to play her part under those circumstances. He was waiting until she reached the safety of the square before pulling the trigger. He didn't know when he had first decided to kill the colonel if he got the chance. Perhaps it was when Ardanza was killed. Perhaps it was before that, when he heard from Suarez that Jackson was involved with biological weapons. It didn't matter when he had decided. What mattered was that Jackson deserved to die. He'd betrayed the trust of his country and its people.

There was no need for Karen to know he'd killed Jackson. By the time she reached this room he'd have dismantled the rifle. They'd collect their things and disappear. If things went wrong he'd take his chances. Karen would be in the clear.

Karen was cutting across the square as Leon leaned over the rifle. He eased the stock into his shoulder. He looked through the scope and picked out Jackson's forehead, nestled his finger around the trigger and slipped off the safety catch. He hesitated. A car had stopped in front of Karen. Two policemen had grabbed her. He recognised Suarez.

He looked through the scope at Jackson. Now the bastard was smiling. Leon slowly tensed his finger.

'Stop,' cried Karen. 'Don't shoot Jackson.'

Leon faltered. He wondered how she knew he was going to kill him. He aimed again. He had his own agenda and would stay true to his own beliefs. He squeezed the trigger.

'Please don't shoot,' he heard Karen plead.

It stopped him cold. He wondered why she was begging for Jackson's life. If it mattered so much she could have it. He stepped towards the window so she could see him and raised his hand in acknowledgment.

He turned back to the rifle on the table, flicked on the safety catch and started dismantling it.

7

Karen saw Leon at the hotel window and breathed a sigh of relief. It would have been a mistake for him to be arrested for an unnecessary murder. 'There was an accident,' she said.

Suarez nodded. He misunderstood her. 'We know about it. We know about the bomb and what happened to Michel Ardanza. We know you were not involved.' He smiled understandingly.

'There was an accident involving the viruses. I put them into the plastic bags and tied them up. Somehow the nozzle on the aerosol jammed when I was transporting it. Colonel Jackson opened the bag just now.'

'What do you mean?'

'The virus was released inside the plastic bag. None of it

could have escaped until Colonel Jackson opened it just now. Fortunately the wind's blowing offshore. So long as he stays where he is we're all safe.'

Inspector Suarez stared at her. Slowly the smile left his face. He looked past her to the end of the quay. Karen followed his gaze. Colonel Jackson was still sitting where she'd left him. Suarez issued a stream of instructions to the policemen, then turned to her. 'I wish you had not done that,' he said quietly. 'But I can understand your reasons.'

'Done what?' asked Karen innocently.

They stared at each other.

'There will have to be an inquiry now,' said Suarez.

Karen smiled. 'I know, it's only right that justice should take place. It would be a pity for Michel Ardanza to have died in vain, don't you think?'

Suarez considered that. Then he nodded.

POSTSCRIPT

Sometimes on warm summer nights the nurses sat Colonel Jackson in his wheelchair across the porch from Hank. 'Here's some company for you,' they said to Hank. Jackson stared across the lawn while Hank muttered. The nurses didn't know whether it made any difference to either of them.

Jackson couldn't care less. He was a prisoner in his own body. The past played endlessly on his horizon, day and night, like a tape on a loop. There was nothing else to occupy his thoughts.

He knew there was something wrong when the policemen cleared the quay and told him to stay where he was. It was cold when the sun went down. It was lonely too, out there. Not as lonely as it was going to get, he knew that now. By then he'd guessed what the girl had done.

He tried to remember what Dr Rampton had told him about the virus. Something about it mutating in the optic nerve, causing damage to the brain and a loss of all motor function. If only Ardanza had stolen a genetically targeted virus he'd probably be in the clear, but this was a fusion virus with no limiting parameters.

Rampton had quoted the odds. They weren't so bad.

Thirty out of seventy per cent meant eighty in a hundred people would walk away from the virus. It obviously hadn't been stored in optimum conditions so he added a few more points in his favour.

It was nearly midnight by the time they brought a truck down to him. He was surrounded by Spanish marines dressed in biochemical suits with red and yellow flags stuck on their sleeves. A fish jumped in the moonlight. Strange, the details he remembered. It was a night like this with a full moon and stars. They put him in an isolation tent and shipped him home.

The virus felled him two days later. He lay on the hospital bed unable to move, sweat pouring off him. That was the moment of truth. That was when he knew he had it. The doctors stuck needles in every vein, and tubes in every orifice. They changed his blood a dozen times and filled him up with anti-virals. They kept him in the isolation tent for six months until he was no longer contagious, but by then he couldn't speak or move.

Eventually there was an inquiry. They wheeled him into court and propped him on the stand as if he was some freak. He listened to months of bullshit evidence. The drugs made it hard for him to concentrate and he couldn't remember details, but it made no difference because he couldn't testify.

They accused him of implementing the programme for the genetic manipulation of the viruses, as if it had been all his own idea. He knew they were only pretending to see justice done. Winners wrote the history books and he'd played his part. The inquiry was a charade, of course. General Tyler and Dr Rampton were conspicuous by their absence.

Jackson accepted he was the fall guy. He had nothing left to lose now. They found him guilty of abusing his position and misusing public funds, then stripped him of his rank.

The thing that hurt the most was hearing Karen Guttman give evidence. She wasn't charged with causing his condition by deliberately releasing the virus into the plastic bag and handing it to him. She'd pulled a trigger and sentenced him to a living death. He last saw her when he was carried down the steps after the hearing. These days his memory played tricks on him but he was sure that Garrick had his arm around her shoulder.

Then they shipped him to this nursing home in West Virginia.

Weeks had turned into years. He still couldn't walk or feed himself. Probably never would. In a while the nurses would come out, wheel him back inside and ask, 'What were you thinking about?' Same damned question every night.

They knew he couldn't answer.

He had a hundred secrets but he'd take them to the grave.

Not like Hank across the porch, who was an open book. Every night he counted the women he'd slept with in the past. Sometimes he got excited, forgetting that the girls were old folk now, and called out their names. Then the doctors sedated him.